MERCILESS DEFENDER

CHICAGO MAFIA DONS

BIANCA COLE

CONTENTS

1. Maeve — 1
2. Gael — 15
3. Maeve — 29
4. Gael — 41
5. Maeve — 55
6. Gael — 67
7. Maeve — 77
8. Gael — 87
9. Maeve — 97
10. Gael — 107
11. Maeve — 117
12. Gael — 127
13. Maeve — 141
14. Gael — 155
15. Maeve — 167
16. Gael — 179
17. Maeve — 189
18. Gael — 201
19. Maeve — 215
20. Gael — 227
21. Maeve — 239
22. Gael — 251
23. Maeve — 261
24. Gael — 271
25. Maeve — 283
26. Gael — 293
27. Maeve — 303

28. Gael	315
29. Maeve	331
30. Epilogue	343
Also by Bianca Cole	361
About the Author	363

Merciless Defender Copyright © 2021 Bianca Cole

All Rights Reserved.
No part of this publication may be reproduced, stored, or transmitted in any form or by any means, electronic, mechanical, photocopying, recording, scanning, or otherwise without written permission from the publisher. It is illegal to copy this book, post it to a website, or distribute it by any other means without permission.

This novel is entirely a work of fiction. The names, characters and incidents portrayed in it are the work of the author's imagination. Any resemblance to actual persons, living or dead, events or localities is entirely coincidental.

Warning: the unauthorized reproduction or distribution of this copyrighted work is illegal. Criminal copyright infringement, including infringement without monetary gain, is investigated by the FBI and is punishable by up to 5 years in prison and a fine of $250,000.

Book cover design by Deliciously Dark Designs

Photography: James Critchley Photography

Proofreading: Norma's Nook Proofreading

1

MAEVE

Two years ago…

Despair claws at my insides, threatening to drown me in a sea of darkness so black it feels like there's no escape.

The ornately carved coffin probably cost a fortune. My father's answer for everything is to spend money, but it won't bring her back. Within a matter of minutes, she'll be buried in the wooden box in the cavernous hole next to it.

Perhaps I was a fool to be so blissfully ignorant of the danger surrounding our family. I never imagined my world could turn upside down this fast. My mind can't stop repeating one sentence over and over like a broken record.

She can't be dead.

Four words I wish were true with all of my heart. Maybe it's the reason I can't stop replaying them, as I don't want to believe that she's dead.

It feels like yesterday that I sat in the kitchen, eating her pancakes and joking with her about the neighbors. That was a week and one day ago. The same day that my father returned home and gave us the news. It's hard to comprehend that is the last memory I'll ever have of her.

Your mother is dead.

Father said those four simple words and nothing more. No explanation for her death or tears shed as he told the four of his children. The solemn tone of his voice was the only sign that her loss moved him. As always, his dark eyes held no emotion and were dry, even though he had lost his wife of thirty-two years.

It feels like I've been free-falling ever since. Grief is the most unexplainable sensation in the world. No one and nothing can prepare you for the hole left when someone close to you dies.

I glance briefly at my father, noticing he has the same emotionless expression on his face. He keeps his arms crossed over his chest, staring into the deep hole. I've known for a long time my father is a broken man. His demons have haunted him for as long as I can remember.

My mother always used to defend him, insisting that he loved my brothers and me. I never felt his love, so I can't believe it exists.

My two older brothers, Rourke and Killian, are the spitting image of him: the same blank stares and brooding expressions. Neither one allows the tears to fall as we put her to rest. Only my younger brother, Kieran, shows his emotions. He clutches my hand, crying as the priest talks of holy things and her passing to a *better place*. I can't believe that for one second. My mom was better here with our family and me.

We all are mourning her loss and handling it differently, but I can't fathom how my older brothers can keep the tears back. Father taught them to harden their emotions from a young age, training them to fill top ranks within the clan.

I return my attention to the coffin which is waiting to be lowered into the hole in the ground. After father gave us the news, he left it to Gael, his friend and second-in-command, to explain what happened to our mom.

The Italians killed her because of a war my father

was fighting, and she became collateral in his bid for more power.

I'm not naturally angry, but I've never felt so much rage toward another human being before. Her death is my father's fault, and it should have been him we are burying today, not her. Mom was the glue that held this family together. Now, we're hardly a family at all.

My brothers won't talk to me about what happened. Even Kieran has been shutting me out. Mom was the only person I could talk to, and we were the best of friends. The relentless stream of tears flood down my face as the pain is unbearable.

Gael squeezes my other hand tightly. If it weren't for him, I don't know what I'd do. He is the chief of the clan and one of my father's closest friends.

He has barely left my side since her death, supporting me while my family pushes me away. It's a dangerous game since my desire for him has simmered for years. As we spend more time together, I find it impossible not to long for a deeper connection with him. The intensity of my feelings for him is growing daily.

The priest finishes the blessing, calling my brothers and father forward to lower the coffin into the grave. The sexism that rules this family shines through, as I wanted to be involved, but my father dismissed the idea.

They each take the end of an emerald green rope under the coffin and lift the weight, lowering her into the hole. I struggle to draw the air into my lungs as I watch her disappear into the ground. The river of tears flows faster down my cheeks.

I watch as my brothers move away from the hole. My father glances at the coffin for a few brief moments before turning his back without a word.

Life without my mom seems pointless. When you lose someone so close to you so suddenly, it is hard not to question what the point of it all is.

My uncle Blaine steps forward and throws some flowers into his sister's grave. He is so much like my mom in both looks and temperament. Blaine is hurting badly over this, and the tears streaming down his face are a testament to that.

Torin, my father's brother, steps forward and does the same.

Gael wraps an arm around my shoulders, pulling me against him tightly. "Do you want to throw some flowers in?" he asks, holding out a small bunch of yellow roses, which were her favorite.

I nod in response. "Yes, but I'll wait until people

leave." I need time alone with her coffin to say goodbye.

Her death and then the funeral happened too fast. Four weeks ago, we were out shopping for my prom dress to wear. I went to prom and finished my senior year at high school. We had lunch before heading to the mall, having a great time trying on clothes together. I'm not sure I'll ever come to terms with the fact we'll never do that again.

Once it's just Gael and me, I move closer. It's an unreal feeling, staring at a box in the ground housing the body of a person I loved so much. I don't know how to say goodbye.

Gael gives me space, standing at a distance from me. I try to find the words I want to say to her, but the pain blocks my throat. Slowly, I sink to my knees at the edge of the hole, trying to get closer to her.

"I already miss you so much, Mom," I sob, shaking my head. "I can't believe you're gone. It's not fair." Tears stream down my face relentlessly, as I wish I could float away and no longer feel the pain. "Please come back."

I hear Gael approach, his shoes crunching on the dried fall leaves littering the floor. "Careful, little dove," he says, his voice softer than I've ever heard it.

"The edge could fall in." He sets a hand on my shoulder firmly, urging me to stand.

I swallow hard and rise to my feet, taking one step back into his warm embrace. For a while, I remain there, staring, unable to let go. I wish with all my heart this were a terrible nightmare that I'll wake from any minute.

It feels too real. My mother is gone, and she's never coming back.

It's all my father's fault.

Anger mixes with grief as I find his figure in the distance, walking away without a backward glance. He did not say one word over her grave or shed a single tear, making me wish he was the one in the coffin and not her more than ever.

Gael keeps his arm around me, holding me silently as I drop a few flowers into her grave. A pillar of support holding me up, as I feel like I could drift away into nothingness if he wasn't here.

SIX MONTHS LATER...

"Morning, sis," Kieran says as I enter the kitchen.

I nod at him. "Morning." I glance around and

find Gael isn't here. He's normally always here by now. "Have you seen Gael?"

Kieran's brow furrows. "Didn't he tell you?"

My stomach twists at the tone of his voice. "Tell me what?"

He shakes his head. "Obviously not. He left for Europe last night, as dad assigned him a job over there."

Numbness spreads through my flesh like a disease. I blink a few times, wondering if I heard him correctly.

Europe.

"How long for?" I ask, wondering why Gael wouldn't have mentioned it yesterday morning.

Kieran's expression turns pitiful, which irritates me. "A year or two but it's not set in stone."

My heart pounds painfully in my chest as I quickly take a seat on the nearest barstool. I rest my head in my hands, trying to process the news. "Are you sure?" I murmur.

Kieran stands and wraps an arm around me. "Dad confirmed it with him three days ago, and I thought he would have told you."

Tears flood my eyes as I stare at the island surface, wishing I could disappear into the floor.

How could he leave me without a word?

I hold back my tears, knowing how pathetic it would be to cry in front of my brother. Gael means the world to me, and I can't believe he would leave without a goodbye. We've been getting close, but perhaps it was all one-sided.

"You okay, little sis?" Kieran asks.

I swallow hard, forcing away the tears. "Yeah, I can't believe Gael left without telling me."

"It is weird." Kieran takes a seat next to me, brow furrowed. "I know he's been there for you since we lost Mom."

Gael has been part of the family for years, which means no one finds it odd how much time I spent with him. None of my family realizes how I feel about him. He wasn't only helping me mourn; he was making me fall for him harder than ever.

The crushing sorrow over my mom's death, along with Gael's abandonment, is almost too much to live with. I grab a bagel off the counter, nibbling on it to distract my mind.

"What are you two talking about?" Rourke asks, entering the kitchen. He grabs a bagel off the counter and sits across from me.

Rourke is my eldest brother. He's always been my protector growing up. The harsh, violent man takes after his father, but the only difference is he cares about me.

Kieran shakes his head. "Why don't you mind your own business, Rourke?"

Rourke's eyes narrow. "No need to get your panties in a twist, knucklehead."

Kieran and Rourke are opposites, and they have always struggled to get along. Kieran grabs a bagel and heads out of the room without a word.

I sigh. "Why do you always have to wind him up?" I ask.

Rourke smirks. "It's not my fault he's so sensitive."

I roll my eyes and sip my coffee, leaving the half-eaten bagel. My stomach is too much of a mess after finding out Gael left.

"What's bothering you, Maeve?" Rourke asks.

It's strange for him to ask, as he is rarely up for talking. I shake my head. "I just found out Gael left."

Rourke's brow raises. "Aye, are you telling me he didn't tell you?"

I shake my head.

Rourke's crystal blue eyes almost shine in the spotlights as he stares at me with that same irritating pity. "It's probably for the best, though. Don't you think?"

I search my brother's eyes. "I don't understand. Why is it for the best?"

"Only an idiot would miss the way you look at him." He runs a hand through his golden-brown hair. "And the way he looks at you."

My stomach twists. Rourke has always been so perceptive. "I don't know what you are talking about."

Rourke waves his hand dismissively. "Deny it all you want. You should put Gael out of your mind for good." He grabs another bagel, taking a huge bite. "Father will arrange your marriage, and it won't be to Gael Ryan."

Tears prickle my eyes as I know my brother is right. He never sugarcoats the truth. That's not his style, but it doesn't make it hurt any less. "You don't understand," I murmur.

Rourke shakes his head. "No, I doubt I do." He reaches for my hand and squeezes it. "Try to put him out of your thoughts, and it won't be as hard while he's across the Atlantic."

I meet Rourke's gaze. "Did you send him away?" I ask.

Rourke's eyes flash with anger. "No. I may be a bastard, but I'm not our father. Gael was the one who put himself forward to go."

Gael wanted to leave, and the revelation makes it hurt more. I stand and turn away from him without a word.

"Maeve, where are you going?"

I don't turn around to face him as the tears stream down my face. "I need to be alone."

Rourke doesn't say another word as I charge out of the kitchen. My heart is pounding so hard as I rush up the stairs to my room. I can hardly see where I'm going as the tears cloud my vision, and I knock into Jane, our housekeeper. "Oh, I'm sorry."

Jane notices me crying. "Are you okay, Miss Callaghan?"

I shake my head. "Fine. I'm still struggling after my mother's death."

Her eyes flood with pity.

Why is it that everyone looks at me like that?

"Of course. If you ever need to talk, I'm here."

I force a smile. "Thanks." I dodge around her and open the door to my room, slamming it behind me. A river of tears spills down my face as I struggle to draw the air into my lungs.

After my mom's death, I didn't believe it could get worse. Now it feels like I'm grieving for Gael too. The pain doesn't match what I felt when my mother died, as he's still alive, but it only adds to my grief.

I dig my cell phone out of my pocket, hoping this is a mistake. My finger hovers over his name for a moment before I press it. The dial tone doesn't sound as it instantly goes to messaging.

'It's *Gael. Leave a message, and I might get back to you.*'

My tears fall faster as I swallow my pain. "Gael, it's Maeve." I try to steady my breathing. "Kieran just told me you left for Europe. Is that true?" My throat is in agony as I speak through the pain. "Why didn't you say goodbye?" I ask, unable to hold the tears back any longer as I cry down the phone. I feel utterly pathetic. "I need you to call me back, please." I cancel the call and drop my phone to the floor before slumping down next to it.

The pain I feel is intense. It has been six months since my mother died, but Gael leaving brings it all back, and it threatens to tear me apart again. It feels like I'm riding a wave of grief, struggling to find any stability in a world that no longer makes sense.

2

GAEL

Present-day...

Slowly my plan to move Ronan Callaghan out of the way is falling into place. The boss of the Callaghan Clan should be careful who he trusts.

The moment I fell for his daughter three years ago, I knew I would have to eliminate him from the equation if I wanted to claim her for myself.

As Ronan's second-in-command, I have a unique position that gives me more power than most realize. I spent my time in Europe undermining Ronan's efforts for revenge over the Morrone family on the other side of the Atlantic. Now I've been back for six months, and my plan to force him toward an alliance with the Bratva is working.

Twenty years ago, Ronan gave me meaning and a place to belong. He took a lost and damaged eighteen-year-old boy and turned him into a merciless killing machine. An act that will backfire on him in the months to come.

I can't deny the undercurrent of guilt I feel at my intention to betray him, but there is one thing I learned while spending two years away from Maeve. I can't live without her.

Ronan wouldn't entertain the idea of a coupling between his daughter and me because he wants her to marry a man who will further the clan's political and financial power. I fasten my tie, checking my appearance in the mirror.

The bright amber eyes staring back at me are no longer recognizable. I have turned into someone I no longer know, yet there is no stopping the path I walk. The reason will be in attendance at tonight's party.

Maeve Callaghan.

The Callaghan princess and only daughter of the clan's boss, she has been the bane of my existence ever since we got too close over two years ago. Maeve is my single weakness on this earth.

When I volunteered for the job in Europe, a part of me had convinced myself the reason was to sever ties with the forbidden beauty.

Deep down, I knew it would give me a power Ronan would never expect. He sent me to Europe to execute his plan for revenge by locating the Morrone's extended family and annihilating them.

Instead, I aggravated tensions from across the Atlantic, ensuring the pressure in Chicago heightened as I fed Ronan my side of the story. If I am to remove him from the equation, the only workable way is to start a war without anyone knowing I'm the cause.

I returned six months ago from Europe, having failed my task of locating the Morrone family's relatives. As I'd hoped, the city of Chicago was more unstable than ever.

I disappointed Ronan, but he believed me when I told him they were impossible to find despite my hunting in every corner of Europe. The man is a ruthless leader, but he has a weakness that I can't explain when it comes to me. Perhaps he saw a man just like him, broken and in need of fixing.

Tonight's party is going to be at Ronan's pub, The Shamrock, which is odd because he rarely uses his business establishments for clan parties. I don't know what this important announcement is that he has to make, which makes me uneasy. Ronan rarely keeps things from me, but he insisted I don't need to know prior.

All I know is that if it is a clan event, Maeve will be there, whether or not she wants to be. Ronan may not be big on caring for his children, but he likes to project this image of a happy Irish family behind the clan, even after Eloise's murder.

I crack my neck as there has been damage to the relationship I had with Maeve ever since my disappearance to Europe. Damage that I'm struggling to repair.

The first moment I saw her after two years apart was at her twenty-first birthday party. Ronan called me to the house to discuss business a few days after I'd returned, proving how little he cared about his daughter's milestone birthday.

My world stood still when I looked into her eyes again. Maeve Callaghan had morphed from a beautiful teenager into the sexiest woman I'd ever seen. I knew at that moment all my efforts to undermine Ronan were justified. The sparks between us were as intense, if not more so.

Then I saw she was on the arm of another man, and rage coursed through my veins as it turned me into an animal. I couldn't do anything about it since I abandoned her without a word, until I walked into the library to find him forcing himself on her, despite her pleas to stop. The man ended up in hospital with a few broken ribs, but I made sure he kept his mouth shut.

There's one thing I'm certain of: I would kill for Maeve Callaghan.

After one last look at myself in the mirror, I turn away. Staying away from Maeve is becoming increasingly difficult as I try to ensure my plan goes off without a hitch. If it is successful, then Maeve will never know who was behind her father's downfall.

There is no dousing the blazing heat of our undeniable connection despite her anger with me. The fire rekindled the moment our eyes met, perhaps hotter than ever as rage always intensifies other emotions.

I grab my car keys off the side table in my entrance hall and walk out of my home, locking the door. Apprehension prickles over my skin as I walk into the unknown. Ronan rarely keeps things from me, but he has been increasingly unpredictable the longer time passes since his wife's murder.

I unlock my car and slide into the driver's seat of my SUV. The roads are busy as I turn over the key in the ignition and pull out onto the street. My cell phone rings over the hands-free, and I answer it.

Seamus speaks, "Gael, do you know what this announcement is about tonight, then?"

Seamus is one of my closest friends and one of

only two people who knows my insane plan. It makes him jittery, though. "No, Ronan wouldn't tell me." I rub a hand across the back of my neck. "He insisted on keeping it a secret until the announcement."

There's a few moments of silence on the other end. "You don't think he knows, do you, lad?"

That is one thing I'm confident of. "No. I'm certain he doesn't."

I hear Seamus tapping something on the other end. "I hope you are right. I ain't going to make it tonight. Can you fill me in?"

My brow furrows as all the clan members have to attend. "Won't Ronan notice you're missing?"

Seamus is the head enforcer of the clan, and Ronan always expects him to attend clan events. "Nah, I explained to him my wife is sick, and I have to look after the kids."

"Sorry to hear that. I hope she feels better soon." I pull off the main road, taking a shortcut to Beverly, where the pub is. "I'll fill you in tomorrow."

"Thanks." He cancels the call.

I focus my mind on keeping my head in the game. When planning a takedown like I am, you have to be hyper-focused on everything around you. Unfortunately, my mind is distracted by one thing: seeing Maeve.

She hates my guts after I left her without a word while she was grieving her mom. I knew full well that her feelings for me were as strong as mine were for her. It was too dangerous to flirt with such a forbidden line without a plan in place, even if it was what we both wanted.

Ronan isn't a forgiving man. He would have killed me in a heartbeat if he knew the sick thoughts I have every time I so much as look at Maeve. I pull into the pub's parking lot and park at the front, noticing Ronan's town car nearby.

Maeve and her brothers would have accompanied their father here. My brow furrows when I see Spartak Volkov and his two children entering the pub too.

Why the fuck would Ronan invite the Volkov Bratva?

I wanted him to make an alliance with them, but on my terms. If I can't control what he agrees to with them, then I have no power to eradicate the alliance, either. Anxiety claws at me as I'm always in control, but Ronan is throwing me a curveball.

I get out of my car and march toward the pub, where loud Irish music plays. As I enter, the heavy drum of people chattering underlines the music. I clench my jaw as I can barely hear myself think.

Instantly, I find Ronan standing near the back of

the pub with Spartak, Maxim, and Viktoria Volkov. There is no way that I can question him over his guests in front of them. I sigh and turn my attention to the bar. I need a drink to focus my mind.

The bar is busy, but I catch Aisling's eye. She gives me a nod, pouring my favorite without me having to ask.

"Jameson whiskey on the rocks." She places it down on the bar.

"Thanks." I smile, but it feels forced.

"No worries. Have a good night." She winks.

Aisling has had a thing for me for years, but I've never indulged her. There was never a spark between us, at least, not that I felt.

Someone claps me on the shoulder, making me tense. "Hey lad, what's this all about then." I relax as I recognize Tiernan's voice, the other man who knows about my plan. He's also head of security for the clan.

I meet his questioning gaze. "I'm afraid for once I'm as clueless as you are."

His brow furrows. "Unusual." I can tell he has the same thought as Seamus, but he doesn't voice it. If Ronan knew of my betrayal, he wouldn't be throwing a party, and it would be far more sinister than this.

I glance at Ronan and nod. "I think it must

involve the Russians, though."

His eyes widen. "What the fuck is Spartak doing here?"

I take a sip of my whiskey, enjoying the fiery burn as it slides down my throat. "I'm sure we'll find out soon enough."

A sense of awareness prickles over my skin as I glance toward the pub's entrance. Maeve Callaghan walks in wearing a stunning powder blue evening gown that highlights the blue in her vibrant eyes.

I'm surprised that she arrived after her father.

She looks around the pub, and her eyes stop the moment she finds me by the bar. A small smile twists onto her luscious red lips as if she knows what she does to me, turning up looking so damn beautiful.

"If you would excuse me," I say to Tiernan.

His eyes follow mine. "You're in too deep, lad." There's a serious glint in his eyes. "It's a dangerous game you're playing."

I meet my friend's gaze. "I know." I have known the dangers for long enough, and it is why I'm taking precautions to cement our fates together. Tiernan is right though; I should keep my distance until such time, but it is impossible. Maeve is like gravity, pulling me to her.

I walk away from Tiernan.

Maeve is trying hard not to look in my direction, which is adorable. I can't deny I enjoy the little game we play.

"Hello, little dove," I murmur, making sure no one else can hear.

Her lips purse temptingly, and she moves her dazzling blue eyes to me. "Hey, Gael," she says, clenching her jaw. She tries so hard to maintain that anger toward me, but she's not very good at it.

"Do you have any idea what this party is all about?" I ask, struggling to keep my eyes from wandering over her flawless body, a body I long to explore every inch of. The intensity of my gaze makes her squirm as tension flares between us.

Her slender neck moves as she gulps. "No, Father has told none of us. At least, that's what my brothers say. It won't surprise me if everyone knows except for me." Her brow furrows. "Don't you know?"

I shake my head. "No. Your father didn't fill me in on this one."

"That's strange," Maeve muses, twirling a strand of hair around her finger. "Why are the Russians here?"

"I don't know. It must have something to do with the announcement." I meet her gaze, which burns with a longing that matches my own.

"How have you been?" I ask, trying to prolong our conversation as much as possible. Merely being in her presence helps ease the frantic thoughts racing through my mind.

She sighs. "Fine. I get bored since Father insists I can't get a job."

Ronan has always been overly protective of Maeve, which puzzles me. He rarely shows he cares about his daughter, but he sticks his nose into every aspect of her life. "Can't you get a job online nowadays or something?"

She rolls her eyes. "That is too dangerous for a Callaghan."

I shake my head. "That makes little sense."

There's a sadness burning in her beautiful blue eyes. Sometimes, I wish she knew the plan I'm meticulously working on to free her from the prison her father traps her in.

"He's forcing me to remain bored, unemployed, and single until he marries me off to someone," Maeve says.

The suggestion makes my blood boil. "I don't think so," I say quickly, dismissing the idea. "Your father has never mentioned an arranged marriage to me."

A flash of hope enters Maeve's eyes. "Really? He's

always hinting at it to me."

It's not necessarily a matter Ronan would consult me on, as it isn't clan business. "I couldn't say for sure." I swallow hard, wondering if Ronan would be insane enough to pair Maeve up with Maxim Volkov. "He hasn't ever mentioned it to me, is all."

Our eye contact lingers as the conversation stutters, heightening the tension between us. I could drown in her beautiful eyes, forgetting everyone and everything around us. Maeve licks her bottom lip, drawing my attention to it.

I feel my cock harden and bite back a groan that tries to escape my mouth. Clearing my throat, I ask, "Shall I get you a drink, little dove?"

It is hell on earth being so close to someone you want so badly but not having the power to take her.

"Sure, I'll have a glass of champagne."

I smile. "Always have had expensive taste, haven't you, lass?"

She blushes and shrugs. "I guess."

After a few moments of lingering eye contact, I force myself to turn away from her. Aisling's brow hitches when she sees me approaching again. "Slow down, Gael, if you want to walk out of here tonight."

I chuckle. "I'm ordering for someone else." I rub

a hand across the back of my neck. "Can I get a glass of champagne, please?"

Aisling's expression turns stern, as she knows I'm getting a drink for a woman. "Sure." She turns to retrieve the drink. I get a few irritated glares at the bar since I skipped the queue, not once, but twice.

She places the glass down on the bar.

"Thanks." I turn back into the crowd, searching for Maeve.

I'm sidetracked by the sound of my boss's voice over the microphone. "Can I have everyone's attention for a few minutes?"

Maeve's blue dress catches my attention as she stands near the stage, facing away from me.

I hasten my steps toward her as everyone turns silent, listening to Ronan.

"Thank you." He gazes out over the crowd like a king looking down on all his subjects. "I'm sure you are all wondering why I've brought you here tonight." He pauses for effect. "I have an important announcement to make."

My brow furrows as all of his attention moves to Maeve.

"My little girl is engaged to Maxim Volkov."

Over my dead body.

My footsteps falter a short way from Maeve as I

stare at my boss, wondering if I heard him right.

"Their union will strengthen both the Volkov Bratva and Callaghan Clan, giving us more power over the city together," he continues.

I don't listen to any more of his bullshit, continuing to walk toward Maeve. The desperate need to reach her drives me. The rage inside of me is an inferno. I will not stand by while her father sells her off to the Russians. Maxim is renowned for his brutality.

"Come up here, Maeve," Ronan commands.

My stomach churns as I stop inches from her. Maeve turns to flee, only to bump into me instead. Our eyes meet, and the sorrow in hers cuts me to the core. All I want to do is assure her she will not marry Maxim, not so long as I'm still breathing.

Instead, under the watchful eye of my boss, I know I have to do what is expected. I can't let her flee. She has to play her part, as disrespecting her father in front of these people is dangerous.

I won't stand by while she marries another man. I would die before I allowed her to be sold to the Volkov family.

Maeve is mine.

I'll bring the city of Chicago to its knees before I let anyone else have her.

3

MAEVE

*H*is announcement has to be a sick joke.

I stare into the soulless eyes of my father, knowing deep down it isn't. Maxim smirks at me, and his smile is enough to make me sick to my stomach. I don't want to know the perverse thoughts spreading through his mind. Numbness spreads through me like a disease.

I won't marry Maxim Volkov. As long as I have an ounce of freedom, I'll fight this every step of the way.

My father's eyes narrow. "Come here, Maeve."

I shake my head, knowing I can't stand up there and play a part in my father's bullshit plan. When I turn around, my heart skips a beat. Gael blocks my way, staring at me intensely. "Maeve, indulge him, as disrespecting him in front of all these people will anger him."

I search Gael's beautiful amber eyes, wondering if he knew about this engagement all along. The man who left me in my time of need has kicked me in the gut all over again. If it wasn't bad enough that he ran away without saying goodbye, he also lied to me about this. My father rarely keeps anything from Gael, so it's the only explanation.

Resigned to my fate, I turn and drift through the crowd toward my father, a man who has lost sight of everything that matters.

Does he think this little of me?

Spartak and Maxim Volkov are both renowned for their psychopathic tendencies. I have no intention of being tied to the Volkov family, at least not while I'm still breathing.

My father has stabbed me in the back and twisted the knife. I could hardly forgive him for my mom's murder and now this. He's using me as a bargaining chip in the same war that killed her. The man never has and never will care about me.

I stand next to him on the stage, feeling my skin crawl as he grabs my hand. "To Maxim and Maeve," he says.

I've never hated someone as much as I hate

him. It's a disease that threatens to consume me. The rage is so acute it makes me wish I could kill him, but I know I can't. Murder is something I could never pull off. It may be in my DNA, but I can't imagine what it takes to actually murder someone.

The cheers and clapping of the crowd fade into the background. My thoughts are so loud I can hardly register anything around me.

Maxim Volkov is Bratva. The Russians, along with the Italians, are our natural enemy. My father thinks a marriage between our families can wipe away years of animosity, but I know it won't work. Alliances in the city of Chicago are fleeting.

It proves how disposable I am to my father. My fate as the bride to a Volkov will be brutal. I find my brothers standing together in the crowd. Kieran's eyes are wide, which proves to me this engagement is news to him.

I turn my attention to Rourke and Killian, who both look unmoved by the news. They knew about this, and I remember Rourke's words the day Gael left for Europe.

Father will arrange your marriage, and it won't be to Gael Ryan.

Rourke knew this would happen a long while ago,

even if my father hadn't chosen my fiancé at the time.

My father turns to me. "You will not fight this, Maeve."

I look into his dark eyes and shake my head. "No, I won't."

A flicker of surprise enters his expression. "Really? I expected some snarky comment at least."

I raise a brow. "Oh, sorry to disappoint you." I have no intention of fighting this, as there's no point. By the morning, I will have left town. I'm not sticking around to be offered to Maxim like nothing more than a sacrificial lamb.

My father turns to Maxim and Spartak. "There are no objections from my daughter."

Maxim smirks. "It wouldn't matter if she objected, as she doesn't have a choice." The evil glare he gives me chills me to the core.

"When is the wedding?" I ask my father, glancing away from Maxim.

"Four days from now." He narrows his eyes. "It should be plenty of time to make all the arrangements."

Spartak approaches me and grabs my chin between his finger and thumb, forcing me to look him in the eyes. "Such a pretty girl," he muses, his Russian accent thick.

I swallow hard at the unreadable look in his almost black eyes. He turns to his son, speaking to him in Russian. It's unnerving not knowing what he says, even more so when they both laugh.

"You will do nicely," Spartak says, releasing me from his grasp.

I try to claw back the fear, knowing that whatever he thinks he's going to do with me, it won't happen. My father's subtle hints that at some point I'd be married off prepared me. Not to mention Rourke's warning that father would choose my husband.

I have enough cash to start over, find a job, and escape Chicago forever. My father will hunt me, but I'll keep moving. Life on the run is far kinder than a life beholden to a man like Maxim.

"Well, it was nice speaking with you both." I glance over at Maxim. "I guess I'll see you in four days."

Maxim smirks. "I can't wait." The tone of his voice is enough to make my stomach churn. I won't marry him unless they chain me to the altar. Knowing my father, he would take those precautions if necessary. However, I have no intention of getting near enough to the pulpit.

I don't reply to him and turn away, walking off the stage into the crowd. My heart is pounding in my ears as I move through people chatting, searching for Kieran. I have to know if he was aware of this.

A forceful hand wraps around my wrist, and I'm dragged from the main pub area to a small, empty dining area at the back. My brow furrows as I glance at Gael, who looks manic. His amber eyes are glowing with what I can only describe as rage. "You can't marry Maxim."

I narrow my eyes, finding it difficult to believe he didn't know about this. "Don't pretend that you didn't know about the engagement." A lump forms in my throat. "It is not the first time you have betrayed me, and I'm sure it won't be the last."

"Betrayed you?" Gael growls. "You know nothing, little dove." He drags me further into the shadows, away from prying eyes, pushing me against a wall. "I did what I had to do."

Two years ago, he hurt me in ways he'll never understand. "You abandoned me when I needed you." My brow furrows. "You told me to go up on to that stage when all I wanted to do was run."

"Running wasn't the sensible option." He grabs my hips possessively, lighting me on fire. Gael has never touched me the way he's touching me right now. I forget everything and lose myself in his amber eyes, wishing this were all a nightmare. "What are you going to do?" he asks.

I search his eyes, wishing I could trust him with the truth. He would stop me if he knew my plan to run. "Nothing." I free myself from his grasp, ducking under his arm. "A Callaghan woman must behave and do as she's told." I glance back at him, memorizing his face. This moment is the last time I will set eyes on the man I've wanted for so long. "Goodbye, Gael."

His eyes flash with anger, and he shakes his head. "No, it is not goodbye, little dove." He walks toward me, lowering his voice. "I'll find a way out of this for you. Trust me." He grabs my hand, trying to get me to listen.

I wish I could. Since he abandoned me, the most important thing I've learned is that no one will look out for me. The only person I can rely on is myself. I yank my hand free. "You've never given me a reason to trust you." I turn away and pace through into the main pub, heading toward the exit.

After tonight, I'll never see him again. Once I'm on the run, I'll leave behind everyone I care about. Staying isn't an option, though. Maxim doesn't strike me as a man who would allow his wife any freedom to visit family or friends. I lose them either way, but running means I won't be subjected to a life with a man who is certifiably insane.

I lost Gael once, which is why I know I can do it again.

My father underestimated me, but that has been the story of my life.

If he thinks I'm going to lie down and accept Maxim as my husband, he can think again. I won't be here by the morning. Ever since I was eighteen years old, I knew my father could pull something like this.

He made comments about me stepping up and doing my duty for the family, so it prepared me to run at any moment. I grab the rucksack out from under my bed, which is always packed with my fake ID and a supply of cash to get me up and running somewhere new.

Maddison City, in Wisconsin, is where I plan to go. I even have the train schedule and can get a train out of the city before midnight tonight. I check my watch, noticing I have an hour and a half to make it to the station. I've booked an Uber to meet me at the bus stop just half a mile down the street.

This part of the city is riddled with Callaghan Clan members, which means I need to be unrecognizable. I head into the bathroom and grab some makeup wipes, taking off the light makeup I wore to the party. The opposite style of mine has to be grunge, so I put on heavy eyeliner and loads of mascara. It's amazing how different makeup can make you look.

Once satisfied I don't look like myself, I turn my attention to my clothes.

I walk into the closet and pull off the blue evening gown, hanging it up. I grab a pair of jogging pants and an oversized sweater, which belong to Kieran.

Once dressed, I return to my room and check myself in the mirror. There is no way anyone would recognize me now. I grab the rucksack off the bed and shrug it onto my shoulders.

A sadness weighs on my chest as I do a final spin, taking in my childhood bedroom for the last time. I've never known a home away from Chicago. It feels like I'm leaving my mom since all our happy memories were here, but if I stay, I'll be ripped away from here, anyway.

I hate my father for doing this to me. Since Mom died, our fragile relationship has been strained, but this is the icing on the cake. I'll never forgive him for it.

The worst thing is I have to leave my brothers without saying goodbye. I love all of them, but Kieran and I are the closest. It hurts that I'm about to lose the three of them.

The window of my room looks over a flat roof below. It's an escape route I've used many times when I was younger, sneaking out to parties while my father was unaware. I force the window open and glance out, ensuring none of my father's guards are down on the ground.

Once I'm confident, I jump out of the window carefully and onto the roof below. I scale to the ground from the roof, sighing once I'm in the yard without falling. The yard is clear, and there are no flashlights between me and the hole I cut in the fence when I was in high school.

No one has ever found it since I chose an overgrown area. I take a deep breath, not looking back at my childhood home, and sprint toward the gap. Getting caught is not an option, and until I'm out of the city limits, I'm in danger of being spotted.

I'm thankful when I get to the fence and find the hole, chucking my rucksack through first. Then, I climb through it, wincing as the thorns pierce through my jogging pants. Finally, I make it through to the other side and grab my rucksack, slinging it over my shoulder.

The walk through the park is longer than on the street, but I must stay out of sight. Once I'm in the Uber, then I will feel more comfortable.

My heart skips a beat as I notice two dark figures walking toward me. I keep my face down and walk faster, hoping that they aren't my father's men.

A familiar voice hits my ears. "Ronan can't sell her to the Russians. She's his blood, for fuck's sake."

My stomach dips as it's Gael.

"Aye, the guy has lost the plot. Who wants to get in bed with the Russians, anyway?" Tiernan, one of my father's men, replies.

I keep as far over as possible on the path as Gael will recognize me if he sees my face.

"I have to stop the wedding."

Hope and sadness mix as I realize there is nothing Gael can do. If he did something, my father would kill him. That's something I'm sure of. The only reason I feel hope bloom is because I've always clung to the possibility that he feels the same for me as I do for him.

"You will end up dead, lad. It's too risky." Tiernan replies as I walk past them.

Neither of them glances at me, almost unaware I'm there. I march away from them, knowing that lingering and eavesdropping won't help.

Gael will know by tomorrow that I ran away. My father will have an army searching for me, but I'll ensure they don't find me. I won't sit by while I'm sold as a pawn in a war that cost my mom her life.

4

GAEL

Six months later...

The weight of Maeve's decision still rests heavily on my shoulders as I walk toward the Callaghan Corp headquarters.

It frustrates me. I couldn't assure Maeve I'd get her out of the engagement. Instead, she ran without a word. Our last moment together replays over and over in my mind. I should have known she was going to run by the way she said goodbye.

Ronan has resources trying to locate her, and in the end, they'll succeed. I hate being separated from Maeve again, but it's bought me time. He rang me an hour ago, requesting I meet him at his legitimate business headquarters. He didn't want to detail the reason on the phone.

I walk through the sliding doors into the modern, striking entrance hall of the office block. The secretary on the front desk smiles at me, and I smile back. A few men in suits give me an odd look as they pass by out of the building.

I don't fit in here. I may wear an expensive suit, but the neck and hand tattoos are impossible to hide. Ronan rarely requests clan members visit the corporation's headquarters since he likes to keep the legitimate part of his operation separate from the criminal part.

I walk to the elevator and call it, feeling anxiety twist my stomach. Confidence has always been my forte, but the longer I silently work against my boss to undermine him, the more nervous I am that he'll figure out my plan.

The elevator dings, signaling its arrival. Three women filter out of the elevator, passing me. I slide inside and hit the top floor, where Ronan's office is located as CEO. The only way up there is if you have the security code, which it requests. I tap it in, and the elevator rises.

Once it arrives on Ronan's floor, I step out and walk toward his office. It's late, so all of his staff have gone home. The door to his office is ajar, and I see him standing at the window with his back to me.

I clear my throat and push it open. "You wanted to see me, sir?" I ask.

He continues staring out over the city of Chicago. Few people have such amazing views. "Yes, I have a task for you." He turns to face me, dark eyes blazing with purpose. "It's a task I can only entrust to you, Gael."

Little does he know I'm the last person on this earth he should trust. "Aye, what is it?"

Ronan draws in a deep breath. "The PI has located Maeve."

I feel my pulse skitter beneath my skin as I stare blankly at my boss. The eyes are the window into the soul, and I have learned how to black out that window. I hide the rising turmoil inside of me. They located her faster than I expected, but I'm ready for this.

After Maeve disappeared the morning after her father announced her engagement, my plan changed. Maeve offered me the perfect catalyst for a breakdown in relations between the Russians and the clan.

I clench my jaw. "Do you want me to retrieve her?"

Ronan runs a hand through his hair and walks toward the safe in the corner.

His silence unnerves me, but I watch as he opens

it and pulls out a large manilla envelope. He walks toward me and places it in my hand. "Yes, this is her location." Ronan has handed the man who has plotted his downfall for three years the fucking key.

As I look into his dark eyes, I don't feel the guilt I expect. Ronan took me in and gave me a place to belong when I needed it. He saved me from a life on the run. I didn't believe the day would come that I'd happily betray him, but it's crazy what love can make you do. "I will not let you down," I lie.

Ronan claps me on the shoulder. "I know you won't, lad."

There's a small twinge of guilt as I stare into my mentor's eyes. "When do you want me to leave?"

"As soon as possible. We don't want to risk Maeve leaving Madison." Ronan's expression turns stern. "I've already alerted Spartak that I found her. He expects his son to have a bride any day now, and we can't disappoint him."

Idiot.

The smart thing to do would've been to keep his mouth shut until he had Maeve here in Chicago. His impatience will benefit me. The tensions between the two powerful organizations will heighten when he doesn't deliver on his promise. "Got it."

The sooner I can get my hands on her, the better.

I have to ensure she is somewhere safe, away from her father. A ridiculous notion as fathers are supposed to protect their daughters. Instead, he is selling her to a monster, all so he can gain an advantage over the Morrone family.

Who will protect her if I don't?

I know that it's not only a need to protect her that drives me and that I want her for my selfish reasons. Maeve is my obsession, my world, and I intend to take her for myself, no matter the consequences.

Although I respected Ronan at one time, he lost it when he announced Maeve's engagement to a man known for beating women.

Some women enjoy the rough treatment, but Maxim takes it a step too far. Maeve doesn't strike me as that kind of woman. Although I, too, enjoy the darker side of sex, I can change for her. I can learn to be gentle for the woman who has held my heart for three years.

"I'll leave for Madison tonight," I say, running a hand across the back of my neck. "Is there anything else?"

Ronan nods. "Yes, don't let her get in your head, Gael." He shakes his head. "I know you two are close, but she has to do her duty for the family."

Bullshit.

The engagement isn't about duty. It's about Ronan's warped quest for revenge that knows no bounds. "Aye, I won't." She doesn't need to get in my head, as I have made my mind up.

Chicago will burn for his mistake. Ronan will burn for his mistake.

Once I carry out my plan, the entire city will be in chaos, and I will claim my prize: the Callaghan princess.

I'M one sick son of a bitch.

I fix my attention on her pert, firm breasts bouncing in her too-tight top as she serves dirty perverts their drinks. Six months without seeing her has only deepened my sick obsession with the Callaghan princess. Maeve doesn't suit this place, but she looks happier than I've ever seen her.

I feel a little jealous that she's found happiness away from me, and it angers me she works here every night as other men look at her like a piece of meat. No man is allowed to look at what is mine.

Her golden, long hair flows around her shoulders in elegant, soft waves, and her bright red lipstick emphasizes her deliciously pouty lips that I have longed to kiss for far too long. I feel like a predator stalking its prey in the shadows, waiting for the opportune moment to pounce.

Maeve is unaware that I'm here. If she knew, then she'd run. I can't risk her running as I'm here to save her from Maxim, not bring her to him. Other than my two closest friends, no one knows the plan that has been in motion for three years.

Ronan is blissfully unaware of my feelings for his daughter, unlike his son, Rourke. Rourke has taken the role of protector to Maeve, which is why I can't understand him accepting her marriage to Maxim. He's confronted me frequently to keep my hands to myself when I'm with his sister.

I have resisted temptation no matter how difficult, knowing that I had to bide my time. Three years of resisting have finally ended. The moment Ronan announced her engagement to Maxim, the prospect of another man touching her, let alone a fucking Russian, made my blood boil.

Maeve turns to grab a bottle off of the bar, drawing my attention to her beautiful, firm ass. An ass I have wanted to spank for so damn long. I grit my teeth, trying to focus my mind on anything but her body.

My problems started when the Morrone family

murdered Maeve's mother. Remy Morrone, to be exact: the don to the powerful Italian crime family residing in Chicago. Before her death, Maeve and I had little to do with each other.

Ronan, as always, was emotionally unavailable. Hellbent on getting his revenge rather than taking care of his children. In her father's absence, I expected her brothers to help her through it, but the loss shocked them too. They weren't in a place to support their sister, so Maeve leaned on me.

It was impossible not to feel the life-altering chemistry that flared between us as we got to know each other better. I knew Maeve felt it as well, and she wanted me with as much conviction as I wanted her. It got to a point when I knew I had to put some distance between us before I crossed a dangerous line with no plan in place.

Ronan mentioned the job he needed doing in Europe, and I saw an opportunity. An opportunity to get some distance but also remove the one thing standing between us getting together. Her father. It was a week before Maeve's nineteenth birthday, which is another reason she was so angry with me.

I told myself the reason I took the job was to sever my connection with Maeve, despite knowing it was so I could work against my boss from thousands of miles away.

The connection I share with the beautiful Irish princess is unbreakable. It was cowardly to leave and not say goodbye to her. I repeatedly listened to the desperate voicemails she left on my cell phone, begging me to come back. No matter how badly I wanted to, I knew I couldn't. Not until the groundwork of my plan was in place.

Not to mention, Maeve didn't know how out of control I was—on the precipice of making a grave mistake that would put both our lives in danger. Ronan would kill me for touching his daughter, who he views as a valuable asset.

I'm a tortured man with tastes that no innocent young woman like Maeve would ever desire. It didn't matter that I'd put thousands of miles between us. For two years, she remained the object of my obsession and the solo star in all of my twisted fantasies.

A guy bumps into my table, spilling half of my Irish whiskey. "What the fuck?" I growl, glaring at the drunk idiot.

He holds his hands up. "Sorry, I didn't see you there." He pales as his eyes glide to the tattoo on my neck. "What were you drinking? I'm on my way to the bar to order another round. I'll replace it for you."

I narrow my eyes at him. "Jameson whiskey."

He nods. "I'll bring it to you."

I don't say a word, returning my attention to the object of my obsession. Maeve's smile drives me wild as she speaks to one of her co-workers.

Damn it.

My cock is hard in my pants, and my heart is pounding like a beating drum in my head. Maeve is a drug. A drug that I can't give up.

I've sat in the shadows on the mezzanine of the club for two hours now, watching her like a perverted stalker. I could watch her forever.

I knock back the rest of my whiskey, shutting my eyes. I pinch the bridge of my nose, feeling the conflict inside of me weighing heavily on my soul. I'm not conflicted over my decision to double-cross Ronan. I'm conflicted over revealing my true nature to the woman I love.

The beat of my heart is frantic. It's the same every single time I'm in her presence. It's as though she calls out to the most basal, primal male part of me, driving me wild. I get wound up by every damn thing she does.

I know how wrong it is to want this girl. She's

seventeen years younger than me, and I've known her most of her life. Maeve is beautiful both inside and out. My past is dark, and I'm not sweet like her. I'm a monster dressed in a suit.

My cell rings, breaking through my chaotic thoughts. I dig it out of my pocket, and my stomach dips at the name on the screen.

Ronan.

Ignoring his call will only make him nervous.

"Hey, Ronan," I say, clenching my jaw as I speak. It's hard to hold up a charade with a man who mentored me, and, ironically, the one person who took a chance on me will end up regretting that decision.

He never used to be so hellbent on power and money. The family used to be important to him, but he lost sight of that.

If his plan to unite the Callaghan and Volkov families brings ruin for the Morrone family, what happens then? The Russians won't wait for us to turn on them, leaving Maeve's fate in their hands.

"Are you in Madison now?" he asks.

I swallow hard. "Yeah, I've tracked Maeve to a club, and I'm waiting for the right moment to snatch her."

Ronan lets out a breath of relief. "Grand news. I knew I could count on you, lad."

The lead weight of guilt sinks deeper into my stomach. He can't count on me, and once everything comes to a head, he'll wish he never gave a chance to Gael Ryan, the broken eighteen-year-old kid he saved from prison, seeing potential in him.

The danger I'll bring to the clan will be unprecedented when I remove him from the equation. I can't find it in me to change my mind, no matter how much loyalty I have to the clan. Maeve is more important to me than anything else on this planet. I'll burn down the entire city of Chicago if it means she stays with me.

"Sure, is there anything else, sir?" I ask.

Ronan is silent for a moment. "Remember, don't let her get in your head, whatever you do," he warns.

That ship sailed a long time ago. Maeve is ingrained in me so deeply there's no way I can ever get her out. Even spending two years thousands of miles away from her couldn't get her out of my head.

"Of course not. I'll update you shortly." I grind my teeth, knowing that in a matter of hours, he will panic. My disappearance will shock everyone.

"Thanks, lad. See you soon." He cancels the call.

I clutch my empty whiskey tumbler, wondering

where that asshole is with my replacement. I have to resist the urge to throw it against the wall. Rage has always been my go-to emotion—an emotion I struggle to get a handle on. The situation I'm in riles me up.

I shake my head and let go of the glass, glancing up in search of my angel.

When my eyes find her, she's talking to the asshole that bumped into my table. Her eyes are wide in surprise and lips pursed, which tells me the guy is hitting on her or being a jerk.

The rage coils through me again, infecting my bloodstream. Whichever it is, he'll regret it. I'm done watching my little dove from afar. It's time for me to trap her in my cage and never let her go.

5

MAEVE

The neon lights flash around me as I spin to grab the bottle of bourbon off the top shelf.

It's busy tonight, but then it always is.

Ever since I fled Chicago six months ago, I've worked at Jive, a nightclub in Madison. It's a refreshing change to have so much freedom and control over my own life. Despite missing my brothers very much, I know I made the right decision.

The regular jerks are here trying to get into my pants. Tonight is especially bad as I've had six men hit on me, and it's only ten o'clock, which is a sign that tonight will be a long one.

I pour two double jacks on the rocks and set them down in front of the customer. "Ten dollars, please."

The man grins at me in a way that makes my stomach sick. Jerk number seven, it would seem. "Of course, sweetheart. How about a date too?" His eyebrow rises.

They have taught us to flirt harmlessly with the customers, but I struggle with it "Unfortunately, we have a strict no dating customers policy here."

His brow furrows. "Wouldn't that mean you can't date any guy in Madison?"

I laugh. "Of course not. I'm sure there are plenty of guys in the city who have never been here."

He shakes his head and then places the cash in my hand. He grabs the drinks and walks away, mumbling to himself under his breath.

I can hear Ally, my best friend, back in Chicago, badgering me about getting laid. She insists it is the reason I'm so uptight. She is probably right, as it's not exactly normal for a twenty-two-year-old to be a virgin.

My father micromanaged my life, ensuring I never got too close to any men. The one boyfriend I had, Chad, didn't last long, as he was a jerk. I think the fundamental problem is that I've wanted one man for as long as I can remember.

Gael Ryan.

No other man has made me feel desire the way he

does. He's ten years younger than my father at thirty-nine, but he's been a part of the Callaghan Clan since he was eighteen years old. His story is sad as he had no family for most of his life. My father saw potential in him and took him under his wing, training him to be the clan chief.

I know deep down he is the main reason I ran. The mere thought of walking down the aisle and marrying Maxim Volkov while he watched was unbearable. It was easier to leave and never look back, even if I miss him every single day. I miss my brothers too, but for once, I put myself first.

One of the senior bartenders, Alexa, walks toward me with a frustrated look on her face. She gestures for me to follow her toward the back of the bar.

"What's wrong?" I ask.

She turns and crosses her arms over her chest. "Maeve, you need to work on your customer service skills." She shakes her head. "I've had a complaint from two guys already tonight."

I sigh. "Are you serious? Just because I don't want to flirt with some guy who thinks he's God's gift to women doesn't mean I'm bad at customer service." It's crazy the way this world works.

Alexa sighs. "Maeve, that's part of the job, girl."

She rubs her forehead. "You work behind the bar of a club, and you've got to be flirty with the guys."

I purse my lips together. "Okay, I'll try harder."

She smiles kindly. "I'm sorry to pull you up on it, and I get flirting isn't always natural for people." She shrugs. "Hank expects me to pull people up on any complaints we get." She holds a hand out to me. "No hard feelings, right?"

I nod and take her hand, shaking. "Of course." Alexa is nice and has always been supportive since I started working here. I understand she is only doing her job.

Alexa returns to work at the bar, and I follow. A customer spills a drink, and I grab a cloth to wipe it off. "I'll clean that up for you."

The lady smiles. "Thank you."

"Don't mention it," I say, throwing the cloth down and returning to the bar. A lull in customers gives me a welcome break as I grab my water bottle and take a sip. I worry the most about Kieran as we've always been close, but I know he can take care of himself. My younger brother is twenty years old now, and I have to stop worrying about him.

"Hello, did you hear me?" A man waves his hand in front of my face, pulling my attention away from my wandering thoughts.

"Oh, I'm sorry. What was it you wanted?"

"Bitch, don't make me say my order again," he growls at me, making me recoil.

I swallow hard and search for the manager, Hank. He must be out the back as he's not behind the bar. "I'm very sorry, sir. I didn't hear you."

The guy slams his hand on the bar, shocking me. "You're a fucking whore that should get a job in a strip club since you can't do this one," the man says.

A sudden sense of dread sweeps over me, drawing my attention behind him. My heart stills in my chest as amber eyes meet mine from across the room. Eyes that haunt my fantasies. They steal all the air from my lungs in an instant.

Gael Ryan is here.

If he's here, then it means one thing. They've found me. I'd hoped to remain in Madison, Wisconsin longer than this, lying low. It's no surprise my father didn't have time to come to me himself, sending his second-in-command instead.

His eye contact doesn't waver as he moves closer. They are expressionless as he makes his way toward the bar. My mouth dries as I take a moment to admire his rough beauty. The dark tattoo on his neck disappears below the collar of his crisp white shirt. He is wearing a dark checkered suit that fits him like a second skin. I feel desire tighten in my stomach. Gael doesn't know what he does to me.

The only emotion I should feel for him is anger. For the two years that he was away, I was furious at him. I swore I hated him and always would. Then twelve months ago, he strolled into my home to meet with my father as if nothing ever happened. He spoke to me in his normal, easy way, as if it he didn't leave without a word. As if it weren't difficult enough losing my mom, I had to lose him too.

It's so hard to hate him. A woman steps in his path, sending red-furious jealousy through me and breaking our lingering eye contact.

I tear my eyes from them and force myself to focus on the angry customer. "S-sir, I don't think that's fair." I shake my head, knowing that the best way to deal with assholes like him is to deescalate the situation fast. "Please repeat your order, and I will get right away for you." I don't want to find out what Gael will do to this guy. He's scary when he's angry.

I glance up to see Gael heading this way again. His dark eyes are fixed on me, but now they're burning with rage.

He curls his lip in disgust. "Two vodka tonics and a Jameson," he says, shaking his head. "Don't make me wait, bitch."

I clench my jaw and turn to grab his order. This guy is one of the biggest jerks I've encountered yet. Although, it isn't unusual to get abuse from drunk customers.

I get his drinks and bring them over to him. "Twenty-two dollars please," I say.

He narrows his eyes at me, and I know he's going to make a fuss about paying.

My stomach dips as Gael appears a foot behind him, glaring at the man.

He keeps his facial hair short, but there's still a peppering of stubble that gives his angular jaw a rugged appearance. And those eyes, I could lose myself in those eyes. The simmering inferno in them tells me this will not be fun to watch.

Gael is a dangerous man.

"Not sure I should pay full price since the service was so shit." He takes a swig of one drink I got him. "I'd say this order is on the house."

"Pay her," Gael booms, his voice sending goosebumps prickling over every inch of my skin. A tightness coils in my stomach as I stare at the rough, handsome man coming to my rescue.

"Or what?" The guy spins around with his fists clenched. "Stay out of this. It has nothing to do with you, jerk."

The look in Gael's eyes fills me with dread. He's rough, ruthless, and doesn't care who he hurts. His entire body is stiff with tension as he glares silently at the man who disrespected me.

It brings me right back to the time he attacked Chad, putting him in the hospital. The first time I'd seen him in two years was when he came rushing back into my life and heart, even stronger than before.

Gael followed us into the library that day, when Chad tried to take things too far and wouldn't stop. A shudder pulses down my spine as the memory of blood and cracking of bones hits me. His savage nature should scare me, but the way he protected me got me hot under the collar. Something tells me he's about to do the same thing to this guy, right here in the club I work at.

"I said, pay her," he says again, his voice quieter but even more lethal.

My heart is pounding in my throat as I watch Gael's eerily still form and expressionless eyes boring into him. Finally, the guy turns around and throws the cash at me. "Fine, here you go, whore." He leers at me with an upturned lip. "Get a job at a strip club or massage parlor where you can please the customers."

I turn my attention to Gael, who now has bloody murder in his eyes. I know he won't let that slide. The guy turns to leave, but Gael is blocking him with his wall of hard muscle.

"Get out of my way, douchebag."

A muscle ticks in Gael's jaw, and the look in his eyes is more dangerous than this idiot can comprehend. "Apologize to her now," he growls. The sound gets my heart racing and my panties wet. I can't understand how the sound of Gael all riled up like this gets me going.

"No fucking chance. What's your problem?"

Gael strikes like a viper, so fast that the guy didn't have a chance in hell of defending himself. He grabs his collar, spins him around, and smashes his head against the bar so hard that he cuts it open. Blood spills onto the bar, and my stomach twists with sickness. The one strike knocks the guy out as he slumps to the floor in a bloody heap.

A few women gasp, and one cries out in shock, staring at the blood pooling on the bar. I move to grab a cloth and wipe it away, trying to still my thundering heartbeat. Gael is insane, and he doesn't care who he hurts, kills, or maims. It should make me want him less, but I'm as twisted as him.

The throbbing between my thighs is unbearable

as I turn back around. Gael stares at me with an intensity that melts my resolve. His eyes dip slowly to my exposed cleavage and linger for a moment, setting my nerves on fire. There's fiery anger in his eyes as he moves close to the bar.

His strong and protective nature drives me wild. I clench my thighs together to stop the desire coursing through my core and soaking my panties.

He's about to get me fired. Not that he cares, and there's only one reason he would be here, and that's bringing me back to Chicago, kicking and screaming.

"Out now," he orders, his voice stern.

I shake my head. "I'm working."

Gael slams his hands down on the bar, glaring at me. "No, you're coming with me." He runs a hand across his stubble-dusted jaw. "Don't make me come behind there and drag you out."

I sink my teeth into my bottom lip at the thought of being dragged out by him, and it's tempting.

"Jamie, what on earth is going on here?" Hank asks, staring at the guy and then at the bloodied cloth in my hand. Jamie Evans is my false identity in Madison. I hoped it would make it difficult for my father to find me. "Who's blood is that?" His brow furrows.

I glance between Hank and Gael, wondering how

to explain this. How am I going to get away from him? Then an idea forms in my mind.

"This guy attacked one of our patrons," I say, feeling a smirk tug at my lips. "He knocked him out."

"Sir, you better leave or I'll call the police," Hank says, squaring his shoulders despite being shorter than me.

Gael doesn't even look at him, glaring at me with a rage that could bring most people to their knees, but I know he'd never hurt me. "Out now, Maeve. Don't make me ask again."

Hank steps forward. "Who is Maeve? Do you know this man, Jamie?" He glances at me, and it feels like my world is crashing down around me. All my efforts to build a new life here are pointless now that Gael is here.

Even if I could get him arrested, it wouldn't buy me enough time to throw him off my scent. But I have to try. "I don't know the guy. Maybe he's a crazy stalker?" I say, playing dumb. "You better call the police."

Hank nods and rushes toward the phone behind him, leaving Gael and me alone.

A deep rumble vibrates through Gael's chest. "Don't think you'll escape that easy, little dove." He moves toward the hatch at the side. "You are coming with me whether or not you like it."

The tension crackles in the air as we stare into each other's eyes. Gael will never know how angry I am at him for leaving, and he will never know how desperately I ache for him.

Gael is here to deliver me to another man. It hurts more than I can ever put into words. I don't want to marry Maxim. I want to marry the man standing in front of me. I want him with every fiber of my soul.

6

GAEL

My prey remains unearthly still, staring at me as if I've startled her. The tension in her shoulders is clear, warning me she's readying herself to flee. Her bright blue eyes are dilated as they remain fixed on me.

I move closer to the bar, shoving the unconscious, bloody man out of the way. Pain floods her blue eyes, and I know the reason. She believes I'm here to retrieve her and bring her back to her father. A ridiculous notion, considering I promised her I'd get her out of the engagement to Maxim when we last spoke.

I know my actions in the past have hurt her, but she'll come to understand everything I've ever done is for her. I abandoned her when she needed me in her eyes, and now I'm here to deliver her to another man. She doesn't know how wrong she is.

Maeve Callaghan has always been mine. There's no chance in hell I'd let her marry Maxim Volkov. Since she was eighteen years old, I have held the claim on her heart, body, mind, and soul. Ever since we got too close while I tried to ease the pain of her mother's passing, it is a claim that I will never give up while there is still a beat in my chest and breath in my lungs. I'd die before I let another man take her from me.

I observe her as she takes a few steps away from the counter. Her eyes dart from side to side as she plans her escape. They land on her cell phone a few feet away and then return to me.

I can't let her call the cops. Instinct drives me as I open the hatch to the bar and step forward, closing the distance between us.

"You can't come back here," she says, her eyes wide.

I smirk at her. "Oh, Maeve. You know I can do whatever the fuck I want."

She takes a few more steps backwards, her face pale as she tries to work out an escape plan.

There is no escape. I corner my little dove against the bar, setting my hands on either side of her. Desire so acute blazes inside of me, taking on a life of its own. I lean toward her, inhaling her sweet jasmine scent. "Don't make me carry you out of here," I say.

Maeve searches my eyes, her chest heaving up and down violently. She bites her bottom lip, drawing my eyes to the perfect, plump flesh. My cock hardens in my pants as I think about kissing her.

Fuck.

This isn't the time or place. I clench my jaw and force myself to focus, glancing into Maeve's steely blue eyes. "Leave with me now, little dove." I move my hand to her hip, squeezing gently. "Or I'll drag you out."

Maeve's eyes harden. "I'd rather you go to jail," she spits.

The dark, sadistic side of me loves that she's putting up a fight. I take a step back, wishing she would accept the inevitable. She's coming with me, and she knows it.

Her boss returns, noticing I'm behind the bar. "What the fuck are you doing?" He marches toward me. "You can't be back here. The cops are on their way."

I turn toward him, straightening to my full height. "What are you going to do about it?" I ask, glaring at him.

His face pales, and he takes a few steps back. "The cops will be here any minute."

I narrow my eyes, wondering if he's bluffing. We shouldn't stick around to find out.

"Maev—" I turn around to find Maeve is gone. "Motherfucker," I growl, glaring at her boss.

He moves further away from me, shaking.

I search the crowd and notice her dashing through it elegantly. The sight kicks adrenaline through my bloodstream as the chase starts, and I rush after her, pushing my way through the crowd.

Maeve does not know the monster she is dealing with. She believes she knows me, but she doesn't understand the darkness I was running from when Ronan found me and gave me a chance. He nurtured the darkness, but it will backfire on him.

I keep my pace fast but don't run as I dodge drunk idiots. Never once do I lose sight of her as she moves for the exit. Maeve makes it to the exit and glances over her shoulder, finding my gaze in the crowd as if we're the only two people in this club. Fear is all I see in them as she sprints out of the door, leaving my sight for the first time.

I know how sick it is that the chase is a turn-on for me. She's pure and innocent, and I'm broken and twisted. I adjust my straining cock in my pants, trying to ignore my questionable urges.

Maeve darts down an alleyway seconds after I step onto the sidewalk. It's a mistake, as her best chance would have been to remain on the busy streets. It's as if she wants me to catch her, as if she wants me to push her up against the wall of a dark alleyway and take her roughly, the way I've craved.

I clench my fists by my side, trying to ignore the perverse thoughts entering my head. It's no use. With Maeve Callaghan, I'm a lost cause. I stride to the alleyway and follow her, feeling my heart rate speed up the moment I see her from behind.

The feral need to claim her rears its ugly head as I take in the sight of her too-short skirt. It shows off her pale, exquisite thighs. I groan softly as more blood courses south, making my cock so damn hard it hurts. The way her ass sways from side to side is impossibly tempting as she rushes away on her high heels. My little dove is entirely unaware that I've caught her already.

"I would give up now, little dove," I call.

Maeve freezes on the spot. I expect her to turn and face me, but she doesn't. She's like a statue stuck in one position. Then she suddenly kicks off her shoes and sprints with bare feet down the alleyway.

I growl, irritated that she'd be so stupid. Taking her shoes off in the center of a city down a dirty alleyway is ridiculous, as she'll end up with cut-up feet from broken glass in no time. I break into a sprint, closing the distance between us.

Once I'm inches away from her, I wrap an arm around her waist. I jerk her to a stop. "Not so fast." I lift her from her feet. "It's foolish to run barefoot in a city center. You'll cut your feet." The need to care and protect her has always been strong inside of me.

"It's better than marrying some Russian bastard." She tenses against me. "Let me go, Gael."

My name on her lips is sensual, and I want her to scream it while I bury myself to the hilt inside of her. I tighten my grip on her at the mere thought of being inside of this angel. "Don't fight me, Maeve," I growl, feeling my need for her overwhelm my senses. It's so hard to keep a handle on my control when she drives me insane.

She turns limp in my arms. "My life is over," she exclaims, her voice utterly devastated. It makes my chest ache, hearing her so broken.

"Maybe it's just beginning," I mutter, knowing that I'm walking a dangerous line. The feel of Maeve's soft body against mine clouds my judgment, as she is my weakness and the only thing on this earth that can unravel me.

"I don't fucking think so," she says, shaking her head frantically. "Once I'm married to Maxim, my life will be over." She shudders. "I hate to think of all the terrible things he'll do to me."

There's no way in hell she's marrying him, as I'd kill him and the rest of his worthless Russian family to have her. "Over my dead body," I growl, making her still in my arms.

"Gael?" There's a question in her voice, and it's a question we both know the damn answer to. I'm not here to take her back to Chicago, as that was never my plan.

"Little dove," I say her nickname softly, keeping her back pressed against me. "Put your shoes back on," I order, letting her back down on the asphalt.

She sighs heavily and grabs her shoes, putting them on.

I watch her, feeling the chaotic storm brewing inside of me. For too long, I've resisted these earth-shattering urges that almost destroyed me.

Maeve puts her shoes on and turns to face me. The question that she wants to ask me hangs heavily between us as she searches my eyes. "Why did you say over your dead body?" she asks.

I clench my jaw, knowing that revealing everything right now isn't the plan. First, I have to get Maeve somewhere safe and pull off a plan so crazy most men would never attempt it, but I'm not most men.

Instead of answering her question, I move closer to her.

Maeve takes a step back with each of mine. Her back hits the wall, and her breath escapes her. "Gael?" she says my name as a question again, her eyes flooding with fear.

I press my hands on either side of her against the wall. Her sweet jasmine scent calls to the inner darkness that wants to infect her innocence and turn it black.

Maeve's chest rises and falls fast as her breathing speeds up. The sound of her raspy breaths is enough to drive me wild with need. I can hardly control myself any longer as I stare down at the woman I've wanted for three long years.

My plan is going to throw the whole of Chicago into chaos, but I don't care. Chicago can burn down as long as I have my little dove alive and safe by my side.

"Tell me what you mean, please," Maeve begs.

When I don't say a word, I notice the fear increasing in her eyes. "Please, just let me go, Gael."

All I can do is stare at her, knowing that her request is an impossibility. I'll never let her go, no matter the consequences. Not as long as there's still air in my lungs. Maeve is my world, and she's about to understand what that means.

7

MAEVE

I feel captivated by his angry eyes as he glares down at me. Gael's warmth radiates through my skin as his hard body boxes me against the wall, making it impossible for me to escape.

I inhale a deep breath, filling my senses with his musky, masculine scent.

"Why do you have to push me, little dove?" He brings a finger to my chin and strokes my jaw tenderly.

I shudder, wishing he wouldn't call me that. The nickname he gave me when we started getting close feels wrong now. We're not close anymore. Instead, we're worlds apart. I'm not sure I know the angry, brutal man standing in front of me.

"I won't come back with you to marry that Russian dickhead," I spit, wishing he'd explain why he said I'd marry Maxim over his dead body. Gael won't answer my question.

His lip pulls up at the side in a half-smirk. "No, you won't."

My brow furrows as I stare into his dark, smoldering eyes. It feels like we're going around in circles. "What do you mean?" I ask again, unsure whether he will answer. A shiver of unease courses through me as I wonder if my father has changed his mind. Then, I remember the last conversation I had with Gael after the announcement.

I will find a way out of this for you. Trust me.

He doesn't want me to marry Maxim either, but he can't work against my father. It's suicide.

Gael's jaw tenses, and I notice a torn look enter his eyes. Before he abandoned me, I was sure he felt the same way I felt about him. That was before he broke my heart in two and didn't so much as pick up the phone to explain why he left me when I needed him the most.

"There's been a change of plan," he rumbles, his voice so deep it makes need pulse through me and sets my soul on fire.

I tilt my head to the side. "Let me guess. You're

going to tell me my father won't force me to marry anyone. I need to come with you, and everything will be fine." I shake my head. "I'm not a fucking moron."

He moves even closer to me, pressing his muscular body against mine. "No, you're not."

I hate the way my nipples harden against the fabric of my shirt. I hate the way he's always so cryptic with me. I hate the way he makes me burn for him so damn easily. "Stop being so vague and tell me why you are here if it's not to bring me back to marry Maxim." My breaths come in short rasps as I try to get a handle over my crippling urges.

Gael continues to stare at me, unyielding.

I feel wetness sliding down my legs as my arousal increases, clenching my thighs together instinctively. "Gael?" I murmur his name for the third time.

His eyes flash with fire. "I'm here to save you."

My brow furrows. "Save me from what?"

His eyes dip to my lips, sending shudders through me. Is it possible to hurt from a desire so desperate it feels like it might tear you apart? It sure as hell feels like it. "Please let go of me," I beg, feeling more slick arousal sliding down my thighs. I'm practically dripping with need for him.

"Why, Maeve?" he asks, a smirk twisting his lips.

"Is it because I'm getting you wet?" he asks, his voice husky.

Fierce heat floods through every vein of my body, setting me on fire. I try to retreat into the cold bricks behind me, wishing they'd swallow me. Gael knows how badly I want him, and he's teasing me. "Don't be cruel," I say, wishing my voice didn't sound so vulnerable. He's toying with my desires, and it hurts.

His dark eyes soften. "Is it cruel to give in to what we both want?"

I stop breathing for a moment, wondering if I'm dreaming. "What is it we both want?"

He smirks and slides a hand to my exposed thigh, groaning as his fingers skate over my slick thighs. "Fuck, baby, you're soaked."

I bite my lip, watching the god of a man I've longed for regard me with hunger so deep it scares me. His lips move toward me, and it feels like time slows down. They collide with the column of my neck as he slowly kisses me there, lavishing attention on my skin so gently it sends tingles through my entire body. "Fuck," I gasp, clutching onto his powerful arms for support. My knees turn to jelly as he moves his hand higher and higher up my thigh.

I tense at the prospect of being touched, even by

Gael. I don't know how to let go of my inhibitions. "Gael, wait."

He doesn't listen to me and slides a finger through the fabric of my panties. "So damn wet, Maeve," he growls before sliding a finger beneath the gusset and shoving it inside of me.

I moan softly, unable to organize the insane thoughts in my mind. Gael has lost control as he bites my neck and collarbone, thrusting his finger in and out of me with careful strokes.

"I want to hear you moan for me, little dove," he growls into my ear before biting my earlobe hard enough to hurt.

I yelp in pain, but he quickly covers my mouth with his. Our lips meld together as he probes his tongue through my defenses, demanding my submission. It's impossible to resist as I open my lips and allow him to plunder my mouth with his tongue. The raw need pulsing in the air stifles the oxygen and makes it impossible to breathe.

I can't hold back anymore. Every dirty fantasy that has played out in my mind for the last three years is coming true, and it's better than it ever was in my dreams.

Gael continues to finger me roughly as he kisses me as if his life depends on it.

Has he wanted this as badly as I have all this time?

When he finally breaks the kiss, I draw in a long gulping breath of oxygen. It feels like I'm free falling as Gael's finger continues to assault the most intimate part of my body. He gropes my ass with his other hand and holds my gaze. "My little dove is all grown up," he murmurs, eyes full of fiery lust that burns me to the core.

I watch him as he pulls his finger out of me and brings it to his mouth, sucking my juice from it. I can't help but moan at the erotic sight.

"Sweeter than sin, baby," he murmurs. "I've wanted you for too damn long, Maeve."

I stare at him in shock, unable to find the words to reply to him. Before I say anything, he drops to his knees in front of me. "What are you—"

Oh my God.

Gael lifts my skirt and buries his nose against my panties, smelling my scent. I reach for his shoulders to steady myself, feeling lightheaded as the man of my dreams loses control with me. He pulls my panties down, making me tense.

"Wait, don't—"

Gael sucks my clit, making me forget what I was about to say. My body coils with desire as I clutch onto his shoulders even tighter. My pussy gushes, and he licks at me, lapping up every drop.

I moan loudly, feeling the tension in my shoulders easing. I writhe in pure ecstasy as his tongue drives me to somewhere I've never been before, with anyone. "Gael, oh my God."

His tongue delves into my pussy hungrily. It's as though he's a beast, starving for me. "Fuck, little dove. You taste better than I ever could have imagined."

His dirty talk gets me hotter than I ever believed possible. I think I died and went to heaven tonight. Gael's finger accompanies his tongue as he slides it deep inside of me, moving his mouth to my clit.

"Fuck," I cry, unashamed of the fact we're in the center of Madison.

The incredible pleasure building inside of me surpasses anything I've felt. I roll my hips instinctively toward him, fucking his tongue as he continues to finger me. The pleasure is unbelievable as he nips my clit with his teeth before rolling it between his lips and tongue. He's a master of desire, and I'm his slave right now.

"Please," I whimper, feeling myself on the edge of release

He stops, glancing at me with those sensual dark brown eyes. "Please, what?" he rasps, his hair disheveled.

"I need to…." Heat pulses through my cheeks as my inhibition hits me again. I wish I weren't so uptight.

He smirks at me. "You need to come, baby." He shakes his head. "You can say it."

I swallow hard and nod.

"I want to hear you say it, or I won't let you come." There's a glint of evil in his eyes, as though he gets off making me uncomfortable.

"Please make me come," I whisper, only loud enough for him to hear.

He growls, a throaty sound that almost sends me over the edge. He sucks my clit into his mouth and sinks two fingers deep inside of me, making me spasm. My body tenses as the rush of pleasure washes over me in waves. A gush of liquid floods out of my pussy and into his mouth, making me instantly embarrassed.

Gael groans and laps up every drop, devouring me with more hunger than before. He stands and captures my lips, making me taste myself on him. It's unbelievably erotic, and I feel myself turning to jelly again as he possessively holds me against him.

The zip of his pants coming undone makes me tense, and I freeze as he hoists me in his arms against the wall. Frantic passion overtakes his eyes as he captures my lips again. I feel the hot press of his cock against my entrance and instantly panic.

He's so strong as he holds me against the wall. "Stop, Gael," I cry, my heart thudding so hard it feels like it might tear through my chest at any moment. "Stop."

He groans like an animal, his eyes dilated and dazed with lust. It's like he's drugged on desire and no longer with me. He drags the tip of his cock through my slick, aching entrance. This isn't right. Not here.

I claw at his neck so hard that I draw blood. "Stop," I cry louder. "I'm a virgin." Tears flood down my cheeks as he suddenly snaps out of it. His eyes go wide as he notices the tears, and he quickly puts his cock away, dropping me to my feet.

Guilt floods his amber eyes. "I'm sorry. I—" He shakes his head and rubs a hand across the back of his neck, wincing at the spot where I dug my nails into him and drew blood. "Come with me," he orders, turning his back on me.

I stare after the man I've longed for, wondering what got into him. He lost control with me, ready to take me no matter what I said. Perhaps Gael isn't the man I thought he was and he's like all the other men my father surrounds himself with—selfish and misogynistic.

My chest aches as I follow him to my fate.

The question is, what does he have in store for me?

8

GAEL

ontrol.

It's always been one of my positive attributes, and I lost it with her. With Maeve Callaghan, control isn't in my vocabulary. My little dove has finally stopped crying after I lost myself to my beastly instincts.

Maeve sits silently in the passenger seat of the charger I rented. She has barely looked at me since I almost fucked her in that alleyway, despite her telling me to stop. I couldn't hear her. It was as if I were no longer in control of my body, governed by a primal need to make her mine.

I run a hand across the back of my neck, feeling the cut where she drew blood. It was the only way she could snap me out of it. When that word hit my ears, it felt like she'd slapped me in the face.

A virgin.

I know Ronan has been protective of her over the years, but I was sure she must have had sex with that piece of shit I put in the hospital on her twenty-first birthday. It never occurred to me she may be untouched.

It should make me reconsider my plan, but I'm not a good man. Instead, it makes me want her even more. My Maeve is as pure as can be, and I want to be the only man to touch her for the rest of her life. There's a palpable tension between us.

She's angry that I almost fucked her against her wishes, but perhaps she underestimated the man I am. A feral beast cloaked in an expensive suit. The suit, the fancy watch, and the car are all a rouse. None of us are any better than monsters, but I know for sure her life would be better with me than with Maxim.

When she dug her nails into my skin, the pain was enjoyable, and it's sick that I delighted in her reluctance for a moment. Maeve almost became a casualty of my darkness, and I almost lost her in that alleyway for good.

As I glance over at her, I wonder if my actions

have lost her, anyway. I crossed a line I never should have crossed with her, and I did it forcefully and unapologetically.

"Where are we going?" she asks without taking her eyes off the window.

I force my attention back on the road, tightening my grip on the steering wheel. "You will see soon enough." The plan to secure my future with Maeve is reckless and bordering on insane.

Chicago will burn for my actions. The clan will face a war so intense no one will have seen the likes of it, but I can't find it in myself to care. My friend shouldn't have been so selfish, using his daughter as a bargaining chip with the Russians.

I intend to drive Maeve into the mountains, where I own a log cabin that belonged to my parents, which remained in my name after they died. No one knows about it or where it is, meaning it's the perfect hideout from the storm that is brewing.

I ditched my cell phone in a trash can back in Madison, leaving a blood-stained rag with my blood on it. It should send Ronan chasing his tail for a while, giving me time to get the plan into motion with my contacts. I adjust the bandage on my arm which covers the knife wound I inflicted on myself.

Maeve looks at me for the first time since we got

in the car, hugging her arms around herself. "You are scaring me, Gael."

She is right to be scared, as I'm a loose cannon with her. I say nothing in reply.

What can I say?

I've never been great with words, and I don't know how to ease her fears or tell her the truth. Maeve's my angel, and she needs to understand that she belongs to me.

My lack of response to her last statement seems to shut her up as she hugs herself even tighter before returning her attention to the window. The sniffling starts again as she cries, making my stomach twist with guilt.

The gas station on the right appears, signaling we're about an hour from my cabin. I indicate and turn off, pulling into a parking spot next to the shop. "Wait here," I order.

Maeve glares at me with red, puffy eyes in silence as I get out of the car and head into the shop.

I need to get enough supplies so we can remain in the mountains for a while, giving me enough time to get everything off the ground. I also need a burner phone, as Tiernan and Seamus are waiting for my instruction back in Chicago.

I walk into the shop, and the guy behind the

counter gives me an odd look. I guess I'm a little overdressed for a dive like this. Ignoring his stares, I grab a basket and walk down the aisles. I'm quick to grab everything we will need, filling my basket high with food.

The guy rings up my stuff. "That's one hundred and five bucks. Can I get you anything else?"

The liquor behind him catches my attention. "Two bottles of Jameson and a burner phone, please."

He grabs the two bottles and a phone, bagging them. "One hundred and eighty-five bucks."

I pay the guy with cash and head back into the parking lot, carrying the heavy, ladened bags. It feels like my heart stops beating the moment I set eyes on the car.

Maeve is gone. I rush over to it and dump the bags in the back before turning and searching for her. There's no sign of her. Other than the gas station and a small diner, there's nowhere else for her to go.

I run a hand over my stubbled jaw and groan in frustration. The longer we're on the road, the more chance we've got of being spotted by someone who knows who Maeve is.

I grit my teeth and head for the diner, hoping to God that she's in there. When I get inside, I see her standing at the counter. The panic inside of me eases, but my anger at her blatant disregard for my order kicks up a gear.

Maeve knows how to wind me up. I charge to her side, glaring at her as rage courses through my veins. Maeve reels off her order to the server without a damn care in the world. She doesn't realize the danger we're both in.

I notice her credit card in her hand, which would have been a fucking beacon to Ronan if she had used it here, since he knows about her fake identity in Madison. "I told you to stay in the car," I growl.

She glances at me briefly. "I'm hungry."

I grind my teeth. "I got us food in the gas station."

Maeve shrugs. "I wanted a bagel, a donut, and a coffee. Do you want anything?"

It's as though she's purposely obnoxious to piss me off. "Get in the car now. No food."

The lady behind the counter clears her throat. "So, do you want the order or not?"

"Ignore him. It's a free country, and I'm getting my food." She twirls a strand of golden hair around her finger. "I'll take a large vanilla latte, too, please." She shoots me an irritating glare that makes me want to bend her over the counter and spank her perky ass right here in front of everyone.

I grab her wrist and pull her toward me. "Don't use your card unless you want your father to find you." I thrust twenty dollars into her hand, snatching the card from her. I control my urges to punish her in public and say nothing more on the matter. "I'll be waiting in the car." I walk away from her, trying to hold it together. Maeve needs to learn some discipline, and I'm happy to be her teacher.

I sit in the driver's seat of the rental and grab the burner phone out of one of the grocery bags. The phone powers on. I pull a piece of paper out of the glove box with Tiernan's number and Seamus' number on it. I enter them into the phone, tapping my foot impatiently as I wait for Maeve.

Seamus and Tiernan have agreed to help me with my plan. They don't have any love for Ronan and understand why I have to do this. I intend to rely on them to get my plan into place to run smoothly on my return to Chicago.

Maeve comes out of the diner, holding a bag and coffee cup. She walks over to the car, throws open the door, and sits down as if she's done nothing wrong. She pulls out her bagel and nibbles on it, frustrating the hell out of me. After a few long moments of silence between us, I've had enough.

I grab her wrist hard, making her drop her bagel.

"Hey, what the—"

"You'll regret disobeying me," I say, cutting her bratty protest off.

She glares at me. "Is that a threat?"

I reach for her throat and grip it tightly. "Stop pushing me, little dove."

Her eyes widen, and she stares at me in shock. Maeve hasn't seen this rough, dominant side of me. "Who are you?" Her eyes brim with unshed tears as she searches my face.

No doubt looking for an ounce of regret at my actions since I stole her from Madison, but she won't find any. I don't regret taking her because she is mine and has been since I fell for her three years ago.

I release her throat and turn the key in the ignition. There's no way I can answer her question. Maeve has this idealist vision of me in her mind, but she does not know who the real Gael Ryan is.

I notice Maeve worry her lip out of the corner of my eye before glancing out of the window. The light sound of sniffling signals she's crying again.

I clench my jaw, resisting the urge to soothe away her tears. Maeve needs to learn a hard lesson. The dark and dangerous world she was born into isn't easy, even if her father shielded her all her life.

I keep all my attention on the road, knowing that I can't worry about her right now. All that I'm doing is for her, and in time she will come to understand that. I may be rough, but I'm her savior from a life of hell with a Russian Bratva heir.

In time, she will understand that everything I'm doing is for her.

9

MAEVE

Gael terrifies me.

He never used to scare me, but I've not seen this side of him. He's feral and out of control. Dark and vindictive in ways I never knew he was capable of. They say be careful what you wish for, and perhaps that saying is true for my fantasy with Gael.

I always knew there was darkness in him. The way he so roughly tried to fuck me against the wall was terrifying. A man I trusted shouldn't have lost control like that, and yet a small part of me wanted him to do it. A tiny part of me buried deeply wanted him to fuck me, despite my pleas for him to stop. It's a rather confusing and sickening sensation that I'll never understand.

I'm exhausted as we continue to drive miles and miles from the gas station, but I don't feel safe enough to shut my eyes. Gael used to make me feel safe, but right now, I feel vulnerable with him around.

The way he devoured my pussy in that alleyway was the single most erotic experience of my life, but also the most shocking.

Gael turns off the main road onto an off-road path heading up into the mountains. It's scary that he is taking me somewhere so remote—somewhere no one can hear my screams.

I don't believe he wants to harm me, but if his behavior in that alleyway outside the club was anything to go by, he wants me in a primal way and had little control over his urges.

Before he appeared in the club, spending time alone with him in a remote area would have been a dream come true. Right now, it feels more like a nightmare. I don't know this man at all or what he's capable of.

After about half a mile up the track, we come to an abandoned cabin. It looks creepy, surrounded by forest, and hidden. I glance at Gael, who hasn't said a word since we left the diner. "Where are we?"

He glances at me. "It's best you don't know the details."

I bite my tongue, swallowing my fear as Gael gets out of the car and walks toward the cabin.

Instead of following, I remain in the passenger seat, too scared to follow him in there. The fear coils through my blood and makes it impossible to move.

Who is this man?

He glances out of the door and signals for me to follow, but I can't will my limbs to move.

I see the irritation ignite in his amber eyes when I don't get out of the car. His jaw tightens. He glares at me with such a fiery expression it both scares and excites me.

The past few hours since he snatched me from the club, I've honestly questioned whether I ever knew him at all. Gael has always been a little scary and overprotective, but he's acting feral now.

If he thinks staring at me like that will get me to move, he's mistaken. Gael huffs and then marches to the car. I consider locking my side, but he grabs the handle fast when he sees me move to push the lock.

"Out now," he barks, fists clenched by his side.

I stare at him. "What is going on here? You at least owe me an explanation."

His eyes dance with dangerous anger. "I owe you fuck all." The vehement in Gael's voice sets me on edge. I unbuckle my belt and try to climb over the center console to run out the other side.

Gael growls and grabs my ankles, dragging me out of the car and onto the ground.

My head slams into the hard dirt, making me wince. "What the fuck?" I scramble to my feet and grab my head. "You're a fucking psychopath."

His eyes are frantic as he moves slowly toward me. I step away from him faster, hearing the voice in my head screaming at me to run. He's insane, and maybe he lost his mind while he was in Europe.

I turn around and dash into the woods, hoping I can hide from him in there. It would be less scary if he turned up and dragged me back to Chicago to marry Maxim. I'm not sure why I'm here in the mountains with him, but the way he's acting is freaking me out.

I rush into the foliage with no idea where I'm going. The thud of following footsteps makes my heart pound faster. The light of day is dying as I push deeper into the forest.

"Maeve, stop," Gael growls, breathless as he chases after me. He's too damn close.

"No," I cry, feeling tears welling in my eyes that I ever trusted this man. "Stay the fuck away from me,"

I shout, veering off right and heading down a wild, overgrown path.

For all I know, he intends to torture me for some sick and twisted pleasure he gets from it. Gael, the man I fantasized about for years, isn't the man chasing me. He's different in a bad way.

My foot gets caught on a rock on the path, and I fall flat on my face, wincing as I cut open my legs on the rocky ground.

Gael's footsteps slow. "Shit, Maeve. Are you okay?" he asks, his voice suddenly concerned.

"Stay away from me," I say, forcing myself to my feet. My head swims as I hit it on the rocky ground, and I bring my hand to my forehead. When I pull it away, I find blood on my fingers.

"Maeve. Your head is bleeding. I need to look at it." He holds his hands out. "Come back with me, and I will explain everything. I promise."

I squint at him, knowing he'd probably say anything to get me to come with him. "How can I trust you? I don't know who you are anymore."

His jaw clenches, and his dark eyes flash with hurt. "I know I've been acting like a madman since I took you from Madison." He runs a hand across the back of his neck, his shoulders slumping. "All I want to do is protect you."

It's hard to believe that statement. Especially since Gael almost took my virginity in an alleyway when I explicitly told him to stop. I knew he wasn't a good man. He's a criminal, for fuck's sake, but I never expected him to take things that far with me. Perhaps I'm a fool. "Fine," I murmur, wrapping my arms tightly around myself. "I'll come back with you."

Gael looks relieved as he pulls his jacket off his shoulders and wraps it around me. "You look cold. Come on." The scent of him clings to the fabric, wrapping me in its soothing embrace. Although, I'm not sure anything about Gael Ryan is soothing anymore. He has a darkness in him I underestimated.

He steers me back onto the path I ran down, keeping a steadying hand on my back. His touch only serves to confuse me further. I've wanted him for too long, and now reality is turning out to be far different from fantasy, making my urges even more difficult to wrap my head around.

I shouldn't want him anymore, not after what he did to me back in that alleyway. My stomach sinks as I know despite all of that, I want him as much as ever.

A silence so deep cloaks us as we move through the quiet woods surrounding the cabin he drove up to. When it comes back into view, anxiety floods through my veins. The idea of spending any time alone with Gael in such a small, secluded building scares me.

"Where are we exactly?" I ask as he opens the car's trunk to get out the supplies he bought at the gas station.

He grunts. "It's better you don't know the details."

I sigh heavily, wondering if I was a fool to believe he'd explain anything to me once we're inside.

He leads the way into the cabin, unlocking the door and pushing it open. It's basic, but cozy. An enormous fireplace sits pride of place on the far wall, with two plush couches positioned perfectly around it.

On the left-hand side is a small, open-plan kitchen. Gael takes the grocery bags in there and sets them on the countertop.

I stand in the doorway, feeling unsure of what to do.

"Sit down so I can check your injuries," he says.

I walk over to the couch and flop down, twiddling my thumbs.

Gael walks over with a first-aid kit and opens it on the coffee table. He sits next to me and sighs as he pulls out some cotton gauze and saline solution. "I wish you would listen to me, little dove." He dabs the wound on my head, making it sting. "I hate seeing you hurt."

I swallow hard, allowing him to clean up the wound. "Is it bad?" I ask.

He shakes his head. "Luckily, no." He pulls out a small Band-Aid and places it on the cut. "That should stop the bleeding, but don't lie down." His brow furrows. "You might have a concussion."

I sit back on the sofa. "Are you going to explain everything now?" I ask, looking into his troubled amber eyes.

He shakes his head. "I will, but first I have to take a walk up the mountain to ensure there's no one else here. I'll be about an hour."

My brow furrows. "Can't I come with you?" The prospect of staying in this cabin alone gives me the creeps. There's no TV, which means I can't drown out the silence with noise.

His dark eyes find mine. "No, it's not safe. Please be patient, and I'll be back shortly." Without another word, he heads out of the door, shutting it and locking it behind him.

I shake my head and glance around the cabin again, noticing a bookshelf on the far side. I stand

and approach it, hoping to find something to read. I notice one old romance book and dig it out. I love reading, but I've had little time for it ever since I ran away from Chicago.

Life under my father's watchful eye meant I didn't know the true meaning of hard work. The shifts at the club barely covered my rent, let alone my food expenses. So I've been working two jobs: the club at night and a job at a local bookstore in the day. It has been exhausting but a good life lesson.

I can't understand why Gael hasn't taken me straight back to Chicago. A part of me hopes he intends to keep me for himself, even if that is ridiculous because my father will search every corner of the United States to find us both.

There is no hiding from Ronan Callaghan. I knew that when I moved to Madison with a fake ID. It was merely a move to buy me some time, hoping my father would drop marrying me off to a Russian.

Maxim Volkov is a nasty piece of work. I've met him a few times, and I have no desire to marry him. Gael is showing me his true colors. I'm not sure that I'm going to like the man he is under it all. Only time will tell.

10

GAEL

The air is cool as I walk the path from the cabin further into the mountains. I need to clear my head and get some distance from the woman turning me into a feral beast, as well as ensuring that we're alone on this part of the mountain. The last thing I need is for some bandits to show up.

The mountains are remote and difficult to navigate, making them the perfect spot for convicts to hide. As I walk, it's impossible to keep my mind off of Maeve no matter how hard I try. The two-mile trek up the mountain took me less time than I expected.

A part of me is reluctant to turn back, but the path becomes more dangerous, and the night is quickly drawing in. I turn around and navigate my way back toward the cabin. It was my father's, but I don't remember ever being here with my family. It's small, which will prove problematic considering Maeve is in there. I can't trust myself anywhere near her at the moment. However, it was the only safe place to bring her. No one alive today knows about this cabin except for me.

Once I'm about half a mile from it, I notice a billow of smoke rising above the treetops.

Fuck's sake.

The only place that could come from is the cabin which means Maeve has lit a fire. I grind my teeth, knowing that she has potentially put us in severe danger with her ignorance. The smoke is a signal for miles around that people are hiding up here. I don't expect Ronan to be on our tails yet, but anonymity is key to the success of my plan.

I hasten my steps, desperate to make it back to the cabin and put out the fire. The last few hundred yards, I break into a jog. I storm into the cabin, making Maeve jump at my sudden appearance. "What the fuck are you doing?" I growl.

Her eyes widen. "What do you mean?"

I shake my head and rush over to her. "The fire.

Are you insane?" I grab the wet cloth off the kitchen counter and throw it over the flames, starving it of oxygen.

Her mouth hangs open as she stares at me in shock. "I was cold."

"Fuck's sake, Maeve. We're hiding and you've lit a goddamn beacon to the world that we're up here." I grab her wrist and drag her to her feet. "Do you want your father to find you and drag your ass back to Chicago?"

Her brow furrows. "No, but I think you are overreacting about a fucking fire." She yanks her wrist from my grasp, irritating me.

I pinch the bridge of my nose and let out a deep breath. "First, you disobey me at the gas station, and now this." I open my eyes and meet her gaze. "It's about time I taught you a lesson."

Her eyes widen, and she takes a step away from me. "What are you going to do?"

I step forward with every step she takes back until she knocks into the sofa. "Gael," her voice is fearful as the soft column of her throat bobs.

I hold her gaze before grabbing her wrist and yanking her close. "Bend over."

Maeve pales and shakes her head. "No."

I clench my jaw. "Now, or I'll force you."

Her eyes search mine as if looking for a shred of goodness or mercy, but she won't find it. It's time Maeve met the real man she wished had stayed three years ago.

She yanks her arm away and jumps over the sofa, trying to escape. Maeve will learn that running only makes everything worse. I stride around the sofa and chase her down the corridor. I slam my foot in the bedroom door before she can shut it on me.

I force it open, making her squeal.

"Stay the fuck away from me." She rushes toward the bed and grabs a pillow, wielding it in front of her.

I can't help but find her choice of weapon amusing. "What are you going to do to me with that?"

"Batter you," she spits.

I laugh. "Come on. You are irrational. Accept your punishment for your disobedience."

She shakes her head. "I got some food, and you didn't tell me not to light a damn fire." Maeve sets her hands on her hips. "You are an asshole."

I growl and launch toward her, only to receive a smack in the face with a soft, feather-down pillow, but it doesn't slow me as I tear it from her hands and throw it across the room before grabbing her hips.

Maeve glares at me with a mix of desire and rage. "Let go of me."

I say nothing and turn her around, molding my chest against her back. "You'll learn to obey me, baby girl." I press my lips to the back of her neck. "I know deep down you long to be submissive and to be dominated by me the way you've always craved."

"You're a cocky bastard." Maeve leans against me, allowing me to take her weight. "I never said I wanted you."

I nibble at her earlobe. "You didn't have to say it. I sensed it three years ago when we got too close."

The mention of my fleeing the country makes her tense again. "You mean when you abandoned me?" Her voice cracks.

I know that's what it seemed like to her, but she must understand that I was working to ensure we could end up together. Not to mention, I was on the edge of losing control with her and landing us in terrible danger. "I couldn't stay, Maeve. The way I'm losing control with you now, I would have done the same back then." I run my hands down her hips. "I needed a plan."

A palpable tension crackles through the air. "Why now?"

I can't answer that question, as I know it's too

soon to reveal the plan I have in place. My time away from Maeve only deepened the draw she has on me. "I can't stay away from you any longer, little dove."

Maeve releases a shaky breath. "Why do you want me to bend over?" she asks, her voice uncertain.

I kiss beneath her ear. "Because I need to punish you," I murmur into her ear.

Maeve trembles in my arms before slowly bending over for me.

"Good girl," I groan, lifting her skirt to get a perfect view of her firm, round ass cheeks. My cock strains in my boxer briefs at the sight of her skimpy panties, barely covering her soaking wet cunt.

I run my hand over the soft, pale flesh of her ass. "You need to learn what happens when you disobey, little dove."

Maeve visibly shudders.

I bring my hand back and spank her right ass cheek firmly, coaxing a yelp from her.

"What the—"

Before she can question me, I spank her left cheek even harder. It entices a soft scream from her lips, which turns on the darker side of me.

"Gael, stop," she murmurs, her voice vulnerable and quiet.

I clench my jaw, holding onto the reins of control. Maeve deserves to be punished, and no matter how much she begs me to stop, I won't. "No, you need to learn who is in control here." I spank her ass again, and this time her cry is laced with unmistakable arousal. My little dove enjoys being spanked.

I grind my teeth to stop myself from slipping my hand into her panties. The last time that happened, I almost fucked her against her will. Maeve means too much to me, even if I'm not showing it right now.

I'm acting the damn opposite, but I can't chain the beast inside of me. I guess that's what happens when you try to bury a craving so deep it runs through the core of your soul.

My desire for Maeve has turned into something sick. Not to mention, I've never been good at expressing my emotions. After a few more firm spanks of her ass, I know it's time to stop. Her skin is red and welted, meaning anymore and I'll cause too much damage.

"I think you've learned your lesson." I straighten up, pulling her skirt back over her ass. "Get cleaned up. Dinner will be ready in twenty minutes."

I need to get myself in check. Maeve's punishment was cruel and unfair since I didn't warn her not to light a fire. The darkness inside of me has a life of its own.

I tear myself away from her, walking back into the main cabin. The pasta I bought at the gas station will make a quick and easy dinner, coupled with a homemade tomato sauce. I get to work making the food, listening for any movement from Maeve.

Maybe my rough treatment of her will break her spirit, something I don't want to happen. The sauce is quicker to make than I expect as I dish it up, wondering when Maeve will come out of the bedroom.

After twenty-one minutes, I feel my patience wearing thin. I like punctuality which has never been Maeve's forte.

I'm about to drag her out, but she appears, wearing one of my shirts which reaches down to her mid-thigh.

I almost lose my shit when I see her in it, clenching my jaw. It's a sight so perfect and a vision I've imagined so many times.

"Come, sit," I say, signaling at the bowl on the table. "I cooked us some pasta."

Maeve doesn't say a word, sitting down in her chair. She keeps her head down, picking up the spoon and dipping it into the bowl hesitantly.

"I said I'd explain why you are here, Maeve."

My voice draws her beautiful blue eyes to mine. "Yes. Why are we here?"

I draw in a deep breath. "I have a plan to get you out of your arranged marriage to Maxim, and this place is somewhere to keep you safe while I put that plan in place."

Her brow furrows. "So you will return to Chicago and leave me here?"

I search her eyes, knowing that she'd hate me going back to Chicago. It's necessary, though, and I have to eliminate the one person who stands between us. The one person who I've stood by through thick and thin for twenty years. "I will return, yes, as I have people I trust putting the arrangements into place."

She swallows hard, looking down at her bowl again. "Why would you do this?"

It's a question I don't wish to answer right now. Although the main reason is to save Maeve from a life with a man who does not love her, I know the true motivation is to keep her to myself. "It's the least I can do after I left you three years ago."

The mention of my disappearance after her mother's death quiets her. She nods and tucks into the food. A tense silence fills the room as we eat together, both aware that my answer isn't the entire truth. We both know I plan to claim her for myself.

The important question is: does she want me now that she's seen the monster that lies within?

It may not matter what she wants as I'm on the edge of the light, stumbling into the darkness the longer we play this game.

11

MAEVE

I wake the next morning and get out of bed, wrapping a robe around me. The cabin is small, and I can hear voices coming from outside. I walk out of the bedroom, noticing that the front door is ajar. Footsteps echo as Gael paces up and down.

"Can you do that for me, Seamus?" he asks.

I linger by the front door, listening to Gael on the phone outside. Despite insisting he'd tell me what is going on, he was rather vague. All he told me last night was everything that he is doing is to protect me from Maxim and that he has a plan to get me out of the engagement.

All he does is stare at me with toe-curling hunger and clench his jaw every time I ask him about the plan. I think I know the answer after his crazy stunt in the alleyway and then again in the bedroom yesterday evening.

Gael doesn't intend to give me to Maxim, but it's crazy that he thinks he has a choice. My father will murder him as soon as he learns Gael wants me instead, as it will screw up the merger between the Volkov Bratva and the Callaghan Clan, leaving my poor excuse for a father at their mercy.

I should be ecstatic that Gael wants me for himself, but I'm not sure I know him at all anymore. He's turned from the caring, affectionate man that only wanted to be my shoulder to cry on into a feral, growling animal that only seems to want me for a very dirty reason. I want him in that way too, but I fear what it means.

"Thanks, lad. Keep me updated. I'm counting on you." I hear Gael walk toward the door and scuttle onto the sofa, diving for it just in time.

Gael's eyes narrow the moment he sees me. "You were eavesdropping, weren't you?"

I shake my head. "No idea what you are talking about."

He stares at me, unwavering, as if trying to break my resolve. I won't buckle or break for him, even if that's what he wants.

"Come here," he orders.

I shrug. "I'm pretty comfy here, thanks." I notice the flash of rage in his eyes at my disobedience. Gael treats me differently here. He's demanding and dominant, and it's a side to him I've never seen before. I can't work out whether I like it or hate it.

"I said come here," he says, his voice slower.

I narrow my eyes. "I said I'm comfy here."

It seems my defiance only throws fuel to the blazing fire of rage that is culminating inside of him. He marches toward me and grabs a fistful of my hair, yanking me to my feet with it.

"Ow, that hurts," I whine.

He moves his face to within an inch of mine. "Didn't you learn your lesson yesterday?" His warm breath falls on my face as his eyes search mine frantically. "I'm in charge, and if I tell you to do something, then you do it."

He's acting like a self-righteous dick right now. I can't understand why his ordering me around makes me want to disobey him more. I spit at him out of instinct, not wanting to give him the easy satisfaction of my submission. There's something wrong with me for wanting him to treat me the same way he did yesterday.

The growl from his chest is bordering on feral. "It

looks like you learned nothing." He sits on the sofa and grabs me hard, forcing me over his lap.

The position is more intimate than yesterday's punishment. I feel the hard press of Gael's cock against my abdomen as I remain still over his knee, waiting anxiously for the pain to follow. It's insane how good it feels being taken in hand by a man I've longed for all these years.

I feel his warm, large hand caress my bare ass as he pushes my skirt up.

He growls, and I feel his cock pulse beneath me. "No panties?"

I swallow hard, feeling the slickness building between my thighs. "I don't have any clean ones," I say.

Gael's muscles tense beneath me as he brings his hand down on my right ass cheek with less force than he did yesterday. The sensation is more pleasurable than painful as I squirm on his lap, desperate to feel friction against my clit.

He does the same to my other cheek, switching between them as he doles out my punishment.

I moan as the need and desire heighten.

The sound stops Gael in his tracks. He stiffens beneath me. "Are you enjoying this?" he asks, his voice full of lust.

I swallow hard, feeling ashamed that I'm enjoying my punishment. "No."

"Liar," he growls, his hand moving from my ass to part my thighs wide. "I bet if I touch your pussy it will be soaking wet."

I shudder at the intensity in his voice. A battle rages inside me as I know I shouldn't want him to touch me, not after the way he has acted since he kidnapped me from Madison. The part of me that has longed for Gael for such a long time rises to the surface, wanting him to cross the line.

Gael parts my slick thighs, groaning as he does. "I can see you're soaked without even touching you, naughty girl." I feel his finger slide through my slick entrance as he bumps the pad over my sensitive clit.

"Fuck," I breathe.

He spanks me again. "That's for the dirty language, little dove."

I shudder as the pain only amplifies the all-consuming need burning inside of me. "Gael," I moan his name as he slides a finger inside of me, teasing me with it. Memories of yesterday when he had me against the wall flood my mind, as he made me orgasm harder than I ever have before.

Suddenly, he stops touching me and spanks me

again. "I don't think you've learned your lesson yet, have you?"

I swallow hard. "I think I have."

Gael growls, sending pleasure through me. "Then why are you so wet? A punishment isn't supposed to be enjoyable."

I'm not sure why I say the next words. "I enjoy anything that requires your hands on me."

He tenses beneath me, his breathing turning deeper and raspy. "Fuck, little dove." He forces me onto my back on the sofa and captures my lips, kissing me passionately. "I can't hold myself back any longer." He wraps his arms around me and lifts me off the sofa, forcing me to wrap my legs around his waist.

"Gael, what are you—"

He kisses me again, silencing my question before I can finish it. My mind is racing as he kisses me frantically. Fear and excitement mingle as I wonder if he'll take things too far again. Despite the man I've longed for being the one to kiss me, I'm unbelievably anxious about the way he lost control.

I've fantasized about losing my virginity to him for so long that I fear the reality won't live up to the fantasy. Gael carries me into the bedroom and sets me down on my feet, staring at me like a man possessed.

"On your knees," he growls, sending shivers down my spine.

I search his handsome face, wondering if this is real. Slowly, I sink to my knees in front of him, longing to please him in every way possible. All the shit that went on between us in the last couple of days is forgotten.

Gael looks manic as he stares at me, bringing his fingers to the button on his pants and undoing it before slowly unzipping the zipper and pulling them down.

My heart skips a beat at the enormous bulge outlined in his tight boxer briefs. It looks too large, and I've never done this before. Suddenly, I feel out of my depth as I wait for Gael to do something or say something.

His dark eyes hold such passion as he stares at me. "Take it out, little dove."

I swallow hard, glancing between his face and the bulge. "Gael, I'm worried I'll do it wrong."

A gut-wrenching groan escapes his lips. "Are you telling me you've never sucked a cock before?"

I raise a brow, searching his face. "When I said a virgin, I meant it in every sense of the word."

"Fuck," he curses, shutting his eyes. "There's no way you can do it wrong, baby."

I feel my stomach tighten and arousal increase, hearing him call me baby. "Okay, sir," I murmur.

He growls softly, lacing his fingers in my hair.

I reach for the waistband of his boxer briefs and pull them down, gasping when the hard, impossible length bobs free. For a moment, I stare in awe at the thick girth and ridiculous length. The thought of fitting it in my mouth makes my jaw ache. "It's too big for my mouth," I point out.

Gael chuckles. "Don't worry. It'll fit, little dove."

My heart is pounding hard as I reach for it, barely able to wrap my fingers around the shaft. Slowly, I tug it up and down, feeling the hungry desire building inside of me. My thighs are slick with arousal.

I move my mouth toward him, and that's when he jerks me to a stop. His hand tightens in my hair, holding me back from taking his cock into my mouth. I swallow hard and stare up at him.

When he says nothing, I break the silence. "Gael?" I say his name questioningly, gazing up at his beautiful, chiseled face.

Gael's hands remain laced in my hair, gripping hard enough to hurt. His chest rises and falls with heavy, frantic breaths. He looks like a man on the edge. I'm not sure whether the way he stares at me excites or scares me.

The desire I feel builds in my stomach as I wait for his response, wondering what demons haunt the man I've longed for all this time. I fear he harbors darkness beyond anything I can imagine.

I know how wrong it is that the darkness is also what draws me to him. It's like tempting bait that I can't resist taking despite knowing the danger that lurks once I do.

12

GAEL

Blood pulses through my veins so hot it feels like I'm burning from the inside out. My name on her lips, although innocent, turns me animalistic.

Maeve looks up at me from her knees, waiting for my next move.

What is my next move?

I have this beauty kneeling for me, her dainty little hand barely wrapped around my shaft, her pouty lips inches from taking me inside of her mouth. Yet, I have my hand in her hair, hard, stopping her from moving.

My mind and body are at war with each other. I'd promised myself I wouldn't touch Maeve until I knew I could pull this off. That it was easier to keep a distance until I could be sure my plan would work. I know I'm scaring her with my hot and cold actions.

"We shouldn't do this," I murmur, not letting go of her hair.

Maeve licks her lip nervously. "Why not?" She shakes her head. "I assume you've brought me here to keep me for yourself, right?"

I try to fight the red-hot urge to thrust every inch of my cock through her lips. It's almost impossible. "You've always been mine," I rumble.

Maeve's eyes flash with heat. "Always," she murmurs. "It's why I'm still a virgin."

That remark breaks all my resolve. Maeve has been saving herself for me. "Fuck, baby," I groan, shutting my eyes as my last thread of resolve disappears. I loosen my grip on her hair, wanting nothing more than to feel her mouth around my cock. There's no use fighting it anymore.

The hold on my control is slipping as she stares at me. I fight against the need to grab her hair and plunge every inch down her throat.

"Put it in your mouth," I order, my voice barely recognizable.

Maeve hesitates, staring up at me with those big blue eyes of hers.

I force it forward, breaking through her thick red lips.

She grunts as the head hits the back of her throat, choking the moment I block her airways. Her body tenses, and she gags all over my cock. I can't control myself as I ram it in and out of the back of her throat, struggling to rein in the beast.

She claws at my thighs frantically, but I'm too strong. Tears prickle at her eyes, but I can't stop. I've lost control as I plow every inch inside of her mouth. Her body thrashes out at me as she tries to get me to stop. What is happening between us now is one reason I ran away three years ago. I'm unable to control myself at the best of times. When I'm with Maeve, I'm untamable.

I give her a moment's reprieve, allowing her to gulp oxygen before thrusting back into her throat. Saliva spills down her mouth and neck. The mere sight of her at my mercy on her knees like this makes me lose my mind.

My breaths come in deep rasps as I fuck her throat roughly, driving myself toward the edge of explosion. Maeve has stopped trying to fight me as she continues to take my cock down her throat. I can feel my release driving closer with each violent thrust of my hips.

She drifts her hands to my thighs and grips onto them, feeling my muscles contract as I fuck her throat. "Take every inch, little dove," I rasp, realizing how wrong it is being so rough with her. She's a virgin. An innocent, beautiful virgin.

I slow the force of my thrusts, but I still can't control that lewd hunger that turns me into a beast. My hard cock swells against her perfect little tongue. I roar as my balls tighten and my release washes over me.

Maeve chokes on my cum as it floods down her throat.

"Swallow it, baby," I order, keeping my hand laced in her hair.

Maeve's face is a mess, covered in saliva. Drops of my cum spill onto her chin as she swallows the rest of it.

"Let me see," I order, moving my hand to her chin.

Her eyes are dazed with lust as she opens her mouth, letting me see that she's swallowed it all.

"Good girl," I groan, wrapping my arms around her waist and lifting her to her feet. Maeve clutches to me for support, her legs like jelly.

"Are you going to fuck me?" she asks.

I grit my teeth as I search her eyes, wondering if that's what she wants. "That depends."

Her dainty hands shake as she moves them to settle on my chest, using me as support. "On what?"

I draw in a deep breath. "Whether you want me to."

Her brow raises. "That didn't seem to matter in the alleyway by the club."

A soft rumble pulses through my chest. "I have no control when I'm with you."

Maeve sinks her white teeth into her red lips, drawing all my attention to her luscious mouth. "That's why you tried to choke me with your dick?"

I cup her face in my hands and gently caress her bottom lip with my thumb. "This is the reason I had to run to Europe, Maeve. I'm too rough for you."

The column of her throat bobs. "You're not."

I shake my head. "How can you know what you like?"

"I know I like you," she murmurs, making hope ignite in my gut. Despite my diabolical treatment of her, she still wants me. "No matter how rough you are, Gael. I've wanted this for so long."

My body collides with hers roughly. I pull Maeve's lips to mine, devouring her with the strength of my passion. A passion that has been bending and twisting into something so unruly for three years.

I lift her and carry her toward the bed, knowing nothing will stop me now. Since she was eighteen years old, Maeve has held my heart, and nothing could stave my hunger for her.

Maeve's confession that she wants me as well means there's no stopping this. I drop her lithe, small body on the bed and take a step back, admiring her beautiful form. "Perfect, little dove."

Her eyes flash. "Why do you call me that?"

I loosen the buttons on my shirt before pulling it off. "I'll call you what I like, Maeve." I remove my pants and boxers next, standing in front of her naked. "I own you, baby girl."

Maeve's expression turns lustful as her eyes drop to the hard length between my thighs.

I grab her hips and pull her close to the edge of the bed before tearing her blouse open.

Maeve gasps. "Gael, what the hell? That's my only top."

"Fuck the top. I'll get you a new one," I growl before unhooking Maeve's bra from the front and freeing her perfect breasts.

I devour them with my mouth, softly biting her nipple between my teeth.

Maeve gasps at my assault, reaching for me and threading her fingers in my hair. Her touch is an unusual sensation, as I'm used to a woman being bound and immobile.

It feels good, though, allowing her to touch me. The woman I've longed for so deeply. The beast inside of me and the need to care for and protect her are conflicting.

I unzip her skirt and pull it down her thighs, taking in the heavenly vision of her in nothing. "You are so wet for me," I murmur.

I crawl over her and press my lips to her bare stomach, worshiping every inch of her angelic skin. Slowly, I kiss and lick a path to the soaking wet lips between her thighs. A thread of resolve is all that holds my control.

Maeve moans deeply, shutting her eyes as I move my lips higher up her waist. Goosebumps raise over her skin as I move toward her perfect, pert breasts. I lavish all my attention on her right nipple, sucking the hard, puckered flesh into my mouth.

"Fuck, Gael," Maeve breathes, making my balls draw up at the sound of her crying my name.

"No naughty words, baby," I murmur, moving my lips further down as I kiss her stomach softly.

She shudders in anticipation, entirely aware of

where I'm taking this next. The last time I tasted her, I lost my mind. This time I have to rein in the beast at all costs. I almost lost her heart down that alleyway, but I won't risk it again.

I plunge my tongue into her, desperate to taste every drop of her juice. A wild rage rules me as I sink my fingertips into her hips so hard I know I'll leave bruises. Hell, I want to leave marks all over her. The violence of my feelings for this woman is primitive, and it has no rhyme or reason.

I plunge three thick fingers inside of her, continuing to lick her clit frantically.

Maeve moans, and it's the most delicious sound I've ever heard. A sound I've longed to hear from her lips for three long years.

"Gael, I'm going to—"

I stop abruptly, leaving her on the precipice of ecstasy.

She stares at me with wide eyes as I pull my fingers out of her and wipe my mouth.

"Open your mouth for me, baby girl," I order

She stares at me for a few seconds before doing as I say.

Slowly, I place my two fingers into her mouth. "Taste yourself for me."

A wrenching moan escapes her lips as the desire

pulsing between us reaches a crest I've never experienced before. It's all-consuming, as we have turned each other into ravenous animals.

"Good girl," I purr, making her shudder.

Maeve bites her bottom lip, waiting for my next move. It gives me a rush to have her squirm for me.

"What do you want, Maeve?" I ask.

She contemplates the question in silence, leaving me waiting for what feels like an eternity. "You," she breathes.

I groan, stroking my hard cock in my hands. Maeve watches me with a lustful look that drives me wild. "You want this, little dove?" I ask.

Maeve swallows hard, her throat bobbing softly. "Yes, please."

I can't contain myself any longer. The innocent sound of her voice does nothing to slow me. I climb onto her and position my cock at her tight virginal entrance. Her slick juices coat the head of my hard, throbbing dick.

Maeve watches the space between us, waiting for me to push through and pop her cherry. At that moment, I feel like time slows down. Everything I've wanted is right within my grasp, and yet a part of me knows I shouldn't take advantage of her. She's a vulnerable young woman who I've taken captive against her will.

I'm sick, twisted, and broken. Maeve is the exact opposite, and taking her like this might break her too. "Are you sure about this?" I rasp, searching her light blue eyes.

She smiles at me, and it makes my chest ache, as it's such an angelic smile. "Never been more sure about anything in my life." This girl doesn't know what she's getting herself into.

I kiss her deeply before pressing my hips forward. My cock stretches her soaking wet entrance, forcing its way through her tight, untouched channel. Maeve groans in pain as I fill her tight little cunt for the first time. I'm the only man ever to enter her, and that drives me wild with a need so impossible.

I grab hold of her hips, digging my fingertips in so hard. The need to mark her skin is sick, but it lives inside of me. A need to brand her as my own and leave my mark on her so no other man will ever lay claim on her body, mind, or soul engulfs me.

"That's it, baby, take my cock," I murmur, biting her earlobe.

Maeve digs her fingernails into my back, and the pain is welcome. "It's too fucking big," she gasps.

I kiss her lips, tangling my tongue with her own.

"Relax, I need to feel every inch sink inside of you," I murmur against her luscious lips.

Maeve shudders, and then I feel her muscles relax as she allows me inside. Every inch of my cock sinks inside of her. Her moans are a mix between pain and pleasure as I fuck her slowly, trying to claw back the animal need to take her savagely.

I hold myself as deep as possible inside of her virgin cunt, gripping her hips. "Fuck, you are so damn tight," I groan.

Maeve half-moans and half-cries as I move out of her tight heat before slamming back into her. "Fuck," she says.

I bite her bottom lip hard, making her yelp in surprise. "I've wanted this for too fucking long, baby."

Maeve's eyes dilate as she rests her head back on the pillow, moaning in a way that stirs the darkness inside of me. I try to control the darkness and rein it in as it weaves its constricting roots around me. For years I've tried to control it, but I always fail. My fingertips inch harder into Maeve's full hips as I thrust into her with more force than before.

Maeve gasps in surprise as I lose all consciousness of my actions, fucking her like a feral animal.

I can't claw myself back as the real me rises to the surface, dark, rough, and merciless.

"Take it," I growl, biting her bottom lip so hard I draw blood.

Maeve's eyes widen as she brings her fingers to the cut.

"On your hands and knees," I order, pulling my cock from her.

She searches my eyes for a few moments before obeying like the good little girl she is.

I feel my breathing labor as I stare at her perfect body, bent over for me and entirely at my mercy.

Her legs part wide, so I can see her dripping wet virgin pussy nestled between her thighs. The image is one of the sweetest things I've ever seen.

I grab hold of her hips and drag her toward me, sliding every inch of my cock as deep as it can go. For a moment, I hold myself still, clawing onto her hips with all my strength. "I could spend the rest of my life in your tight pussy, little dove," I groan.

Maeve releases a gut-wrenching moan which I feel down deep in my soul. A sound that signifies how badly she wants me. I spank her perfect, round ass cheeks with my hand hard, over and over, longing to see the welts appear.

The desire I feel for her is violent as I fuck her

with all my strength, driving into her so hard despite knowing I shouldn't be so rough. Especially not when it is her first time. All my common sense eludes me because I've resisted for too fucking long, and now my urges are uncontrollable.

"Gael," she cries my name, and it sounds utterly perfect.

I wrap my hands in her soft curls and yank her head back. "That's it, little dove. Take it, every damn inch."

Her eyes roll back in her head as I hold her hair, roughly forcing her to arch her back. "Yes, fuck, yes," she murmurs.

I groan as the intensity of the moment overwhelms it. Three years of desperate longing led up to this moment. A moment that I've thought about repeatedly, but none of my fantasies could live up to the reality. Maeve is better than I've ever imagined, and to top it off, no other man has ever been inside her. She is mine in every sense of the word, now and always.

I feel her muscles contract as she whimpers, warning me she is close to coming undone. "Oh God, yes," she cries.

Grinding my teeth together, I fuck her harder and faster, our bodies melding as one. I lean down over her body and whisper in her ear, "I want to feel that tight, virgin pussy come on my cock, baby."

She fists the duvet cover in her hands, body spasming as her orgasm hits her. A flood of hot liquid coats me as she squeezes even tighter, trying to choke my cock. It drives me to the edge so fucking fast.

My body shudders as I rut into her one last time as deep as I can go, unleashing my seed. The intensity of my release is unlike anything I've experienced.

The release of years of longing for this moment all at once.

Maeve is panting for breath as she falls onto her front, my body weight still over her, and my dick still deep in her cunt.

"I'm not finished with you yet, little dove." I nibble on her earlobe, making her groan.

"What do you mean?" she asks.

I smirk at her adorable innocence. "I intend to fuck you repeatedly tonight until you are so tired you can't keep your eyes open any longer." I bite her earlobe. "Even then, I might not stop."

Maeve hasn't even seen the precipice of my darkness. A darkness that has ruled me for as long as I can remember. She may have given me her virginity, but will she regret it once she gets to know the man I truly am?

13

MAEVE

The melody of birds chirping outside of the window of the cabin adds to my elated mood. Life has more purpose now than it has since before my mom died.

Even the sore ache between my thighs isn't enough to dampen it. The pain serves as a reminder of what happened last night. Gael took my virginity, which I've longed for him to do for years. A fantasy I imagined over and over, and yet it was so different in reality.

Gael is unapologetically rough and feral, like a beast. He takes what he wants no matter the consequences, which should turn me off, but it has the opposite effect. I want him more than ever.

The last thing I expected was to enjoy being

handled so roughly, but I guess you can't know what you will enjoy until you experience it. Losing my virginity to Gael was perfect, and I wouldn't have it any other way.

The blissfulness wears away as I realize this can't continue. Nothing has changed, and my engagement to Maxim Volkov still stands. My father tasked Gael with the job of bringing me back to Chicago.

I know my father too well. If Gael believes that he can evade him and keep me safe, he's gravely mistaken. My father is the most violent and ruthless person I know. He will hunt Gael and me down to the ends of the earth to ensure he holds up his pact with the Volkov Bratva.

Short of taking my father out of the equation, there is no world where this ends well. There is too much at stake for the clan if this merger doesn't go ahead.

Gael doesn't only have to worry about my father, but my brothers too. Rourke, Killian, and Kieran have always been fiercely protective of me as the only girl. I still can't understand why they all seemed so unconcerned by my father's announcement of his intentions to sell me to the Bratva. I didn't exactly stick around long enough to learn their opinion about me being married to Maxim.

I sit up, stretching my arms above my head. Gael's masculine scent clings to the sheets and serves as another reminder of our wild night together. He isn't in bed, and I can't hear him in the adjoining bathroom.

The only positive I can take from this is at least we had this time together. At least the man I'd been saving my virginity for finally took it. If I end up with Maxim, at least I'll always have these memories of the man I love.

Gael clears his throat, making me jump. He stands in the bedroom's doorway, holding a mug of coffee. "Cream, no sugar, right?"

I nod, smiling at him. "Yes, thank you."

He approaches, wearing only a pair of pants. My mouth dries as I take in every dip and curve of his muscles, admiring the dark ink that weaves over his skin like a masterpiece. Gael sits on the edge of the bed and passes the mug into my hands.

Tension floods the room as I sip it in silence, sensing that Gael wants to say something. Maybe he regrets what we did last night.

His amber eyes find mine. "Do you realize the consequences of what I've done?"

I set the mug down on the nightstand and return to meet his gaze. "I'm not entirely sure." All he has done is brought me here and had sex with me. My father will be none the wiser if he takes me to Chicago today.

His shoulders slump as he sighs heavily. "Your father won't rest until I'm dead."

I set my hand on his and squeeze. "I'm resigned to my fate, Gael. Return me to Chicago today. At least we had this time together."

Rage burns in his eyes as he narrows them. "Are you fucking insane?"

I shake my head. "I'd rather marry Maxim than watch you die, or live in a world without you in it, even if we can't be together."

He growls like an animal and grabs my throat hard. "Listen carefully, little dove. There is no chance in hell that I'll ever let you marry that Russian piece of trash." He moves his lips to within an inch of mine, feeding the dark desire blazing to life inside of me. "I would die before I gave up my claim on you. You always have and always will belong to me."

The intensity in his voice knocks the air from my lungs as I remain in his grasp, knowing that his words make no sense. If he doesn't return me to Chicago, he will die.

"I can't stand by while my father kills you." My voice sounds so small.

Gael releases my throat and moves his hands to my cheeks. "That won't happen, little dove."

"How can you be so sure?"

Gael's expression darkens. He swallows hard, his Adam's apple bobbing. "Like you said. Your father won't rest until I'm dead, which means it's him or me."

My eyes widen, and my heart thuds against my rib cage. I may have thought the same thing, but Gael is suggesting doing it for real. "Are you saying that you want to kill my father?"

He lets go of my face and stands, pacing the bedroom floor. "No, I don't want to kill him." He runs a hand across the back of his neck. "I have to kill him, Maeve."

I stare at his tense back, taking in every scar that is etched into his skin. Scars that he must have gotten when he was a child. I know very little about his childhood or past, but I know he has no family.

"Is there no other way?" I can't imagine Gael taking my father's life. They've known each other for twenty years, and my father gave him a place to belong when he was lost.

He turns to face me, shaking his head. "He's lost sight of what is important, Maeve. The desire he has for revenge which will never fill the deep void your mother left in his heart is making him insane."

I know he's right. My mother's death has driven him mad for vengeance, caring about nothing but getting payback on the Morrone family for killing her. I guess that's the way he shows his grief, but it's destructive.

"You realize this is insane, right?"

Gael nods. "It's insane, but it is the only way we can be together."

Deep down in my soul, I know I want to be with him more than anything, but this may be a step too far. My father has never been much of a father to me, but he's still my flesh and blood. All three of my brothers look up to him and respect him, and if Gael kills him, they'll have no one.

"What about my brothers?" I ask.

His brow furrows. "What about them?"

"If you kill my father, then that leaves Rourke in charge. He will want revenge for Father's death."

Gael nods. "I've covered every avenue. No one will know that I killed him, and the Bratva will get the blame, sending Chicago into a war like it's never seen before."

Dread sinks into my gut as it means Rourke will have to handle the fallout. I stand and pace the floor, forgetting I'm naked. My father may not have been present in my life, but I love all three of my brothers.

Can I truly subject them to the pain of loss again, all for my gain?

"It's not fair to them," I murmur.

Gael grabs my shoulders and shakes me. "What about you? Do they care your father intends to sell you to a Russian who will take pleasure in mistreating you?" His eyes are wild. "Do you know how perverse Spartak's son is?"

I shake my head. "He's an asshole." I breathe in a deep breath at the mere thought of sleeping with that man. "I've met him several times, but I don't know him."

Gael lets go and paces toward a briefcase, picking it up. "I'll show you."

I watch him as he pulls some papers out of it and returns, handing them to me.

"That girl was an innocent woman he picked up at one of his nightclubs. After one night with him, she spent a month in the ICU from her injuries."

My stomach churns with sickness as I stare at the beaten-up woman in the photos, wondering how Maxim Volkov could do this to someone who went home with him voluntarily. "Why isn't he in prison?"

Gael chuckles. "Always so naïve, little dove." He

gently runs his finger down my cheek, sending a shiver down my spine. "Maxim would never go to prison for something like that, like your brothers wouldn't if they did something so perverse. The police protect the criminals, as that's how it works in the city of Chicago."

I look at the photos again, realizing what he's insinuating. If he leaves me to marry Maxim, that will be my my future.

"My brothers probably don't realize what he's like."

Gael raises a brow. "Rourke gave me this file the day after your father announced your engagement to him. He had his concerns but agreed with your father that it was for the good of the clan." He paces the floor. "You need to stop protecting everyone else and think of yourself, Maeve." He stops and looks at me with so much intensity. "No one cares about you the way I do."

"That's rich considering you left me," I say, despite knowing he had his reasons. At least, he believes he did. In his eyes, it was to protect us both from doing something we couldn't have explained to my father.

Gael stalks toward me and grabs my throat, angling my face to look at him. "I regret my actions every single day, Maeve." He moves his lips to within an inch of mine. "I can't change the past, but I want to make it right now."

I'm utterly torn as I look into his beautiful amber eyes. He wants to kill my father.

How can I be on board with that?

"Can't we just get on a plane and leave the states?" I suggest, knowing that although my father is powerful, his reach only stretches so far.

Gael shakes his head. "Your father will hunt me to the ends of the earth, Maeve. The betrayal in his eyes will be too great for him to leave alone. Do you want to spend the rest of our lives looking over our shoulders?"

I swallow hard. "No, but I won't ever be able to see my brothers again."

Gael pulls me against him, running a hand through my hair. "Now, that is where you're wrong as long as all goes to plan."

My brow furrows as I search his eyes. "How?"

Gael shrugs. "Remember, I intend to frame the Bratva for your father's murder."

Dread claws at me, pulling me down into its dark hole. There is only one word to describe Gael's plan: dangerous. He is insane if he thinks getting in between two criminal organizations is a good idea.

"You will end up dead." I free myself from his grasp, pacing away from him. "I'll lose you all over again."

Gael follows me. "No, you need to have faith in me." He grabs hold of my shoulder and pulls me around to face him. "I will get this done, and the blame will fall on the Bratva."

I search his eyes, wondering what kind of person I am to consider letting him kill my father. Never have I felt so torn in two.

On the one hand, my father has always maltreated me, never caring about my future. He proved that the moment he announced my engagement to Maxim Volkov. I've hated him more than anyone ever since he got my mom killed.

But he is my flesh and blood, no matter what he has done to me. My brothers need him. If he dies, all the responsibility of running the clan falls to Rourke.

It's all too much to process as I turn away from him again, walking toward the bedroom. I need some space to wrap my head around this news. Gael is right that if we flee, my father will hunt both of us down. For years, I've witnessed the terrible things my father is capable of. When I was ten years old, I saw him kill someone in cold blood. He hardly batted an eyelid that his daughter saw the murder, merely sending me to bed once he noticed me.

Deep down in my heart, I know that if he got his hands on us, he would kill Gael and sell me as fast as possible to the Russians.

"Say something, Maeve," Gael pushes, impatience in his tone.

I hug my arms around myself, turning to face him in the bedroom. "It's a lot to take in. I don't know what to say."

Gael walks toward me. "I'll do what you want, baby. If you tell me no, I won't harm your father." He sets his hands on my shoulders, squeezing gently. "I promise."

I feel torn as I stare at the man who holds my heart in the palm of his hand. It's too much to take in as I try to wrap my head around his plan to assassinate my father. "It will take time to process this."

Gael nods. "I understand."

How can he understand?

Gael opened up to me about his family when we first got close. His parents and siblings died in a car crash when he was three years old. Only he survived the crash, which left him to float between foster homes, never finding a stable home or family. It explains the darkness inside of him. I fear I hardly know the man I've fallen for, even if I have seen a glimpse of his true colors here.

He could never understand the gravity of what he proposes. I wish he had killed him and not told me, blaming the Russians for it.

I have no love for my father, but my brothers are important to me. Brothers who Gael believes don't care for me the way I care for them. I think he's wrong. None of them have any sway over my father. The decision to marry me off to Maxim Volkov was his decision alone.

I walk toward the bathroom. "I need time alone to think." I open the door and try to shut it behind me.

Gael grabs it, holding it open. "I understand how hard this is for you, but don't put up walls, little dove. The choice is yours and always will be."

I search his eyes, finding it hard to believe that Gael would respect my decision. He doesn't take orders from me. "Are you saying if I don't want you to kill my father, you won't?"

Gael's expression is torn as he searches my eyes before nodding. "Yes, that's what I'm saying."

A tense silence ensues between us. "I said I need time." I push on the door, shutting it in his face. My breathing is labored as I rest my back against the door. I can't understand why the idea upsets me so much.

My father has never cared about me, and my forced engagement to an abusive Russian was the ultimate proof. I've wished it were my father who died instead of Mom. Gael knows there can only be one of them standing if we are going to be together.

I can't help but think about my brothers, especially Rourke. He is the one who will have to take the burden of the clan on his shoulders far too early. I know he's capable, but I'm not sure he is ready. I rest my head in my hands, feeling torn in two by Gael's revelation.

What kind of person would I be if I'm okay with him killing my father?

No matter what he has done, he's still my blood and a fundamental part of me. I'm not sure I can get on board with his plan. I'm sure this decision will haunt me for the rest of my life, no matter which path I choose.

14

GAEL

The time is growing closer, making me increasingly anxious. I pace the mouth of the path snaking into the forest, waiting for Tiernan's call.

In two days from now, I'm going to pull off the craziest stunt Chicago has seen. Maeve may have agreed that it is the only option, but I worry she has too many reservations.

My cell phone's ringtone breaks through my thoughts, and I answer, "Is everything in place?"

There are a few moments of silence. "Hello to you too." Tiernan clears his throat. "Aye, we are ready to go two nights from now."

"Sorry, I can't help but feel on edge."

Tiernan sighs. "Understandable."

I continue to pace up and down the leaf-covered path, wondering if what I'm trying to do is insane. Luckily for me, Tiernan is head of security for the clan, and he handles security for Ronan, which gives me easy access to him.

"Ronan will be at Spartak's club on Friday night?" I reiterate, making sure he understands the plan.

I hear him clicking his tongue. "Yes, do you think I'm an idiot who can't follow instructions?"

The club Ronan will attend is owned by the Volkov Bratva, making it easier for me to pin his murder on them. My move will plunge Chicago into chaos, but it's worth it to save my little dove. There is nothing I wouldn't do to keep her from that piece of shit, Maxim Volkov.

"How are tensions within the city?" I ask.

"Similar to when you left, but a little tenser since Ronan couldn't keep his mouth shut." Tiernan chuckles. "The idiot told Spartak he had found Maeve and would deliver her to him by now before he even had her." There's a brief pause. "Stop worrying, Gael. Your plan is genius."

It may be a smart plan, but it's not foolproof, and anything could go wrong. If it does, I already have a safe deposit box with all my money and instructions for where Tiernan is to retrieve Maeve, sending her away on a plane with the cash to set her up for life.

I won't allow her to return to a life of hell in Chicago if I die. If Ronan is the one to emerge from the fight alive, he will sell her to Maxim.

"It's a good plan, aye, but we need to remain vigilant." I run a hand through my hair and glance back at the cabin where Maeve is still fast asleep.

She's been off ever since yesterday morning when I told her my plan to kill her father. I didn't expect her to jump for joy. After all, he is her family. What she doesn't understand is that it is him or me. If I don't follow through and remove the threat, he will hunt both of us to the ends of the earth. Not to mention, he holds leverage over me I can never shake. A dark event from my past that I've been hiding from everyone.

"Of course. I'll keep you posted. Seamus and I will meet you at Lake Geneva, north of Chicago, tomorrow evening."

"Perfect," I reply, canceling the call.

Taking a life is never easy, but it gets easier the more you take. I've never taken the life of a friend, though. A man who gave me a chance when no one else would.

Maeve means more to me than anything in this

world. I know her fate if she is married to Maxim, and I won't watch that happen. Unless she insists she doesn't want me to hurt her father, and then I will back off. The last thing I want to do is lose her forever if she doesn't want me to kill him.

As long as she agrees, I will meet my friends in two days and prepare for the most dangerous thing I've ever done.

Maeve must stay here, and I know she will put up a fight, especially since I intend to take her father out when I leave. She may know it is coming, but she doesn't know when yet. I want to walk the other way to clear my mind, but I am smart enough to know procrastinating never gets you anywhere.

Sighing, I head back into the cabin.

Maeve is sitting in one of my shirts halfway buttoned up, reading a book.

The sight is better than any goddamn painting I've ever seen. Maeve is a work of artistic perfection, and everything about her calls to me in the most instinctive, basic way.

"Hey, little dove," I say, breaking her concentration.

She glances up at me. "Hey." She says nothing more, returning her attention to the book she's holding.

I go into the kitchen and open the refrigerator door, grabbing the milk, eggs, and butter. "I'll make us breakfast."

Maeve continues to read her book, ignoring me. I grind my teeth together, trying to contain my irritation at being so blatantly ignored. The silent treatment helps nothing and gets you nowhere. If she has a problem, then she should tell me.

I open the cupboard and grab some flour and sugar, intending to whip up some pancakes as I know it's Maeve's favorite breakfast. The pan heats while I mix up the ingredients and try to see things from Maeve's point of view.

It can be difficult for me to understand family loyalty since I haven't ever had one. At least, not one I can remember. My parents and siblings died in a car crash when I was three years old, leaving me as the sole survivor. I got trapped in an abusive foster home, never finding a place I belonged. Until I found Ronan, and he accepted me into the Callaghan Clan.

It's the one place I belonged. My brutal killer instincts were perfect for the clan, and Ronan molded me into his chief. Ten years ago, I would have said that nothing could have made me betray Ronan. My loyalty was unwavering and blind.

If it weren't for Maeve, I'd still be the same devoted soldier. However, twenty years since joining the clan, I intend to betray him in the most despicable way.

Guilt coils through me as I cook the mixture in the pan, trying to reason with myself. Ronan taught me never to hesitate to kill first if someone wants you dead. I understand why Maeve is so torn, but it is kill or be killed.

It is necessary for our survival if we want to be together.

The light scent of burning catches my attention, and I shake my head, forcing myself to focus on the food. Once I've cooked all the pancakes and piled them onto the plate, I turn my attention to her.

"Pancakes are ready," I say.

Maeve doesn't turn to look at me, merely mutters, "I'm not hungry."

I slam the two plates down on the table, making her jump. "Don't make me drag you to the table."

Maeve's back tenses at the tone of my voice. "I said I'm not hungry."

Rage coils through me as I try to control my reaction. I pace toward Maeve and grab the book out of her hand, throwing it onto the other sofa.

Her eyes widen. "What the fuck? You lost my page."

"I don't give a shit about your page, Maeve." I set my hands on the armrests of the chair she is sitting in. "You need to eat, and we need to talk."

Her neck bobs as she swallows. "I'm not sure what we need to talk about."

I lean closer to her, moving my face to within an inch of hers. "Are you trying to anger me, little dove?"

She raises a brow. "I just don't want to talk about it."

I slide my fingers around her throat and squeeze gently. "I don't care what you want. We need to figure this out."

Maeve's eyes dilate at my rough treatment of her. I ignore the clawing need grasping at my insides. The need to fuck her roughly on this sofa until she's begging me for more. "Okay, calm down," she spits.

I release my grasp of her throat and take a step back.

She stands and walks past me, sitting down at the table.

I join her and meet her gaze. After I told her yesterday morning, neither of us have mentioned her father again. "I need to know how you feel about my plan, Maeve."

Maeve sits back in her chair. "You mean your plan to murder my father?"

I run a hand across the back of my neck, trying not to lose my cool. "Yes, I told you yesterday. If you don't want me to, then tell me."

A torn expression enters her eyes as she searches mine. "You realize how hard this is for me, right?"

I tilt my head to the side. "Do you believe your father cares what happens to you?"

I regret my question immediately as sorrow fills her radiant blue eyes. "Not really, no," she mutters.

I reach for her hand on the table, but she moves it away. I clench my fingers. "Ronan wouldn't have arranged your marriage to a Russian if he did." Ronan has never cared for her the way a father should care for his daughter, as he has seen her as nothing more than a chess piece in the game he plays.

She nods. "I know."

I point at the plate of pancakes in front of her. "You need to eat."

Maeve rolls her eyes. "I don't think I'm going to waste away, somehow."

I laugh, which lightens the mood. "No, but I made your favorite, baby girl."

She sighs heavily before picking up her fork and taking a small bite. "I don't know why you told me."

My brow furrows. "Would you have preferred that I killed your father and lied to you about it?"

Maeve searches my eyes before shaking her head. "No… I don't know." Her brow furrows. "I wish there were another way."

There is no other way. It's Ronan or me. I'd rather not betray the man who took me in and gave me a purpose in life. Taking his life will be one of the hardest things I've ever done, and yet, I'm certain it is the right thing to do. "There is no other way." I shake my head. "I went through every outcome multiple times in the six months since you ran." I take Maeve's hand and squeeze. "I knew he would find you in the end."

Maeve nods, reclaiming her hand as she forks some pancake into her mouth. "How are you going to explain where you were all this time to my brothers?"

"The most logical explanation is the Russians followed me to Madison and kidnapped us." I crack my neck, feeling the tension build at the thought of trying to pull it off. "I have a plan in place where they will find us. The details aren't important right now.

You will need to corroborate my story, though, so we will discuss it in more detail nearer the time."

Maeve groans. "Great. I'm a terrible liar."

I shake my head. "I disagree. I've witnessed you lie frequently, and you're excellent at it."

Her brow furrows. "When?"

"All the times you snuck out to a party." I smirk at her. "Then blame your hangover on a stomach bug to your brothers." I shrug. "They all believed you."

"And you didn't, so that is proof I'm a terrible liar."

I realize the danger I'm flirting with, revealing the deepness of my obsession with Maeve. I frequently followed her to ensure she was safe, keeping a distance from her so she never detected me. "Let's just say I have kept a personal interest in your safety for longer than you might think."

"Are you saying you stalked me?" Maeve asks.

I clench my jaw. "I wouldn't call it stalking, little dove." I reach for her hand and take it this time. "I wanted nothing to happen to you. I've felt very protective of you for a while."

Maeve's cheeks flush as she glances down at her plate, allowing me to hold her hand. "Right. That's why you almost killed Chad."

I growl at the reminder of that snake. "A bastard

that would have raped you if I hadn't got there in time."

She meets my gaze, and the inferno in her eyes takes me by surprise.

It takes all my self-control not to bend her over this table, but I need to figure out if she is on board right now. The last thing I want is for her to resent me. "Do you want me to do what needs to be done or not?"

Maeve stares at me for a few agonizing moments before nodding. "There's no other option."

The relief I feel is sickening. Maeve had to agree to the plan. Otherwise, I would have to return to Ronan empty-handed, allowing Maeve to run from me forever.

The idea of not seeing her again would have been almost impossible to accept, and I fear the darkness inside of me may not have let it happen. Although I told her she had a choice, I'm not entirely sure she did.

Thankfully, we'll never have to find out.

15

MAEVE

I watch out of the window, waiting for Gael's car to disappear down the track from the cabin. He's leaving for the nearest town to get supplies, about fifteen minute's drive, and I intend to get some fresh air while he's gone, even though he told me not to leave the cabin.

We're in the middle of nowhere, so I can't understand what danger there could be. I grab my coat and rush out of the door toward the mountain path. Gael has kept me cooped up in that tiny cabin for four days, and I'm going out of my mind.

It's about time I got some exercise. I know if Gael comes back earlier than I expect, I'll get punished for disobeying him. I can't deny that the prospect excites me, as Gael's harsh treatment is addictive.

I head up the path, ascending the mountain. The trees' leaves rustle as the cool wind rushes through them, making me shiver. The scenery on the mountain is beautiful, and I take in everything around me, trying to distract my mind from the awful murder Gael will commit.

It's impossible, though.

Every waking moment, his plan is all I can think about. The guilt threatens to tear me apart, but I know we have no choice. As Gael put it, it's kill or be killed. I don't know what my father is capable of. If he learns I slept with Gael, breaking his pact with Maxim, he might kill me too. I would no longer be so valuable to him.

The soft water flow catches my attention, and I follow the trickle, finding a crystal clear stream running down the mountainside. It's a soothing sound that helps clear my head as I focus on it, walking the path along the stream further up the mountain.

I check my watch and see it has only been twenty minutes, and Gael should be gone for another forty minutes, at least. I find a dry stone by the bank of the stream and sit down, resting next to it and taking in the beauty of this place. A fish swims against the current, fighting an uphill battle, and I watch it, mesmerized.

It's hard to believe it doesn't get tired as it slowly makes its way further and further. I glance at my watch, realizing I need to get going to make it before Gael gets back.

I stand and turn the way I came, meandering along the winding mountain path back toward the cabin. After about ten minutes, I hear a gunshot and freeze. My body stiffens as I realize I'm not the only person out here.

A crunch of branches and leaves beneath feet signals whoever shot the gun is heading this way. My heart hammers harder as I try to work out what to do. It could just be an innocent hunter, but I feel anyone up this mountain is probably someone you don't want to meet.

A tall figure appears from further up the path, making my stomach sink. The man's eyes widen when he sees me, and then a sick smirk twists onto his lips. "Hey, Jackson. Look what I've found," his deep voice calls, making my stomach dip. There is more than one of them up here.

"Is it a deer? I'm fucking starving for some veni—" Jackson appears behind him, even taller and bigger than the man before him. He's holding a shovel in one hand and has a rifle over his shoulder. An evil glint ignites in his eyes when he sees me as he adjusts the gun on his shoulder. He licks his lips. "Better than venison, Kev. Isn't this a treat?" He says.

I hold my hands up. "Look, I don't want any trouble, and I'm here on vacation with my boyfriend."

Jackson glances at Kev. "Boyfriend, hey?" he says, glancing around. "I don't see no boyfriend, sweetheart."

I tense, realizing that I need to run for my life. I narrow my eyes. "That's because he's less than four hundred feet away in the cabin we rented."

Kev shakes his head. "She thinks we don't know this mountain, Jackson."

Jackson nods. "The nearest cabin is more than a mile from here, sweetheart."

I take a step backward, realizing I'm royally fucked. Gael will never let me hear the end of this if I make it out alive. "What do you want?" I ask.

The two men smirk, and I already know the answer. They're hunters, and they see me as prey. "I can think of quite a few things I want with you. Starting with that pretty little mouth of yours." Kev grabs his crotch, making me sick to the stomach.

I don't waste another second, turning and running down the path toward the cabin. My heart pounds as fast as my feet thud on the floor.

How could I be so stupid?

Gael told me not to leave the cabin, and I didn't listen. Blood pulses in my ears as I increase the speed of my footsteps, running as hard and fast as I physically can.

The thud of heavy boots hitting the ground close behind me sends dread through every vein. I panic, trying to run faster, but my legs are screaming in agony.

Like the klutz I am, I trip on a tree root protruding from the ground, falling flat on my face. The men grab me and hoist me to my feet.

"Where the fuck do you think you are going, pretty lady?"

I swallow hard at the stench of stale alcohol and cigarettes emanating from the two men.

"Let me go or I'll scream."

They both laugh. "Who do you think will help you out here?"

I yank my arm out of Jackson's grasp. "My boyfriend will kill both of you." I glare at them.

"As we said, we don't see no boyfriend, sweetheart."

I take a step backward, knowing there is no reasoning with these men.

"There's no point fighting it. Why don't you

accept it for what it is and enjoy the experience?" Kev asks.

Is he insane? The man is asking why I don't just enjoy being raped by two dirty perverts.

Kev comes for me, and I scream at the top of my lungs, hoping that Gael is back from town. It's my only chance of getting away from them. He grabs my wrists and pulls me against him. "No one can hear you scream, so do it all the fuck you like. Neither of us is buying this boyfriend shit."

He pushes me to the ground on my back and rips my coat off me. My heart pounds wildly as he stares down at me like a predator watching his prey and toying with it.

Tears flood my eyes as I try to hold it together, wishing I had just listened to Gael.

Jackson takes the place of Kev and tears at my top, ripping it in two. "Move out of the way. I'll get her naked." He moves over me, trying to strip me down to my skin as I struggle against him.

"Get the fuck off me!" I shout.

The crunch of leaves underfoot signals we're no longer alone. My heart soars with hope. I tense as Jackson unzips my pants and tries to pull them down my hips. I feel helpless, but all I can do is hope Gael finds me in time.

The shot of a gun startles me as Jackson falls on top of me, blood spilling out of his mouth, getting it all over my shirt. I glance to the left to see Kev's shocked expression as he turns to face the attacker.

"What the—" Kev stops short as Gael is a foot from him. His eyes are manic as he stabs a knife into his throat and slits it open.

The blood sprays into the air and all over Gael, making my skin crawl. "Fuck," I cry, desperately trying to claw myself from under the heavy deadweight of Jackson.

"Stop," Gael booms, grabbing his body and moving him off me effortlessly. "What the fuck were you thinking, little dove?" he asks, eyes chaotic with a rage so fierce it scares me. "These men were about to defile you, and I told you not to leave the damn cabin." His frantic expression, coupled with blood staining his shirt and splattered on his face, makes him a horrific image.

I swallow hard, knowing I have no explanation. "I thought there would be no one up here and wanted to get some air."

He grabs me and lifts me off the floor, shaking his head. "If it were safe, I wouldn't have insisted you stay in the cabin."

I swallow hard, shaking my head. Blood coats my

clothes as I stand there, feeling pathetic. "I thought you were being overprotective."

Gael growls and moves toward me, grabbing my throat with his hand. "All I ever do is try to protect you, little dove. Why do you fight that?"

I bite my bottom lip. Gael is expecting an answer I don't have.

A muscle in his jaw ticks as he pushes me against a nearby tree. "Did you want me to find out and punish you?" His eyes narrow. "Is that what this was about?"

"No, I just—" I hang my head, knowing deep down, it was exactly my intention. Until those hunters tried to rape me, that's when I realized how stupid I'd been.

"What, Maeve? I can't understand why you'd venture so far away from the cabin if you just wanted fresh air."

I sigh heavily. "Yes, I wanted you to punish me," I murmur, meeting Gael's gaze. "If I'd realized other people were on this mountain, then I'd never have—"

Gael silences me, kissing me hard. Our lips meld in a violent clash as his tongue thrusts against mine with desperation. My heart is pounding as the adrenaline continues to rush through my veins.

He shot one man dead in front of my eyes and

cut the other's throat, and I want him more than ever. Perhaps I'm as sick and twisted as him. After all, I'm the princess of an organized crime family. Violence and danger have surrounded me my entire life.

The blood on Gael's hands should make me sick as he touches me, but it doesn't. He killed them for me, to save me. I believe now more than ever that our desire for each other is a sickness.

When he breaks away, my stomach churns. The blood from the men he killed is smeared over his shirt, face, and hands, giving him a brutal appearance, but it only deepens the need inside of me.

What is wrong with me?

"I'm going to fuck some sense into you right here," he growls, bringing me back to the present.

I can't believe he intends to fuck me here. Despite how ludicrous it is, my pussy gets wetter at the statement. I glance at the two rapists on the floor, feeling nothing but relief that they're gone. "Shouldn't we clean up the mess?"

He tilts his head to the side, smirking at me. "I must admit that I'm surprised how cool you are about this." He moves for me again, grabbing my hips and pulling me against him. "Perhaps we aren't so different after all."

I search his amber eyes, knowing without a doubt

that my love for this man knows no bounds. All I can think about is the consequences of him killing these men for me. "If someone comes up here and finds them, then you'll go to prison."

Gael cups my face in his bloodied hands. "I guarantee that won't happen." He presses his lips to mine in a quick kiss. "Trust me."

I don't say another word as he kisses me, plunging his tongue in and out of my mouth with fevered desperation. My love for this man is a disease I have no control over. He could do anything, and I'm not sure I'd have the power to resist his charm.

He pushes me hard against the tree trunk, pinning me with his weight. The sheer dominance drives me crazy. His fingertips dig into my bruised hips, inflicting sensuous pain as he bites my earlobe.

The adrenaline still coursing through my veins heightens all of my senses. The taste of him, the scent of him, the feel of him against my skin, all of it is ten times more acute as I allow him to devour me, forgetting about the bloody mess he left in his wake.

Gael wraps his powerful arms around my waist and lifts me against the tree, holding me with one arm. "I'm going to fuck you so damn hard, Maeve," he groans, sliding a hand under my panties and dipping a finger into my eager cunt.

"Fuck," I hiss, feeling unbelievably sensitive to his touch.

Gael bites my shoulder so hard he breaks the skin before sucking the wound. "I need to punish you for your disobedience, but right now, all I need is to fuck you." He frantically fumbles with the zip of his pants, freeing his hard cock.

My heart pounds in my ears as his amber eyes find mine. The intensity in them sets my soul on fire and darkens it all at the same time. The darkness that has always lived inside of me rises to the surface. It makes me wonder if I'm not unlike my father, after all: broken and desensitized to blood, violence, and death.

Gael brings out both the best and worst parts of me. I feel the tip of his hard cock nudging against my soaking wet entrance.

"Do you want my cock, little dove?" he asks, searching my eyes with those beautiful amber gems.

I nod in response, clawing into his shoulders in preparation, feeling the raised scars through his shirt. Scars I still don't know how he got.

"Tell me how badly you want it," he teases, moving the tip through my arousal.

"I want it so bad, sir. Please give it to me."

He growls softly. "I'm not sure I believe you, baby girl."

I groan, knowing this is a part of my punishment. Gael is going to tease me until I'm begging him like I've begged no one before.

16

GAEL

I've never felt fear quite like it. An uncontrollable and dangerous emotion that had the power to bring me to my knees.

When I stepped into the cabin and found Maeve missing, every terrible scenario went through my mind. Then, when I heard the scream, I knew my worst nightmare had come true. I ran the entire way to her with adrenaline unlike anything I've felt pulsing through my veins.

Now she stands before me, looking disheveled and covered in the men's blood that I killed. It's sick that I delight in the image. An image that proves I protected her, but only just. Those men should have experienced a more painful death, but I didn't have the time.

I bring my attention to her crystal blue eyes that almost sparkle in the dappled light of the sun broaching the cover of the tree branches. My cock throbs against her dripping wet center as I drag it through her pussy. "Convince me you want it," I tease, my voice hardly recognizable.

The frustration in her blue eyes is adorable. I will teach her what it truly means to be denied pleasure and the tantalizing effects the denial can have.

"I want it so bad, Gael. Please give me your cock," she moans.

I raise a brow, teasing her more. "I'm not sure, little dove." I tilt my head to the side. "Wouldn't I be rewarding you for your unacceptable behavior?"

She bites her bottom lip between her teeth, drawing my attention there. "I'm sorry for disobeying you, sir. I won't ever do it again." I struggle to keep a hold of the threads of my control as I long to be buried inside of her.

I've always been able to delay gratification, but with Maeve, it seems my usual control doesn't exist. "Is that right? How do I know you aren't saying that to get what you want?"

She grunts in frustration, shaking her head. "What do I have to do to prove it to you?"

I bite her bottom lip. "I'll fuck you on one condition. You won't come, no matter how badly you want to, and that's your punishment."

Maeve whimpers. "I'm not sure I can promise that."

I pull my cock away from her entrance. "Then I won't fuck you."

"No, okay, I won't come."

I narrow my eyes at her. "If you disobey me, then your punishment will be ten times harsher."

She nods in response. "Yes, sir, please fuck me."

I search her eyes, wondering how I got this lucky to land Maeve Callaghan. She is too fucking good for me. I push inside of her with one hard stroke, groaning as her tight, wet heat encases me.

Maeve cries out loud, her moans echoing through the trees. "Fuck, it feels so good."

I bite her bottom lip between my teeth hard, drawing blood. "You have such a dirty mouth, little dove."

Her eyes find mine. "Only when you're inside of me, sir."

She knows how to drive me wild.

I lift her lithe frame up and down my length. My muscles are straining as I take her like an animal out in the wild. Maeve calls to the feral side of me. The beast I've tried to keep caged but failed to do so. My escape to Europe was a feeble attempt to contain this dark side of me that threatened to destroy the delicate beauty before me, as we were always going to end up here.

Her reaction to seeing me murder two men wasn't what I expected. Perhaps she has similar darkness lurking beneath the surface, as I know she harbors trauma that even she is consciously unaware of.

Not to mention, her family has exposed her to violence and murder from a young age. Her father never tried to shield his children from his work.

Maeve groans, biting her cut lip as I lift her harder and faster, my desire for her heightening with each thrust.

The way I feel for her only magnifies with every second that passes.

"That's it, take my cock like a good girl and make sure you don't come." I bite her shoulder roughly, making her yelp.

My muscles strain as I continue to hold her against the tree, knowing the bark will graze her skin. I welcome the idea. My desire to inflict pain is deep-rooted in who I am.

"Oh fuck, Gael. How can I hold on?" she cries, her eyes frantic.

"Mind over matter, baby girl."

I stop fucking her and lift her away from the tree, setting her down on the damp forest floor. "You look utterly angelic," I murmur, taking in the image of her sprawled over the leaves and dirt, naked and writhing for me.

Maeve groans, eyes traveling down my body as I kneel between her spread thighs.

"You belong to me, Maeve Callaghan. Never forget that," I murmur into her ear before plunging my cock back into her cunt.

She cries out, her muscles contracting as she fights the orgasm.

"Good girl, fight it for me," I purr, sliding out and then slamming back into her.

Our bodies come together in a fierce clash of skin, dirt, and blood. I feel the rawness of the moment deep in my soul. Neither of us can fight this cosmic pull we have on each other.

Maeve groans, her eyes lulling back in her head as she bites her lip, trying desperately not to let her release come.

I don't give her any mercy, pounding into her roughly. Her firm nipples lure me to lean over and suck on them one by one. Maeve's tortured moans are her response to my tongue lavishing attention on them. I move my mouth away and pinch them forcefully, making her hiss in surprise.

Her cries are laced with anguish as she forces herself not to come. It's a delicious sound I take deep satisfaction from. Despite my protective nature over my little dove, I love to be the one to inflict pain and suffering on her. It's the sadist inside of me rising to the surface.

I claw my fingers into her bruised hips, using my weight to exert my dominance over her.

Maeve groans and wriggles under me, trying to gain control.

She has none with me. Maeve is entirely at my mercy, and that's something I have very little of.

"Oh fuck, I don't know if I can stop myself," she pants.

I grab her throat and squeeze, forcing her eyes open wide. "You will obey me. Do not come."

Her lip trembles as she nods in reply. "Yes, sir."

I feel my cock swell as her eager obedience drives me wild. Obedience I have wanted from her for three years.

"Such a good girl," I muse, thrusting into her with long strokes. I lick her cut bottom lip as the desire inside of me takes on a life of its own.

Maeve's eyes roll back in her head, but she does

as she is told. Every thrilling thrust is driving me closer to my climax, one that I will deny her for now.

She'll learn how amazing I can make her feel once she resists the temptation. I don't intend to let her come until after I've filled her with my seed.

Good things come to those who wait.

"Fuck, this is so hard," Maeve whines, clawing at my chest with her nails.

The pain of her nails digging into my skin is welcome, and it helps ground me when I feel like nothing is holding me to this earth anymore. Maeve is the only thing that makes sense in this world.

If I can't pull off my assassination and successfully frame the Bratva, life as I know it may end. I've always put the Callaghan Clan first, but now I'm putting Maeve and me above all else.

She has become my reason for living.

"I'm going to fill that pretty little cunt with my cum," I growl into her ear. "Is that what you want, little dove?"

She groans, trying desperately to hold on to the threads of her climax and not let go. "I just want to come," she cries.

"Too bad naughty girls don't get what they want. Isn't it?"

I slam into her harder, forcing myself to the edge

of no return. My cock swells, stretching her tight pussy even more as I unleash every drop of cum inside of her.

Maeve whimpers, obeying my command and not letting herself orgasm. "What now?" she pants, eyes wide and frantic.

I smirk at her, knowing that deep down I can't deny my little dove anything. "Now, you need to come for me, baby girl."

Her eyes widen as I continue to fuck her, driving her toward the climax she has fought the entire time. "I thought you—"

I kiss her lips, silencing her. All I need to hear right now are her moans as she has the best orgasm she's ever felt. My tongue plunges into her mouth, gently searching every inch as our saliva mingles.

She groans against my lips, digging her fingernails into my shoulders as I force her to climax. "Fuck," she cries against my lips, frantically spasming beneath me.

Her pussy clenches around my cock as if it never wants me to leave. Hell, I never want to leave her body. If I could spend the rest of my life fucking her, I still wouldn't get enough of my Irish princess.

We rest in the cold, wet dirt for what feels like a lifetime, both of us panting for oxygen as reality slowly returns. I see it in Maeve's eyes as she remembers what happened before we fucked next to two dead bodies, the blood of my prey smeared on both of us.

"Shit," Maeve says, trying to shift me off of her.

I roll away, rising to my feet.

Maeve jumps up and shakes her head, staring at the two dead bodies. "What the fuck are we going to do?"

"Calm down, little dove. You will do nothing." I move toward her and grab her hips, drawing her close. "You will go back to the cabin and have a long, hot bath."

Maeve shakes her head. "No, I have to help you, as it will be quicker."

I stare at Maeve, considering letting her help. She's right, it would be faster, but I can't let her do something so gruesome. I killed these men, and now I'm going to cover my tracks. "No." I cup her face. "Do as you are told." I glance at the men. "We both know what happened when you disobeyed me last time."

A flash of hurt enters her crystal blue eyes. "Are you saying their deaths are my fault?" Her voice is frantic.

My brow furrows. "No. It is their fault for trying

to rape you." I yank her against me. "Please listen to me for once. Return to the cabin."

She searches my eyes before finally relinquishing the fight. "Fine." Her expression turns concerned as she glances at the two dead bodies. "How long will you be?"

I don't know how long it will take me. The ground is hard at this time of year, meaning it will be tough digging the holes to bury them. "Not too long," I lie.

Maeve wraps her arms around my waist and hugs me tightly before turning to leave me. I don't blame Maeve for their deaths. Only I have control over my actions, and the moment I saw that bastard with his hands on her, I snapped.

Love is supposed to be pure, but it becomes diseased when it comes from a man as damaged as me. My love for Maeve is a poison that harms people around us, even if those convicts deserved to die.

I force my troubling thoughts out of my mind. These idiots brought the shovel that will dig their graves, saving me a trip back to the cabin. I grab it and get to work, knowing Maeve doesn't want to be alone for too long.

All I want is to make her happy and keep her safe. It's all I've ever wanted.

17

MAEVE

I stare mindlessly at my bloody clothes in the center of the hardwood floor. My knees held tight against my chest as I rock back and forth gently, trying to soothe the chaos inside. The silence is unbearable as the part of me that has always been broken feels utterly unmendable.

Gael told me to return and take a bath, but I couldn't face doing anything other than stripping the clothes from my body. I can't stop thinking about the gurgling sound as Gael slashed that knife through Kev's throat and the way the blood arced into the sky and splattered over the both of us.

They say that who your parents are doesn't define you, but I beg to differ. For as long as I can remember, I've had a darkness inside of me. I must have inherited it from my father, as my mom was as good as anyone could be.

When Gael killed those two men, all I felt was disgust that their blood got on my favorite shirt. If that isn't proof of how far I've fallen, I'm not sure what is. My mom would be shocked if she could see me now, as Gael brings out that darkness in me.

Sure, those men were about to rape me and have probably raped women before, as it was like second nature to them. However, who am I to say they should die for that sin? Gael could have fought the two men off like he did when Chad got too forceful with me.

Perhaps that would have been enough to save their future victims. They were worthless rapists, but I know that none of us may decide who lives and who dies. Although, both Gael and my father would probably disagree with me, as they have taken countless lives.

My sickness runs deep as a part of me wanted to help him bury the bodies and discard the evidence. Instead of feeling disgusted at my lover's actions, I let him fuck me against a tree as if he didn't just kill two men. There is something very wrong with me.

The click of the lock turning in the cabin door snaps me out of my trance momentarily. Gael is back, and I can't stand the thought of moving as I hug my legs tighter against my chest.

"Maeve?" Gael calls.

I want to respond, but I'm not sure how. My brain has short-circuited as I continue to rock myself.

His heavy footsteps thud toward the bedroom. Panic-stricken eyes find mine the moment he reaches the door. I observe the way the tension in his shoulders eases the moment he sees me.

Thick mud coats his bloodied clothes that serve as a reminder of what he just did. He buried two men out in the woods so no one would ever find them. A part of me wonders if they had any family, but the dark part of me doesn't care.

"Why didn't you answer me, little dove?" He steps closer, eyes darting between my bloody clothes and me.

I shake my head in response, unable to find my voice.

Gael tilts his head, moving ever closer. "Are you okay?"

I search his amber eyes, trying to use him to ground me in a world that makes very little sense. "No."

Gael sighs, walking over to me. He sits down by

my side. "It was a horrific scene for you to witness. I'm sorry."

I meet his gaze. "It's me not finding it horrific that's the problem." I draw in a deep, shaky breath. "I felt nothing when you killed them."

Gael reaches for me, trying to pull me into a hug.

I shake my head. "Don't." The thought of being touched right now makes my skin crawl.

"Fine." Gael moves up the bed and rests his back against the headboard. "Do you want to talk about it?"

I meet his calm, amber stare.

"What is bothering you?" he asks, taking my hand in his. "Do you worry you aren't a good person? Because Maeve–"

"Stop. I don't want you to tell me I'm a good person." I shake my head "I know I'm not. Do you know the first thing I thought when you shot that man?"

Gael shakes his head in response.

"I can't believe his blood just ruined my shirt."

Gael raises an eyebrow. "That was your first thought?"

My stomach sinks as I realize I might reveal how dark my soul is. Gael views me as this innocent and sweet princess who can do no wrong.

I've never murdered someone, but I've witnessed my father and older brothers kill enough times not to be shocked by it.

"Yes, I'm sick," I murmur, hugging my legs tighter to my chest.

Gael rubs a hand across his stubble dusted jaw. "Believe me. You don't know the meaning of the word." His eyes are blazing with certainty. "I'm damaged beyond anything you could ever imagine."

I tilt my head to the side. "How did you get that way?" I ask, genuinely intrigued whether it was because of his rough childhood. Although I know he had no family, I do not know what he went through, as Gael never went into detail. The only glimpse into his past are those horrific scars over his back, which must result from the abusive foster home he got stuck in.

He sighs. "My childhood was rough, as you know."

I nod. "Yes, but you never told me about it."

Gael's jaw clenches, and his entire body turns rigid. "Because some things are best left buried, Maeve." His voice sounds haunted.

"Maybe that's not true." I shrug. "I mean, I'm fucked up because of the death, blood, and gore my father subjected me to at a young age. Is it similar?"

The tension in his frame increases, making me wonder what he went through. "Not exactly." The answer is cold, and I can feel him pulling away from me.

"Okay, I'll stop asking you about it." I continue to hug my legs into my chest. Silence ensues between us, but it's not awkward as it feels like we're both silently wrestling our inner demons together.

Gael breaks the silence, "All you need to know is that I lived with some terrible people growing up." His eyes find mine. "They did unspeakable things to me, and I'm not ready to go into detail about it. Add that on top of the survivor's guilt I felt when I was old enough to understand that I was the only one of my family to survive." His voice cracks with emotion. "I often wished I hadn't, and for years I believed it was my fault they were dead."

My brow furrows. "That makes no sense."

"No, but most emotions don't make logical sense." Gael shifts closer to me, and I allow him to wrap an arm around me, pulling me close. "I don't let my past define my future, Maeve, and neither should you." He runs his fingers through my hair. "You may not have felt bad about me killing those men, but why should you? They were going to rape you, for fuck's sake." The anger in his voice shines through. "It's natural to feel relief that they are dead, even if most people wouldn't admit it."

To a certain degree, I know he's right, but the blood and gore would shock most people. I sat here while Gael dug a hole and buried the bodies, making sure no one will ever find them. I should feel some remorse, but I feel nothing.

"So, we're both fucked up?" I ask, trying to lighten the mood despite the anxiety I feel over my lack of empathy.

Gael laughs, but it's a sad laugh. "Maybe that's why we're so perfect for each other."

My chest aches with emotion. "Maybe." I wonder if we're the worst match for each other. Gael brings out a side of me I never wanted to be uncovered.

Gael lifts my chin, forcing me to look up into his eyes. "We are two broken parts of a whole. When I'm with you, it feels like there is hope I can heal the wounds in my soul."

The intensity in his voice cuts me to the core. "I hope so too," I murmur, wrapping my arms around him and squeezing tightly.

Gael clears his throat. "What was your childhood like?" he asks.

My brow furrows. "It was okay other than the darkness that always surrounded our family." I run a hand over his shirt, feeling his chiseled muscles beneath. "I mean, you were there often, in the background." I meet his gaze, wondering why he would ask. "Our father was often absent, but I didn't mind that, as I preferred it when it was Mom, my brothers, and me. Father's disciplinary methods were harsh."

Gael sighs heavily. "Your father is a good man. He has just lost his way."

I'm not sure I believe that. "If that's the case, why do you want to murder him?"

He stiffens beneath me. "I don't want to murder him. I have to."

I get that there is no world in which we live in America and my father forgets about us, but I'm not sure he can say he has to. "I evaded him for six months, only in a state over from Chicago."

Gael clears his throat. "You don't know what it is like living your life on the run." He sounds like he does.

"And you do?" I ask, glancing up at him.

"Yes, I made some terrible mistakes in my youth." His brow furrows. "The only reason I'm not still on the run is that your father took me in and gave me a place in the clan."

"So, if you don't kill him, he will out you to whoever you were hiding from?" I ask.

He nods. "Yes, the police."

My stomach churns as I stare up at the troubled man I've fallen in love with. "What for?"

"Maeve, drop it." He glares at me with an intensity that would stop most people's hearts.

"I want to know everything about you, Gael. The bad too."

He sighs. "I murdered someone who mistreated me growing up in cold blood."

My heart skips a beat. "How old were you?"

"Seventeen years old. I'd been on the run for a year before your father took me in." His jaw clenches. "Believe me, killing your father is going to be one of the hardest things I've ever done." He glances down at me. "It's worth it for you, Maeve. Why should you suffer at the hands of Maxim Volkov for him?"

I contemplate his words. My father has lost sight of what is important in life: people who love and care for you. He's never shown me the love he should have in my life.

Rourke insists he was different before, as he remembers a time when our father was happy. He is eight years older than me, and I'm not sure why he changed, and neither is Rourke.

"I don't think I should, but do you think there is no reasoning with him?" I ask.

Gael chuckles and shakes his head. "Maeve, I've seen him choke the life out of a man who questioned his choice of suit for a party."

I raise a brow.

"Yes, your father killed a tailor right in front of my eyes. Do you think he'll negotiate with me over you marrying Maxim?" He shakes his head. "He'll kill me before I have the chance to plead my case."

I sit up straighter. "But would he listen to me?"

"You already know the answer to that question, little dove."

I search my soul and know deep down that I do. My father wouldn't listen to me, as he hasn't my entire life. If I approached him and pleaded our case, he'd probably kidnap me and force me to marry Maxim as fast as possible. He won't let anyone stand in his way.

"I do, but I'm not sure how I'm going to face my brothers knowing we were the reason he died." The guilt lies heavy on my chest, and Gael hasn't even killed him yet. I fear the guilt will be unbearable once it is done.

"If you want me to back out, there's still time," Gael says, but I can detect the uncertainty in his voice. He insists I have a choice, but I'm not entirely sure I do.

"No, I want to be with you above everything else." I sigh heavily. "I just worry about my brothers."

He hugs me tighter to his chest and cradles me. "They are adults. They can take care of themselves."

I swallow hard. "I hope you are right." Rourke has been training to take my father's position for years, but he would be the youngest leader Chicago has ever seen at twenty-nine years old.

It's impossible not to worry because I love all three of my brothers. Hurting them is inevitable with Gael's plan, and that is something I will always struggle with.

18

GAEL

I can't help but worry about Maeve. What she witnessed yesterday shook her, and it's understandable. Maeve may be the clan princess, but she's never been that close to the violence.

She believes that makes her a bad person because she felt nothing when those scum died. I think it makes her human, especially since she's so torn up about it now.

I'm supposed to leave this evening to meet Seamus and Tiernan, an hour and a half drive outside the city. Her fragile state makes leaving difficult, especially as I know she won't want to stay in this cabin.

It's mid-afternoon, and I have to tell her sooner

rather than later. Maeve sits on the sofa, reading a book.

"Can we talk?" I ask.

Maeve glances up from the book, setting it down on the coffee table. Her radiant smile has been nowhere to be seen ever since last night. I miss her smile, but I'm not sure how to bring it back, and certainly not with the news I'm about to give her. "Sure."

I crack my neck, preparing myself for her to fight. "I have to leave for Lake Geneva tonight."

Maeve's eyes widen. "What?"

I swallow hard, knowing from the tone of her voice she'll not accept this easily. "I have to leave for Lake Geneva tonight."

She shakes her head. "I heard you. Why did you leave it until now to tell me?"

Originally, I had intended to tell her after I got back from town yesterday, but the chaos that ensued after my return made it impossible. Maeve was not in a stable place. "Because I knew this would be your reaction."

A fierce flash of anger ignites in her eyes, anger like I've never seen from her. "I haven't reacted yet." She stands to her feet and paces forward. "But you're right. I have no intention of staying in this cabin alone."

I sigh heavily. "You'll do as you're told, Maeve. It isn't up for negotiation."

Her chest heaves as the rage mounts. "I'll fucking hitchhike to Chicago if you leave me here."

The threat gets on my last nerve as I close the gap between us, grabbing her wrist hard enough to hurt and pulling her against me. "Over my dead body," I growl, searching her eyes. "Have you not learned from your mistakes?" I shake my head, feeling the rage inside of me take on a life of its own. "Or do you want to be raped by scum?"

Maeve flinches, trying desperately to break free from my grasp. Considering the guilt she's grappling with over our actions yesterday, it's a low blow, but she pushed me to it. "That's not fair."

"It's the truth. If you were stupid enough to hitchhike from here, you would end up defiled or worse." I close the gap between us, feeling my rage and desire merge. "Is that what you want, Maeve?"

"How dare you ask me that?" She spits in my face, shocking me enough to release her. "Do you think I'm a dirty whore that loves being raped like you almost raped me in the alleyway?"

I see red and move for her, grabbing her hips and flinging her over my shoulder. "You're ridiculous. I lost control with you in the alleyway because I had suppressed my desire for too long." I carry her into the bedroom. "I didn't call you a fucking whore. You'll stay in this cabin, and that is the end."

I fling her down onto the bed, and she glares up at me. "What do you think you are doing?"

I unbutton my shirt and toss it to one side. "What does it look like?"

"I'm not staying in this cabin while you risk your life, Gael." She shakes her head. "I'm a grown woman, and you don't get to boss me around."

I growl softly as I drop my pants and crawl onto the bed with her.

Maeve attempts to shy away from me, but I'm too fast.

I grab her throat and squeeze. "Listen carefully, little dove." I move my lips closer to hers, making her tremble. "You belong to me. If I tell you to stay here while I'm in Chicago, then that is exactly what you're going to do." I search her irritated blue eyes. "Do you understand?"

Maeve glares at me. "I understand you are an asshole."

I release her neck and grab her hips, forcing her hard into the bed with my weight. "Why can't you understand I am doing everything I can to keep you safe?"

"Bullshit," she says.

I shake my head. "Don't push me."

"It's bullshit. You don't want me around when you take my father out."

I clench my jaw at the mention of the murder I intend to commit. "If you don't want me to kill him, tell me now." I shake my head. "If that's what you want, I'll hand myself in, and you can go on the run again."

Maeve looks torn as she stares at me.

I'm not entirely sure that I can drop this and turn myself in. The idea feels impossible after I've come so close to getting what I've wanted for so long.

She shakes her head, thankfully. "That's not what I'm saying. I don't want to be left here in this cabin alone with no way of contacting you."

I cup her cheeks tenderly. "If I allowed you to come, it could ruin everything if someone spotted you with me."

"Why? Surely you could say you got back to town with me after being sent to get me?" Her expression hardens. "Plus, I'll make sure I'm not recognizable."

I let go of her cheeks and roll off her, feeling utterly at a loss. "It's too dangerous, and that is not the plan. Seamus will bring you to Chicago once I'm sure the plan has gone off without a hitch."

"You and Tiernan didn't recognize me in the park the night I fled Chicago."

My brow furrows. "The park?"

"Yes, I walked right past you."

I think back to that night and remember passing a woman in an oversized sweater in the park. It's almost impossible to believe I walked right past Maeve, unaware of who she was. "That was you?"

She nods. "I think I've proven my point. Chicago is a large city, and it's easy to blend into the shadows."

I won't take her to Chicago, no matter how much she begs. "No, I am not taking you into a war zone."

Her eyes narrow. "It's not a war zone yet."

I growl as she pushes me to the edge, moving my weight back over her. "You're not coming to Chicago. Drop it now." I press my rock-hard cock into her center, letting her feel how aroused I am right now.

A flood of desire mixes with that dark anger bubbling beneath the surface. "What if I don't?"

I let go of her and push off the bed. She is pushing her luck. I glance over my shoulder at her. "You have left me no choice, little dove."

Her eyes narrow as she watches me disappear into the bathroom.

The darkness inside of me longs to break free. I need her to see the man I am beneath it all.

I rummage through the cabinet on the far wall and find the paddle, gag, butt plug, and body restraint harness.

My cock hardens at the mere thought of her restrained in it for me, but I can't be sure what her reaction to it will be. Maeve displays masochistic tendencies, but I think this may be a step too far.

I return to the bedroom, and her eyes widen when she sees the implements I'm holding. "What are those for?" I don't answer her question. Maeve needs to learn to obey me in all matters, especially ones which involve her safety.

Her slender neck bobs as I get closer to her, remaining silent.

I grab hold of her wrist and yank her to stand in front of me. "Open wide, little dove."

She searches my eyes with uncertainty before opening her mouth for me.

I slide the ball gag into her mouth and fasten it behind her head, making it impossible for her to speak. Quickly, I unbutton the shirt she is wearing and toss it aside, groaning as she isn't wearing her bra. I capture her nipples one by one in my mouth, twirling my tongue around each peak and then sucking hard enough to hurt.

Maeve whimpers behind the gag, and it is the most cock stirring sound I've ever heard.

I groan against her skin before moving my mouth higher to her neck. I bite her hard enough to bruise, making her squirm. My hand moves to her lace panties as I slip my fingers through the waistband and cup her dripping wet pussy.

Maeve's eyes roll back in her head as I slide three thick fingers inside of her, feeling how turned on she is for me.

I withdraw them, making Maeve's eyes meet mine in questioning. Slowly, I bring my fingers to my mouth and suck them clean, tasting her as I hold her gaze.

She quivers with need, her body practically shaking. I tear the panties from her with my two hands, discarding the torn fabric. Next, I fasten the restraint around her body, ensuring the leather also holds her arms tight to her body.

Maeve's breathing deepens as fear brews in her eyes.

I lean toward her and murmur in her ear. "If it gets too much, you ball your hands into fists like this."

I grab her hand and force it into a ball. "Okay?" I return my attention to her eyes, and some of the fear eases.

She nods in response.

Her submission satisfies me in ways I can't explain. My need to dominate and inflict pain is a sickness I've wrestled with for most of my adult life.

I grab one of the leather straps around her hips and pull her close. "You are about to learn how dark I truly am, little dove," I murmur into her ear.

Maeve physically shudders against me, her knees weakening as I support more of her weight.

I turn her around and pull her back against me, making her feel the hard press of my cock through my boxer briefs. Slowly, I push her toward the bed and force her knees up onto it.

My cock jumps, seeing her bent over for me. Her tight little asshole is so inviting.

I clench my jaw and kneel behind her, burying my face in her heavenly cunt. The moment I taste her, it makes me groan. She's so fucking sweet that I could spend the rest of my life happily licking her.

She shudders as I move my tongue to her clit, circling it slowly. Maeve groans behind the gag.

I make out a muffled fuck as I slide three fingers inside of her. Her body reacts to every touch and lick as she grows wetter and wetter. It's clear from her reaction that she enjoys being at my mercy.

I grab the bottle of lube and butt plug, squirting some on the plug before adding some to her ass.

Maeve instantly tenses, her entire body turning rigid.

"Relax, baby. It's going to feel good," I murmur, trying to assure her.

She relaxes slightly, but I can tell she's still stiff.

Using the tip of the butt plug, I work it into her tight, virginal ass. My cock strains at the sight of her muscles giving way. The image of my cock inching into such a tight space makes the desire inside of me surge. Slowly, I ease more of it inside, stopping to add extra lube.

Maeve moans behind the gag, a sound that has the power to undo me.

I force my urges out of my mind and slide the rest of the plug into her ass. "It's inside now, baby girl," I murmur, sliding a finger through her soaking wet cunt. "Does it feel good?"

I know she can't answer me, so the question is part of my torture. All I hear is a muffled groan behind the gag. I focus my attention on the paddle lying on the bed. The sadist inside of me rises to the surface as I wield it in my hand. My eyes land on the soft, unblemished skin of her ass.

I slam the paddle down on her right ass cheek first, making her scream into the gag. She doesn't ball her hands into fists, keeping them outstretched as a sign she wishes to continue. "You're such a naughty girl, always pushing me," I murmur, sliding the paddle over her stinging, red skin.

I use the same amount of force on her left ass cheek, and she squeals behind the gag. Her skin instantly turns red where the paddle hits her, leaving a leather imprint on her skin. I groan and give her five more firm spanks of the paddle on each cheek.

Maeve's screams turn to whimpers the more pain I inflict. Still, her hands remain outstretched as she enjoys it like a natural-born masochist.

Who would have known that we'd be this perfect for each other?

I thought my dark tastes would turn her off, but they have the opposite effect. My cock strains against the confines of my restrictive boxer briefs, so I drop them to the floor.

Maeve groans behind the gag as I slide the tip of my cock through her wetness.

I inch the tip through her entrance slowly, teasing her as my cock slides into her tight little cunt.

Her muscles stretch to accommodate me, and the butt plug moves as I force my way inside.

I grab the leather rope around Maeve's arms and lift her from the bed, using it to anchor myself.

Slowly, I pull out of her wet pussy and then slam back into her with brute force.

Maeve yelps behind the gag, and it's muffled in the most delicious way.

Her muscles flutter around my hard shaft as she comes undone instantly, her body spasming as pleasure racks her.

I grunt like an animal and pick up the pace, fucking her through it. "Such a dirty little girl coming so fast on my cock like that," I growl, spanking her ass with my free hand.

Maeve's ass is still red, and the edges of the paddle are still indented in red lines over her flesh. An image that has the power to undo me.

My cock throbs as I pick up the pace, forgetting all rhyme and reason as I rut into her with as much control as a beast in mating.

Maeve screams behind the gag, her hand constantly outstretched as a sign she wants more.

I stop and grab her, lifting her with the leather straps and positioning her on her back. "I want to look into your eyes while you come for me again, my little masochist."

Maeve's eyes are more dilated than I've ever seen. She looks otherworldly as she stares up at me in a pleasure-filled daze.

I slide my fingers around her pale, slender throat and plunge my cock into her again. The sensation of her body stretching to take every inch is addictive. I feel the butt plug in her ass pressing against me, narrowing her confining channel in this position.

"Do you like having my cock in your tight little cunt and that thick plug in your ass?" I ask, despite knowing she has little way of responding.

Her eyes dilate further as she attempts to nod. The sight of the woman I've wanted for so long enjoying the sicker, darker side of my urges is inexplicably erotic.

I slam inside her roughly, adrenaline flowing through my veins as I make her understand the violence of my desire. It's all-consuming and impossible to satiate.

I continue to apply the right amount of pressure on her throat. Maeve's eyes roll back in her head as she submits to the pleasure for a second time. Her body spasms as I release her throat, allowing her some oxygen.

A flood of liquid squirts around my cock as I fuck her through the pleasure, chasing my explosive release. After three more violent thrusts, I come undone.

I grab the back of her neck and undo the gag, roaring against her mouth. My tongue tangles with hers frantically as I continue to drain every drop of seed into her.

Maeve allows me to take it all, submitting to me in ways I never knew she was capable of.

"Fuck," I pant as I finally finish fucking her. "You're perfection, little dove," I murmur, collapsing onto her for a moment.

Maeve groans. "So good," she pants.

I shift off of her and slowly unbuckle the body harness, freeing her hands. Maeve moves her free hand to her ass to pull out the plug, but I grip her wrist. "No, I want you to keep it in for me, baby girl."

Her eyes widen. "For how long?"

"Until I say." I pull her against me and hold her to my chest, knowing I don't want to leave this bed until the last moment.

We can stay here wrapped in each other for a few hours longer before I have to leave and embark on my most dangerous assignment yet.

19

MAEVE

My stomach churns as I glance over at Gael. He's still sleeping, which means now is my chance. I ease myself out of the bed, searching for the handcuffs and super glue I hid earlier today while he was out for a walk.

Gael will never agree to take me with him, so I have a plan. He's going to be angry, but I'm not sitting in this cabin, waiting for him to return. I tiptoe over to the closet and grab one of Gael's sweaters before pulling on my skirt.

He remains still in the bed, sleeping soundly.

I tiptoe into the kitchen and grab the handcuffs and glue, turning and exiting the cabin toward the car. As always, he has left it unlocked.

I unlock the cuffs and pull the key out, heading

into the forest and throwing it into the stream. Then, I turn around and get into the passenger seat of the car.

Gael mentioned he has to leave tonight, and it's almost seven o'clock, so he can't be sticking around much longer. I clip the handcuffs over my right wrist and fasten it to the grab handle. With the tube of glue, I force the nozzle into the small lock and squirt it in there, hoping it will be enough to stop Gael from picking the lock.

Then I wait for about half an hour until the light in the cabin sitting room illuminates, signaling he's awake. His eyes are wide and panicked as he comes to the door, searching for me. When they land on me sitting in the passenger seat of his car, his eyes narrow.

He is wearing nothing but his tight boxer briefs as he marches to the car, trying to yank open the door. "Out," he barks.

I locked my door so that he couldn't open it. "I'm afraid I can't get out." I glance at the handcuff around my wrist.

Gael's eyes are frantic as he glares at me. "Where are the keys?"

I shrug. "I lost them."

He walks to the driver's side and gets in, leaning

over to yank it off the door. It doesn't budge. He turns the light on and growls when he sees the mess I've made of the lock. "What the fuck do you think you're doing, Maeve?"

I look him in the eye, holding my chin high. "This is the only way I get to come with you."

Gael glares at me. "I thought you'd accepted you weren't coming."

My brow furrows. "Why? Because I had sex with you?"

A flash of fire ignites in his amber eyes. A wicked look that makes my insides churn. "No." He grabs my throat. "As you mention sex, I might use your stupidity to my advantage."

My stomach churns as I squirm under his powerful gaze. "What's that supposed to mean?"

Gael doesn't respond, forcing the passenger seat chair as far back as the cuffs will allow. He kneels in the footwell and forces me back further in the seat.

"What are you doing?" I demand.

Gael glares at me. "Taking what the fuck I want because you've pissed me off, Maeve Callaghan." Gael glares at me. "I'm going to make you pay for this."

A shiver races down my spine, igniting that masochistic need inside of me. My body longs for

Gael to make me pay, as I want him to punish me for being disobedient. My stomach churns as he lifts the hem of the skirt I wore. A skirt that gives him unfettered access to my pussy.

Gael's eyes are dark with both rage and hunger. He tears apart my panties and chucks them into the footwell before releasing his enormous cock from his pants. "You didn't learn your lesson from my earlier punishment."

I swallow hard as my flesh still stings from his merciless assault with the paddle. Butterflies flutter to life in my stomach as I expect another rough fuck from him. He reaches into the glove box and pulls out a bottle of lube, making my heart still in my chest.

No way.

He can't mean anal sex.

Only a few hours ago, I had something put in my ass for the first time in my life. There is no way I'm ready for his gigantic cock in such a tight space. "Are you serious?"

Gael doesn't respond, coating his cock in lube. He then pulls out the plug that he insisted I couldn't take out until he said. In place of it, he squirts lube in my stretched ass.

Panic rises to the surface. "No, don't, Gael. There's no way it'll fit," I say, my voice frantic.

Gael smirks at me. "Perhaps you should have thought better about restraining yourself in my car wearing a fucking skirt, little dove," he says.

I feel the tip of his cock at my tight entrance. "It won't fit."

Gael narrows his eyes at me. "I'll make it fit."

Slowly, he pushes forward. The stinging pain is unbearable as the thick head of his cock forces its way through my tight ring of muscles. The plug wasn't anywhere near as thick as his cock. I bite my lip as the pain surges through me.

Gael stops, adding more lube to his cock and my hole. "You should have thought twice about handcuffing yourself and busting the lock, little dove."

I groan as he continues to force his cock through my tight back passage. My body rejecting the invasion as pain courses through me. "No, please don't," I cry.

Gael wraps his tattooed fingers around my throat and glares into my eyes with darkness like none I've ever witnessed before. "You'll take what I give you as punishment and fucking enjoy it," he growls.

I've never seen this side of Gael before. The darkness that lurks under the surface is pitch black. I draw in a deep, steadying breath to calm myself. "I only wanted to come with you." I protest.

The thick head of his cock breaks through my muscles as he slides deeper. I groan at the foreign feeling of his cock stretching my ass. It shouldn't turn me on, not when I asked him to stop, but it's further proof of how fucked up I truly am.

"Gael," I gasp his name as his cock sinks in all the way.

"That's right. Take my cock in that tight little asshole as punishment, you disobedient little brat," he growls.

I moan as he moves in and out of me slowly.

His eyes are wild as he watches the space where our bodies join intensely. "Your ass looks perfect with my cock in it," he groans.

I moan at how dirty that is. Gael has most certainly erased the uptight part of me, and he has turned me into a dirty, masochistic whore who can't get enough. At least, that's how it feels.

Gael slides out of my ass until the head of his cock is just inside before slamming into me hard.

I yelp, shocked by the sudden change in intensity.

"Take it, take every fucking inch as your punishment," he growls.

I whimper as he fucks me brutally, his cock slamming in and out of my stretched, lubed hole.

"Oh God," I cry.

Gael wraps a tattooed hand around my throat and shakes his head. "Not God, baby, sir," he orders.

I swallow under the firm grip of his fingers, enjoying the way he dominates me so fully. "Fuck, yes, sir," I spit out.

The darkness deepens in his eyes as he moves his fingers to my clit and rubs me there. My nipples are harder than ever as he fucks my ass with more intensity.

I've never felt so out of control and yet so safe as he plows into me.

Gael takes what he wants from me unapologetically, and I fucking love it more than I should. He is so right. We're two broken people that make a whole.

I scream as he increases the tempo. The mix of both pain and pleasure has me on the edge of release already.

Gael's muscles tense as he grinds his teeth, fucking me as hard as he physically can. The violence in his eyes should scare me, but I don't fear him, not anymore.

I love him with all my heart, every damaged part of him. I always have and I always will, no matter what happens.

"Yes, fuck me harder," I cry.

Gael growls like a feral beast. His eyes are so

dilated they almost look black. "Fuck, you are such a dirty, masochistic whore." He leans down and bites my bottom lip between his teeth hard enough to reopen the wound from last night. "My dirty, masochistic whore," he murmurs.

The metallic taste on my lips swirls between us as he kisses me, and the position forces his cock even deeper into my ass.

"I'm going to fucking ruin you, baby."

I groan, knowing he's already ruined me.

"Please," I cry, unsure what I'm even begging him for. I need him as if my life depends on it.

Gael slams into me and holds his cock still, tilting his head to the side. "Please what, little dove?"

I shake my head. "Harder, please, sir."

Gael grabs my throat with even more force and squeezes. "Do you think you deserve to get what you want? After the stunt you've just pulled."

I know without a doubt there is something wrong with me as my nipples tighten and my desire heightens at the anger in his voice. It turns me on like nothing ever has.

"No, sir," I murmur.

He slides his fingers into my soaking wet pussy while continuing to take my ass.

Slowly he pulls them out and then slides them into my mouth. "Suck them clean for me, baby."

I feel so damn dirty tasting myself as I suck them clean without hesitation.

"Good girl," he purrs, grabbing my right nipple and squeezing hard enough to hurt. "So obedient when you have my cock in you, not so obedient when you don't," he growls.

He spanks my thigh hard with the flat of his palm and increases the tempo. He grabs my legs and forces them higher, giving him a better angle to get deeper.

Any pain I felt at the start is gone as he drives me to the edge of no return. All I feel is a blissful pleasure as he grunts and groans above me.

I shut my eyes as the most intense, crippling orgasm I've ever felt hits me. I scream Gael's name over and over again as my body shakes violently as I come undone.

Gael growls as liquid squirts out of my pussy, hitting his bare chest. "Fuck, yes, squirt for me, little dove," he growls.

It feels like my body leaves this plane and floats away as I try to regulate my erratic breathing.

He pumps two more times before roaring and shooting his load deep in my ass. I feel him filling me with his thick cum, and it is the most amazing sensation ever.

Gael pulls his cock from me and pushes it into his boxer briefs. He grabs the butt plug from the center console and adds lube.

My brow furrows. "What are you doing?"

He glares at me. "I'm going to plug my cum deep in your ass, and I want you to keep it in there until I say."

My clit throbs at the prospect. It's so dirty and yet so fucking hot. "Yes, sir," I say.

The glint in his eyes is almost devilish as he slides the plug easily into my stretched, abused hole. "I never thought you'd love anal as much as you just did, little dove."

My cheeks heat at the comment as he gets out of the car, leaving me with torn panties and my skirt up. I watch as he walks back to the cabin. Once he disappears into it, I struggle to get myself back in a sitting position in the seat.

The cuff makes it impossible to use the controls to get it upright again, so I lie back and wait.

After about twenty minutes, Gael returns with a bag over his shoulder. He locks the cabin and then gets into the driver's seat, turning on the engine without a word.

"Could you at least move the seat upright?" I ask.

He gives me a look that could kill before sighing and reaching over me to adjust the seat.

"Thank you," I say.

Gael mumbles something under his breath as he turns the car around and drives down the long, winding mountain road.

Tension so thick clouds the car as I stare out of the window. As the pleasure wears off, I feel a little sickened at how much I loved his rough treatment.

There is a part of me that loves being mistreated. I can't understand why, but it appears to be a fundamental part of who I am.

20

GAEL

Maeve hasn't said a word the entire trip as we get close to Lake Geneva. I lost my cool when I realized what she'd done. Perhaps I went a bit too far by fucking her in the ass while she told me to stop.

There's a suffocating tension in the air which makes the trip uncomfortable. I've been too angry at her to break the silence. Maeve is clueless about the danger she will be in if I fail to kill Ronan. "We're about a minute away from our destination." I don't look at her, keeping my eyes on the road. "You'll obey every command I give you once we're there."

Maeve continues to stare out of the window in silence.

"Do you understand?" I ask, irritation building that she isn't responding.

"Perfectly," she says, a hint of sarcasm lacing her voice.

I growl softly. "You've pushed me to the fucking edge tonight, Maeve. Don't push me anymore, or you will regret it." The violence of my rage is building inside of me like a perfect fucking storm. I don't need to worry about her while I'm trying to pull off the greatest assassination of my career as a killer.

I pull off the main road toward the motel. Seamus and Tiernan should already be there and have our rooms ready. I pull into the parking lot on the right. Seamus and Tiernan stand by their rental car, waiting for me. We selected this motel as somewhere to lie low while we go through the plan.

Maeve has already fucked it up, as she is an equation none of us factored in. It will surprise my friends to see her.

Tiernan already knows there is something wrong, as I called him and asked him to bring a bolt cutter. When he asked why I needed it, I put the phone down on him, as it would make me look weak that I couldn't keep her in that fucking cabin.

Maeve shouldn't be anywhere near Chicago while I kill her father. She insists the city is big enough to go unnoticed, but she'll not make it to the city. I will lock her in the motel until the deed is done, and then Seamus will collect her from here and plant her in a Russian-owned warehouse.

An anonymous tip to the Callaghans will report her there once Ronan is dead. They'll find me with her tied up. It's a warehouse the Russians no longer actively use, so it's perfect. It's a slight change in plans as Seamus was supposed to collect her from the cabin, but the motel is closer to Chicago.

I pull into a space next to their rental car and turn off the engine. The thrum of tension is clear as I glance in Maeve's direction. "Stay here and don't fucking move until I say so."

Maeve doesn't look my way, staring out of the window. It's as if she is trying to anger me with everything she does. Rage filters through my bloodstream like a drug as I grab her wrist. "Did you hear me?"

She finally glances my way, anger burning in the depth of her blue eyes. "Loud and clear," she says, her voice mocking.

I growl as my frustration heightens. It takes all my control to turn away from her and get out of the car. I march toward my friends.

Tiernan's brow furrows. "What the fuck is she doing here, lad?"

Seamus steps forward. "Aye, if anyone spots her with us, then it's all over."

I grunt. "Did you bring the bolt cutters?" I ask. Their question doesn't dignify an answer, as I'm too angry to explain everything to them.

"Aye." Tiernan opens the back door of the rental car and pulls them out, passing them to me.

I snatch them from him, stalking toward the car.

Maeve's eyes widen when I appear at her door, wielding the bolt cutters. I no doubt look like a maniac, and I sure as hell feel like one currently. Maeve tries to use her other hand to lock the door again, but I yank it open before she can.

"You don't want to anger me further, little dove." I pull the door open enough to get the cutters in and cut the chain.

Maeve shudders as she stares at me with wide, fearful eyes.

I drag her out of the car with the cut chain affixed to her wrists.

She struggles against me as I drag her toward the motel.

"What room?" I ask my friends.

"You're in room forty-five." Tiernan chases after me as I follow the signs toward my room. "What is going on?"

I grunt, glancing over my shoulder at him. "I'll explain later. First, I need to get her out of my sight," I growl.

Maeve shakes her head. "It would help if you weren't so aggressive."

I glare at her, feeling uncontrollably angry. "Shut it."

Tiernan pushes in front of me with the key and opens the door to the motel room.

I push her inside before slamming the door. "Lock it."

He does as I say, turning the key in the door. "Fuck, what happened?"

I shake my head and stalk back to the parking lot.

Seamus stands in the same spot, looking confused.

"She chained herself to the damn car, and I didn't have the tools to get her out before I left," I say.

Tiernan and Seamus exchange uncertain glances. "Do you realize the danger if anyone from the clan sees all of us together?" Seamus asks.

Tiernan nods. "Aye, it was bad enough making sure you aren't spotted on the way into the city, but the Callaghan princess is another thing entirely."

I already know what a mess this is, and I don't need to hear it from them. "Drop it," I growl.

Tiernan's eyes widen at my angry outburst. Typically, I'm not the type to lose my cool, but the pressure of pulling off the craziest plan in Chicago's history is getting to me. "Sorry, it is what it is," he says, shrugging his shoulders. "We'll have to make it work."

Seamus nods in agreement.

I run my palm over the back of my neck. "What time do we need to leave tomorrow to make it to the club in time?"

"Seven o'clock," Seamus replies.

Tiernan holds up a folder. "Shall we go through the plan together?"

"Aye, we best make sure we're all on the same page." I glance between the two men. "You didn't bring your cell phones, right?"

Seamus and Tiernan shake their heads. "No, burner only so I can contact my wife," Seamus says.

"Good. Where's your room?"

Tiernan nods to follow him as we exit the parking lot down the same corridor I dragged Maeve. She has a lot of nerve acting so bratty after pulling that stunt on me. Tiernan opens the door to the room next to Maeve's.

I grind my teeth together, knowing she'll be able to hear us through the thin, crappy motel walls. "Couldn't have been further away?"

Tiernan raises a brow. "I can request another room. I don't think it's full."

I shake my head. "Let's get on with this."

Seamus clears the small coffee table, and we sit on the moth-eaten sofa bed that has to be right out of the seventies. He unravels a piece of paper with a timeline on it. "Here it is: Operation Chaos."

He has titled it as that. It's a fitting name since it's going to send the city into chaos.

"Aye, so at seven o'clock tomorrow evening, I will drive you into Chicago," Tiernan says.

My brow furrows. "Isn't it safer if I go alone?"

Tiernan shakes his head. "No, I'm due to meet Ronan at the club. You'll ride in the trunk once we reach the city limits. I'll leave the trunk unlocked once we get to the club, and then you can make your move after I've been gone ten minutes." He glances at my watch. "Set your watch against mine, and that should be at ten past nine."

I check my watch, and it's one minute faster than Tiernan's, so I wind it back. "Okay." I nod as I remember my part. "I enter the club ten minutes after you and head for the VIP section using the name Artyom."

Seamus clears his throat. "Aye, but try to dull down the Irish accent."

"Good point."

Seamus runs a hand across the back of his neck. "In the meantime, I'll follow you to the city with Maeve in the trunk."

"Isn't it safer that you wait to hear the deed is done before bringing her into the city?" I ask.

Tiernan and Seamus shake their heads. "It would be better if we can match the timings and have Maeve in the warehouse ready for your arrival, and I'll have her in the trunk too, so she isn't spotted."

I run a hand over my jaw, knowing Maeve hates confined spaces. "Good luck with that, lad."

He glares at me. "The lass better not give me any trouble."

I shrug. "Can't promise anything. She's a disobedient little thing."

Tiernan clicks his tongue. "Stay focused. Gael, what will you be doing next."

The tension in my shoulders heightens as I think about it. "I will wait in the bathroom of the VIP section." I glance at Tiernan. "After your server drops a drink on him. I'll kill him and leave him in a stall, giving myself enough time to flee the club out the back exit before anyone discovers him."

"Aye, there can be no room for hesitation, Gael. He'll strike first if you give him a chance," Seamus says.

I don't know why he tells me that. I know Ronan better than either of these men, maybe even better than his children know him.

"Do you think I'm stupid?" I glare at my friend.

Seamus pales slightly, shaking his head. "Of course not."

Tiernan claps his hands twice. "Can we focus, please?"

Seamus focuses his attention on the timeline. "I'll drive Maeve to the warehouse building and tie her up after going over her story with her." His brow furrows as he thinks hard. "I'll have a chair and rope ready for Gael to arrive."

Tiernan taps his fingers on the coffee table. "Then?"

Seamus nods. "I leave and head straight to our local as an alibi where I'll meet you."

Tiernan nods. "Perfect. I will leave the club when I can after ensuring my contact has wiped all the CCTV footage for the night. After, I'll meet you at the pub, and then my friend will call in Maeve's location on a burner phone."

It seems like we all have the plan in our heads, but reality doesn't always go to plan. "What could go wrong, though?" I ask.

"Timing could be off, so we need to allow a certain amount of wiggle room," Seamus says.

Tiernan crosses his arms over his chest, leaning forward with a stern expression. "Ronan ends up killing you instead?"

I growl at the idea. "Do you think that little of my skill after all the assassinations I've carried out over twenty years for the clan?"

Tiernan shakes his head. "No, but this one is more personal."

Little does he know that I've been in a similar situation before with my foster parent. However, he is right. I hated James Keane, but I don't hate Ronan. It's an unfortunate situation, and he is the one thing standing in the way of what I want.

"Don't worry about it. I won't fail." I shrug. "If I do, it will incriminate neither of you."

Tiernan narrows his eyes. "Ronan will know I pulled strings to get you in the club."

I shake my head. "How? Didn't you cover your tracks?"

"Of course, but he knows how close we are."

"Aye." Seamus nods in agreement. "If the worst happens and you don't turn up, what do I do with Maeve?"

He says it as if she is a thing to do something with. "For a start, that won't happen. If worst comes to the worst, you go to the address I gave you. There are instructions on how to get Maeve out of the country."

Seamus and Tiernan turn silent as tension clouds the room.

Tiernan stands and says, "Thankfully, I bought a bottle of Jameson Whiskey."

His words are like music to my ears. I need something to take the edge off of the simmering rage boiling beneath my skin, itching to be unleashed.

I watch as Tiernan pulls a bottle out of his bag and grabs the mugs in the room, pouring us each a large drink.

Seamus stands, and I follow his lead, taking my drink from Tiernan.

"To success," I say, lifting my mug of whiskey in the air.

Seamus clinks his mug against mine. "To everything going to plan."

Tiernan's jaw tightens. "To surviving this." He clinks his mug against mine.

We all knock our whiskey back in one. I enjoy the burning sensation as it rushes down my throat, but I know nothing will take the edge off my emotions tonight. Maeve pushed me too far, and the task I will carry out tomorrow weighs too heavily on my shoulders.

Three years of planning and scheming, all for one moment. Failure means death, and I will fight with all of my strength to live for Maeve. The alternative isn't worth thinking about.

21

MAEVE

The darkness in the room threatens to swallow me whole as I lie on the bed, waiting for Gael to return.

I've always hated the dark since I was little. Ever since Father trapped me in a basement for hours on end as punishment for trivial things, but I can't find it in myself to turn on the light.

Gael lost it worse than I expected when he realized what I'd done. I am so conflicted over what he did to me. I asked him to stop, but he wouldn't. That should anger me, but it felt so good to be taken without mercy by him like that.

I'm a masochist. Pain is like a drug, and once you're hooked, you can't kick it no matter what. I should hate Gael for being such a self-righteous asshole, but it only made me fall further in love with him.

My ass still stings from his merciless assault, and yet I love the sensation, reminding me of how good it felt to be stretched by him. The plug remains in place, holding his cum deep inside of me. If that is a punishment, I want more of it.

I glance at the clock on the nightstand, noticing it's almost midnight. Gael has been gone for hours after angrily locking me in this room without a word. I can hear muffled voices on the other side of this wall but can't make out any words.

From the empty car park, I'd assume it's probably Gael, Tiernan, and Seamus. Tiernan has worked for my father almost as long as Gael has, and I'm surprised he wants to help Gael betray my father. Seamus hasn't been with the clan as long, and I've never spoken to him.

I hear a door slam outside the corridor, and it makes my heart stutter in my chest. The thud of footsteps approaching the door follows, and then a key slides into the lock. I hold my breath, waiting for Gael to enter.

He opens the door, and light from the corridor floods into the dark room. Gael walks in and shuts it as fast, turning the lock on the inside with a click. I swallow hard, watching his dark shadow as he approaches.

He was furious the last time I saw him. I'm sure he's probably still pretty pissed.

Instead of approaching the bed or speaking to me, he heads into the adjoining bathroom. I hear the shower turn on and sit up on the bed. My stomach churns as I consider sneaking in there with him. After all, I still have this damn plug in my ass, which he needs to remove.

I shift myself out of bed and creep toward the door, which is cracked open a touch.

Gael stands with his tattooed and scarred back to me, leaning against the wall of the shower as the water cascades down his chiseled muscles.

My mouth dries as I stare at the man I love in awe. He is so breathtakingly beautiful, even with all his scars and rough tattoos. I've never asked him about the scars on his back, and something tells me he wouldn't be open to discussing it. The past haunts Gael, but he won't open up to me about it.

I ease the door open more and step inside the bathroom. Slowly, I unbutton my skirt and drop it to the floor, followed by the top I'm wearing.

Gael doesn't notice me as I continue moving

closer to him. My heart thumps in a steady but fast rhythm against my rib cage.

I drop my bra to the floor and then make the last few steps to the door, placing my hand on it.

Gael notices me then, his eyes snapping over his shoulder as they find mine. They darken the instant he sees me with lust and rage, as it appears the two are often mixed.

"What do you think you are doing, little dove?" he asks.

I shrug. "I'm dirty and need to shower."

He tilts his head slightly. "You've had about four hours to do that."

I lick my bottom lip. "I wanted to wait for you."

He narrows his eyes as I pull open the shower door and step inside.

I let the door swing shut behind me, shutting myself in with the beast of a man in front of me. Some would probably say I'm insane after the way he has treated me since Madison, but his treatment has only cemented one thing firmly in my mind; we are made for each other.

Gael grabs my hips and pushes me against the glass shower screen, looming over me. "Such a naughty girl coming in here uninvited," he muses.

A shiver starts at the top of my head and runs

right down the length of my spine. "I need you to remove the plug from my ass," I say, confidently meeting his intimidating gaze.

A smirk twists onto his lips. "Is that right, baby?"

I nod in response. "Yeah, it's uncomfortable now."

He slides his fingers around my throat, forcing my chin higher. "First, I think I'll fuck you with it in so you have my cum in both your holes."

My stomach flutters with excitement. "Okay, sir," I say.

He growls softly and lifts me off my feet as if I weigh nothing.

I wrap my legs around his hips, feeling the hot press of his cock against my center. The need I feel is insurmountable as he presses his lips to the shell of my ear and bites hard.

"Fuck me," I breathe.

Gael captures my lips with his, plunging his tongue into my mouth with an urgent need.

I lace my fingers in his short hair, drawing him closer. We both realize that this could be our last night together if his plan doesn't work out.

The fear of losing him deepens my need for him as our tongues wrestle in a passionate dance.

Gael pulls away from me and searches my eyes. "Hold on tight, baby girl."

I join my hands together behind his neck as he positions the head of his cock at my entrance. The moment he pushes forward, I groan at the invasion. My eyes slam shut as I rest my head back against the glass wall of the shower. "Fuck," I murmur.

Gael bites my bottom lip softly, forcing my eyes open. "Look at me, little dove." He searches my eyes with those beautiful amber gems. "I want to look into your eyes while I take you."

I shudder as he moves me up and down his cock, holding my gaze intensely. My heart hammers hard against my rib cage as the intimacy between us heightens.

Gael is gentle as he lifts me up and down slowly, allowing me to feel every inch of him slide in and out of me.

I groan, my nipples turning to hard, erect peaks. "It feels so good," I say. Every single time we've had sex, it's always been rough. This time Gael is gentle with me. I'm not sure which I prefer, but all I know is I love having him inside of me.

Gael grunts as he lifts me away from the shower wall and opens the door with one hand. I hold on to him tightly, keeping my legs firm around him as he carries me back to the bedroom.

We're both soaking wet as he lowers me to one of the two beds in the motel room. Gael kisses me softly, his lips tracing a path from my navel to my neck.

I lace my fingers in his hair, savoring how he feels. If things go wrong tomorrow, I need to commit everything about him to my memory.

My chest aches as he captures my mouth with his, pouring every emotion he feels into it. I wish we could remain like this forever, wrapped in each other.

The thick head of his cock nudges against my entrance, and he pushes in without teasing, giving me everything I crave.

"Fuck," I cry as he stretches me around his enormous length. The pressure squeezes the plug in my ass, sending unprecedented pleasure through my body, and I love the way it feels.

Gael nips my bottom lip with his teeth hard enough to hurt before thrusting into me harder. His eyes are wild as he moves in and out of me with a tenderness I've not felt from him before.

I know how he feels about me, but he's yet to say it. Likewise, I haven't said it to him. It doesn't matter, though, as I see the adoration in his eyes every time he looks at me. It's a look that makes me feel like the only other person on this earth.

"That's it, baby, moan for me," he murmurs into my ear before biting the shell.

I feel my orgasm nearing as his slow, hard strokes hit the perfect spot inside of me each time. Gael knows my body better than I do. It's as if we were designed to fit together. Two pieces of a whole.

"Yes, sir," I reply, making him grunt.

His eyes dilate further as they hold my gaze. It feels like he's looking right into my soul. "You are such a good girl," he murmurs, clawing at my hips possessively. Gael's jaw clenches, and he puts more force on my hips. "I need you to get on all fours for me."

I swallow hard at the dark, husky tone of his voice and do as he says. "Yes, sir."

I turn over and arch my back, making him groan.

"You're fucking heaven, little dove." He plays with the plug lodged in my ass, gently tapping on it. "I can't wait to fill you in both holes." He lines his cock up with my pussy and slides inside slowly, allowing me to feel every inch sink as deep as possible.

I arch my back, wanting more from him. "Fuck

me," I moan, desperate to feel the rough dominance that I crave.

Gael's fingers tighten around my neck, and he forces me to arch my back further. "You don't give the commands, baby girl."

I swallow hard under the pressure of his fingers, feeling my arousal increase. "Please, sir," I beg.

Gael grunts. "That's right, beg me for it, little dove."

He continues to hold my throat, choking me as he moves in and out with slow, deliberate strokes.

My nipples tighten and pussy gushes around his thick length as he drives me wild, teasing me. The lack of oxygen as he tightens his grip around my neck is intoxicating. My stomach churns as I wonder if he knows what he's doing, but I trust him with my life.

Gael would never hurt me.

He releases his grasp, allowing me a long inhale of oxygen into my lungs. "You're such a good submissive," he says, spanking my ass with a firm palm.

My stomach churns as the pain only heightens the pleasure. I can't understand why I love it so much. "More, please," I beg.

Gael stills inside of me. "More what?" he asks.

"More pain, please, sir." I arch my back, hoping he'll give me what I desire.

He groans and spanks my other ass cheek harder. I know he will leave marks on me with the force. He does it repeatedly while fucking me, driving me nearer and nearer to the edge of no return.

"Fuck, I'm going to come," I cry.

Gael grunts as he increases the pace, plunging in and out of me with vigor. "That's it, baby. I want to feel your tight little cunt come for me."

His dirty talk is all it takes to tip me over the edge. "Fuck, yes, sir," I cry, my muscles spasming as a wave of irresistible pleasure hits me.

A flood of hot liquid coats Gael's cock as he continues to pump in and out of me.

He grunts above me like an animal, rutting into me while I come for him. "Such a good girl, do you know what good girls deserve?" he asks.

I shake my head.

"Cum in both of their dirty little holes," he says.

I groan, feeling the need inside of me amplify even though I've already climaxed. Gael has this amazing ability to turn me into a desperate whore.

Gael thrusts into me three more times before biting my shoulder hard. He roars against my skin and slides his cock as deep as physically possible, unleashing his cum inside of me.

My nipples tighten as he fills me, both holes now

filled with his cum. I wish this night would never end and we could stay here, enjoying each other for the rest of our lives.

His breathing is labored as he falls onto his back by my side before pulling me down with him. His muscular arms wrap tightly around me, holding me against his chest. "You are perfect, baby," he mutters, pressing his lips to my forehead.

I glance up at him, feeling my chest swell with happiness. "You're perfect," I reply.

He chuckles and shakes his head. "I don't think so, little dove. I'm many things, but perfect isn't one of them."

I sigh heavily. "You are perfect to me." I wiggle, trying to adjust myself as the plug is uncomfortable. "Are you going to take this thing out of my ass yet?"

He smirks a wicked smirk that tells me he has no intention of removing it. "Not until I've had my way with you a few more times."

I swallow hard, my thighs shaking at the thought of feeling that pleasure over and over again. It beats trying to sleep because it's the only way to keep my mind off of what will come tomorrow.

I'm dreading it, so instead, I move my head and allow him to kiss me. The desire ignites again into a blazing hot inferno the moment he touches me.

22

GAEL

I wake in the middle of the night, my heart pounding uncontrollably and sweat beading on my forehead.

I sit up and rub a hand across my face.

It was just a dream.

I repeat the phrase in my mind until I finally accept it. My nightmares result from childhood trauma, a trauma that constantly tries to force itself to the surface, no matter how hard I try to bury it.

Ronan taught me to use my anger and pain from the trauma to mold myself into a stronger man. I'm not sure his advice worked, as my attempt to ignore it has only made it harder to bury.

Maeve rolls over in bed and opens her eyes,

glancing at me. "Are you okay?" Her brow furrows. "You were talking in your sleep."

Shit.

I fear what I said while I slept. "Fine, I had a weird dream." I wave my hand dismissively. "Go back to sleep, little dove."

Her brow furrows. "Do you want to talk about it? You screamed out the name Emilia."

I clench my jaw as her face comes into my mind. Emilia was my sister, and I don't have any memories of her other than the photo my foster parents tortured me with, blaming me for her death. It was the only possession I had when I came into their care, and they used it against me.

"Drop it, Maeve," I say, sliding my legs out of bed and sitting on the edge. I don't need to bring up childhood trauma a day before carrying out my most daring assignment yet. I need a clear head.

Her soft, delicate hand lands on my tense back as she moves her other to my shoulders. Softly, she works out the tension in them. I groan as she kneads my muscles. "Are you trying to turn me on?"

She sighs heavily. "No, I want to relieve your stress." A few moments of silence pass by. "Who is Emilia?"

I growl at her disobedient nature. "What part of drop it do you not understand?"

"I wish you would open up to me, Gael." Her hands continue to work at the knots in my shoulders. "I care about you."

My chest aches at the sincerity in her tone. I swallow hard, wondering if perhaps it's time to stop taking my mentor's advice. "Emilia was my sister's name."

"I didn't think you remembered any of your family."

I shift back and rest against the headboard of the creaky motel bed. "I don't." My brow furrows. "I told you people who did unspeakable things to me raised me."

Maeve meets my gaze and nods. "Yes."

I gesture for her to move closer.

She does, and I hold her against me, pressing my lips to the top of her head. I don't want to keep things from her. Maeve is my future, and we should have no secrets.

"One thing they did was take me into a basement with a picture of Emilia and beat me for killing her. They told me I was the devil's spawn, and that's how I survived. They instilled the idea that I was the reason my entire family died in me from the age of three years old."

Maeve's eyes sparkle with unshed tears as she looks up at me. "That is terrible. How long did it go on?"

My throat bobs as I swallow. "Their abuse continued until I was seventeen years old."

Realization dawns on her face. "When you killed one of your abusers?"

The screams of the man who had beaten and abused me most of my life were the most satisfying sounds I'd ever heard. I delighted in torturing him until I watched the life drain from his eyes. "Yes," I say, as some things are best kept to yourself. Maeve knows darkness thrives inside me, but she doesn't need to know about the psychopathic tendencies that have haunted me ever since my first kill. I think it's the reason Ronan's offer to mold me into a ruthless killing machine was so appealing at eighteen years old.

"I'm so sorry, Gael."

I clench my jaw. "Don't be. I hate being pitied for my past."

Maeve nods in reply and shifts so she can look me in the eye. "Thank you for telling me. I know it isn't easy for you."

Little does she know that deep down, buried under all her sweet innocence, she harbors a secret just as dark. A trauma she experienced as a young girl. I remember when Ronan and I found her, and it made me sick to the stomach. Maeve suppressed what happened to her and possibly has no recollection of the trauma.

I find it hard to believe that you can live through something and then block it out entirely. A part of me harbors envy toward her for that. "It isn't easy to talk about." I meet her gaze. "You're the only person I've told about it." There are three words I've yet to say to my broken little dove. "You do know I love you, don't you, Maeve?" I ask, feeling a tightness coil in my chest because I've never said those three words to another human being in my life.

Maeve's eyes glisten with unshed tears as she nods. "I know. I love you too."

I wonder if she would feel the same if she knew how long I've planned her father's demise. For three years, it's been my sole aim to remove him from the equation, long before he announced her engagement to Maxim. The engagement was a happy accident that gave me a reason to kick my plan into motion.

"We shouldn't have any secrets. Right?" I rake my fingers through her soft, golden hair.

"Right." she agrees.

"I have to confess something, little dove."

She furrows her brow, glancing up at me. "What is it?"

I draw in a deep breath. "I planned to kill your father long before he announced your engagement to Maxim."

Her eyes widen, and she eases herself away from me to search my eyes. "What do you mean?"

I run a hand through my hair, shaking my head. "When I left for Europe, I had an ulterior motive, as I wanted to undermine your father's power in Chicago."

"I don't understand, Gael. What was your reason?"

I squint at her through the darkness. "I knew I loved you when I left for Europe, and I knew the only way we could be together was if Ronan was out of the picture."

Maeve stares at me in silence, her mind working away as she tries to process the news I just gave her. If we're going to do this right, I need to be honest about it. Ronan's death has been my plan for years. A plan I was supposed to keep a secret from her, even after he died. "Let me understand this. If my running away hadn't forced you to come clean, would you have kept your hand in my father's death a secret?"

It's a question I don't want to answer, but there's no escaping it now. "I don't know, but originally I didn't plan on telling you, no."

Maeve turns away and sits on the edge of the bed, holding her head in her hands.

Have I finally destroyed what we have between us? "Are you okay?"

She shakes her head. "I don't know, Gael. Why did you tell me?"

I reach for her and slide my hands onto her shoulders, pressing my lips to her neck. "Because I don't want to keep anything from you." However, I know that I can't mention the trauma she experienced as a child, as Maeve has to remember that for herself when she is ready, if she ever is.

I know about it because I was there when Ronan killed his worthless brother for laying a hand on her when she was five years old. Her mother was hysterical when she learned the truth and forced Maeve into therapy, but the therapist found no evidence she remembered the abuse.

It drove a wedge between Ronan and Eloise from that moment, and I know Ronan resented Maeve for it.

Maeve swallows hard. "Neither do I," she murmurs.

I tilt my head slightly. "What do you have to hide?"

Her brow furrows. "I don't know. Myself?" She says it as if she is asking me a question.

"What do you mean?"

She releases a shuddering breath. "There's a darkness inside of me I can't control." She meets my gaze. "I think it's why I didn't care when you killed those two men in front of me."

"Come here." I sit with my back against the headboard and gesture for her to rest in my arms again. "Everyone has darkness inside of them, and I'm no exception. My soul is as black as they come, but you can't let it define you, little dove."

Maeve's brow furrows as she looks up at me. "Why do you call me that?"

I know she won't like my answer, but she's always been so good and pure in my mind. It's the reason I gave her that nickname, as it felt right for her "Because you are so pure to me, Maeve."

She shakes her head. "I'm not the good girl you believe I am."

"I don't think you're a good girl, Maeve. I think you are perfect for me."

Her eyes soften, and tears form in them. "You are perfect for me too." A stray tear runs down her cheek. "I wish you didn't have to kill my father for us to be together."

I know how much this decision is going to weigh on her for the rest of her life. I fear she may resent me in the end once she realizes the burden our secret will be. A secret she has to keep from the people she loves the most in this world. Maeve has always doted on her three brothers.

"There's still time to call it off," I suggest, despite being unsure whether I could call it off if she wanted me to. Deep down, the darkness inside of me won't let her go. It would have been easier if I'd just left for Europe and forgotten about the princess who held my heart.

Instead, I schemed and plotted, using my knowledge from the man I wished to kill to undermine him. The one thing I'm sure of is that I'm not a good man. I've never pretended to be and never will be. Selfish desire has driven me from the start, even if it turned out Maeve needed saving in the end.

Darkness has thrived inside of me for years, and killing my mentor will only deepen the hold it has on my soul.

Maeve shakes her head. "No, you're right. My

father would throw me to Maxim without a care for my wellbeing." The tears fall freely down her cheeks. "He has never cared what happens to me, so why should I care what happens to him?"

"He cares about you, Maeve, but he has lost sight of what is important." I wipe the tears from her face. "I don't want you to resent me for this decision, as it has to be yours and yours alone."

It's a truth I'm certain of. If Maeve really can't stand me going through this, we will run if it's the only option. I'll keep her safe, even if we have to look over our shoulders for the rest of our lives.

"I want it to be our decision, and I've agreed to it, as I don't want to live without you. No matter how selfish that is."

I nod in response. "Then it is settled." I lift her chin, kissing her lips softly. "The plan goes ahead."

Maeve nods and shuts her eyes, resting her head against my chest. We hold each other close, knowing that the plan is not foolproof.

I could wind up dead instead of her father. Our time together tonight is more precious than I can put into words.

23

MAEVE

"It is time."

Gael has gone over the plan with me several times, and I hate it because we have to split up.

His amber eyes connect with mine, holding an intensity that rocks me to the core. "Are you ready, little dove?"

There is no way I'll ever be ready for what we're about to do. Gael is going to kill my father. A man whom I have no love for, but I can't help but feel guilty.

What kind of person stands by while their lover murders their father?

I guess the answer to that is me. Deep down, I'm as dark and broken as the man who fathered me. I never wanted to face reality, always trying to put distance between myself and clan business.

The fact is that no matter how hard I try, the darkness is a part of my soul and always will be. I think deep down it is why I've always envied Kieran, as he inherited my mother's kind soul. His heart is purer than the rest of us.

"Little dove?" Gael pushes.

I shake my head. "I'm not sure I'll ever really be ready."

There's a sadness in his eyes as if he understands better than anyone. "Aye, neither will I, but it's time."

I push off the bed and pace toward him, letting him wrap a muscular arm around me. "I'm scared that everything will go wrong."

Gael places a calloused finger under my chin and gently forces me to crane my neck to look at him. "Don't think like that. I'll protect you, even if it goes wrong."

My brow furrows, as that's not possible. If it goes wrong, Gael dies, and the mere thought threatens to drown the life out of me. "How can you if you are no longer breathing?"

Gael smiles, but it's a sad smile. "I have my ways, little dove." He presses his lips to mine, kissing me softly.

I lace my fingers in his hair, pulling him harder against me.

He deepens the kiss, his tongue probing against mine with a gentleness that makes my entire body ache with need. It feels like this could be the last time I feel his tongue against mine or his hands on me.

He insists nothing will go wrong, but he does not know that. My father isn't stupid. The moment he sees Gael, he will sense the threat.

I can't stand the thought of him dying at my father's hand. The man has taken too much from me in my life; he can't take Gael.

We break away from each other, breathless.

Gael's brow furrows as he notices the few stray tears that have escaped my eyes. "Don't cry. I'll see you soon."

I swallow hard and nod. "I hope so."

He grabs my hand and pulls me toward the motel door. "Come on. We don't want to be late."

Seamus and Tiernan are already waiting in the parking lot. Tiernan stands with his back to us, impatiently tapping his foot on the concrete. Seamus leans back on the rental car's hood, looking cool and collected.

"Ready, lads?" Gael asks as he pulls me toward them.

Tiernan turns around, crossing his arms over his chest. "About ten minutes ago, yeah."

Gael glares at him. "Watch the attitude."

He runs a hand across the back of his neck. "Sorry, I'm on edge is all."

Seamus pushes off the car and flashes me a friendly smile. "You're riding with me, lass." He nods at the rental car Gael drove yesterday.

I inhale a long breath, hoping it will calm the nerves fluttering to life in my stomach. "Yeah." I glance at Gael. "Be careful, please."

Gael slides into the cocky man I know whenever he's around men from the clan. "I'm always careful." He smirks and it only makes my anxiety grow.

"I'm serious." I move closer to him and lower my voice. "I don't know how I could cope without you in my life."

His expression darkens. "You won't have to find out, trust me." He pulls me against him again and kisses me one last time.

I melt into the embrace, wishing we could freeze in time wrapped in each other's arms for the rest of eternity.

Tiernan clears his throat, annoyance in his dark eyes. "We're already late."

Gael releases me. "Be good for Seamus, little dove."

I walk over to the calm younger man, who gives me another friendly smile. "I don't think anyone has formally introduced us, even though I've worked for your dad for ten years."

I shake my head. "No, I don't think anyone has." I try to smile, but it feels unnatural. "It's nice to meet you."

He chuckles. "Good to meet you too." He unlocks the car, and I slide into the passenger seat.

Heat filters through my cheeks as I remember what Gael did to me only yesterday evening in this same car. Seamus turns the engine over and slides the car into reverse.

"Right, I have a pit stop just outside the city. At the stop, you're going to get into the trunk." His brow furrows. "I assume Gael has already told you?"

I nod in reply, biting my bottom lip at the thought of being in such a confined space. "How long a drive is it from the pit stop to the destination?"

He squints at the GPS in the car as if it will magically tell him. "Hard to say, half an hour?"

Half an hour in a dark, confined space.

My heart rattles against my rib cage as I twist my fingers in my lap. "Great," I mutter.

He glances at me. "Don't tell me you're claustrophobic."

I swallow hard and stare at the road in front of us. "Possibly." When I was younger, I had some unpleasant experiences with being locked in dark, small spaces because Father wanted to teach me a lesson.

My mom didn't agree with my father's archaic methods of discipline, but she didn't have the strength to stop him. I know it's something that haunted her. No matter how much she loved him, she knew the damage he did.

Kieran is two years younger than me, and he got off easier. Father was too consumed with work to bother with disciplining him, but my two older brothers had far longer of it to endure, both being considerably older than me.

"That will be bad." Seamus raps his fingers on the steering wheel. "When you say possibly, does that mean you don't know if you are or not?"

I swallow hard as since I was six years old, I've stayed as far away as possible from confined spaces. "Basically. I had a few horrible experiences with confined spaces as a kid and stayed away from them ever since."

"Shit, well, I don't know how to help with that."

Seamus shakes his head. "We can't risk anyone spotting you in the car with me, lass."

I swallow hard and nod, knowing deep down there's no other way. Facing my fears is the only option. "It will be fine." It will have to be as I don't have any choice.

"I always find music helps, and I'll crank it up when you are in there." Seamus turns on the radio. "Maybe you can sing along." He glances at me. "Although not too loud since we're trying to go unnoticed."

I laugh. "Sounds good."

We sit in silence as we travel toward Chicago. Anxiety has never felt so paralyzing before as it does now. I want this day over with as fast as possible.

I STARE INTO THE CONFINED, cramped space. Panic coils through me as I know that I'm staring my crippling fears in the face.

"Thirty minutes, maximum, I promise," Seamus says.

I swallow hard, as ten minutes would be long enough. "Fuck, okay." I climb into the trunk and lie down, feeling confined before he's even shut the lid. I look up at him. "Please keep the music on."

He smiles. "Aye, you got it, lass." He hesitates for a moment. "Ready?"

I nod in reply.

Seamus shuts the trunk carefully, plunging me into complete darkness.

I dig a flashlight out he gave me and turn it on. I breathe long, slow breaths and try to focus on the music as he turns the engine back on and starts to move.

It's too muffled in the trunk to make out the words, but I try to focus on it.

As we drive for a short while, my heart is racing. Images of the dark basement I fear so damn much flood my mind. No matter how much I try to push them out, the more persistent the visions become.

My breathing becomes labored as I start to panic. "No," I murmur, clawing at the trunk lid desperately as if I can tear my way out of it.

A vision of a dark-haired man with grey eyes standing over me wearing no shirt hits me. I swallow hard, trying to clear his face from my mind. I don't know who he is, but he seems familiar in a horrifying way.

I shut my eyes, but it worsens. "Make it stop," I say to no one in particular. "Please make it stop."

The droning of distant music doesn't seem to help as I try to focus on it, remembering Seamus' advice. The words become clearer as I try to sing along, and it works for a short while until another vision hits me.

Blood and gore. A knife protrudes out of the man's neck as he chokes on his blood. My father grabs the knife and stabs him in the head, putting him out of his misery. The sound is sickening as he falls to a heap on the floor, blood splattering my face as the knife leaves his body. My stomach churns, and I think I might throw up. "No," I cry desperately. "Make it stop." I claw more frantically at the trunk lid with my nails.

My father stands over his body, glaring at me. It's a cold and hateful stare that he has given me for as long as I can remember. I shake my head, trying to shake the images in my mind.

A respite from them comes as they disappear entirely. I relax, hoping they are gone for good. Despite the horror of the images persisting deep in my bones. Whatever visions I was seeing made no sense, as I don't know what they are or who that man is.

The panic hits me again as the visions reappear in

my mind with even more vividity. Blood, gore, and horror are all I see as my breathing becomes shallow and labored.

Dizziness infects me, and I know before it happens that I'm going to pass out. It's been years since I fainted, but I know the sensation all too well. My stomach dips as the darkness surrounding me grows and everything blanks out.

24

GAEL

There's heavy tension in the car as we drive down the highway toward Chicago. The weight of my task deepens with every mile we get closer.

Tiernan side-glances at me. "How are you feeling?"

I crack my neck. "Stupid question, isn't it?" I ask, feeling irritated he would even ask me. I feel like shit right now.

He raises a brow. "Don't tell me you're getting cold feet?"

I glare at my friend. "Never." I've never doubted my ability to do this in the three years I've planned it. "I just know how much is riding on this."

"I don't envy you, lad," Tiernan says, tapping his

fingers on the steering wheel. "I agreed to this because you're my closest friend, and friends help each other out." He sighs heavily. "Make sure you don't fuck it up, though. I have a family to protect."

"No pressure, aye?"

Tiernan's jaw clenches. "Seriously, I can't afford to die."

If I don't succeed, I will not bring Tiernan down with me. My friend, Ely, who lives in the Caribbean, erased any evidence that could tie Tiernan or Seamus to the assassination plot. He's a whizz with computers and owed me a favor. "I've ensured that no one can tie you to this if I fail, trust me."

Tiernan nods and glances my way. "I do trust you." His Adam's apple bobs as he swallows. "Don't fuck it up as I want you around, lad."

He doesn't need to add to the pressure as I'm already feeling it acutely. My entire future rests in my hands.

"Sorry, I don't mean to add to the pressure." Tiernan reaches for the stereo controls and turns it up. "Let's try not to think about it."

I nod and focus on the music blaring out of the speakers, but all it does is add to the chaos swirling around my mind. Chaos I can't seem to control.

"Maeve is a catch, though, lad." Tiernan glances

at me. "How are you going to broach the subject with Rourke?"

I swallow hard, as I haven't thought about it. I have spent all my energy working out how to get Ronan out of the picture. Rourke won't want Maeve to marry Maxim if my plan goes right, but it doesn't mean he will want her with me either.

I remember the warnings he gave me when I was getting close to Maeve before leaving for Europe.

You're not good enough for her, Gael. Please keep away from her before both of you wind up in serious trouble.

He's probably right. I'm not good enough for the beautiful, innocent Callaghan princess. No matter how much she insists she isn't so pure, she is. I'm sure her belief that she has darkness inside of her comes from the trauma she's buried deep down inside.

When and if she finally remembers, she will realize it too.

"I don't know, and I honestly haven't thought that far ahead." I crack my neck as I feel the tension building. "All I know is we'll need to wait a suitable amount of time after her father's death."

"Aye, it would be wise to be careful." Tiernan's brow furrows. "I don't believe Rourke will care who Maeve ends up with, to be honest. He's different to

Ronan even if he inherited his penchant for violence."

I nod in response, no longer wanting to carry on with this conversation. Right now isn't the time to dwell on issues that might crop up in the future, as I need to focus on the task at hand. Killing my mentor is going to be the single most difficult thing I've ever done.

Any man I've killed before I've had no affiliation with, or I hated them. I don't hate Ronan, but I hate what he is trying to do to Maeve. He won't see reason, so I must take his life.

I'd do anything to ensure Maeve is mine, even if it means dying to protect her from Maxim.

The hand on the watch moves to ten past nine. My signal to get out of the trunk. I use my strength to push the trunk upward and climb out onto the street.

The streetlights blind me after being in absolute darkness. I smooth down my crumpled suit jacket, noticing my hands are already shaking from the adrenaline. Podolka is one of the hottest clubs in the city, which means it's always heaving with people.

Tiernan entered the club ten minutes ago. I walk

calmly out of the alleyway that Tiernan parked the car down, cursing under my breath when I see the huge line to get in. As I get closer, I notice a VIP line with no one at it. That's my only chance to get in and make it on time. If Tiernan got me on the list, they should let me in there.

The bouncer's eyes narrow the moment he notices me walking toward him. "Name?"

"Artyom," I say, employing my most Russian accent.

His brow furrows, and for a moment, I don't think he's going to check the list. Finally, he tears his eyes off me and checks the clipboard in his hands. His finger stops on my name, and he nods. "Go on in."

I step past him and enter the club, expelling a relieved sigh as I walk down the dark corridors into the VIP section of Podolka. The first step has gone by without a hitch. I come to the door to the bathroom on my right and stop, glancing in each direction to ensure no one is around.

I slip into the bathroom, feeling my heart pound against my rib cage. The bathroom is empty, and I pull my cell phone out of my pocket and text Tiernan.

All set.

He's waiting for my signal before setting his friend on Ronan. I walk into the stall furthest from the door and shut it, hoping no one else comes in while Ronan is in here. Otherwise, it could get messy.

My cell phone buzzes, and I dig it out, finding a reply from Tiernan.

Headed your way.

Shit. It is all working out like clockwork, which is a little unnerving. I've done this for twenty years, and there hasn't been a job that works out exactly as planned. Somewhere along the line, something is guaranteed to go wrong.

I hear the click of heels outside of the bathroom as the door flings open. "Shall I clean that up for you, sir?" I grind my teeth as I recognize that voice.

Arla.

She is a whore Ronan frequently pays to show him a good time.

Fuck's sake.

I pull out my cell phone and type a response.

Thanks for the heads up on Arla.

The bubbles start as he types back, but I don't wait for his response. Instead, I stow the cell in my pocket and focus on their conversation.

"No," Ronan snaps. "Wait for me at the table, Arla." I hear the door open again and a scuffle on the other side, followed by a harsh slap. Ronan isn't afraid of beating the women he pays. "I'm fed up with you following me everywhere. You know your place. Now stick to it."

Arla makes an irritated huffing noise before the clack of her heels echoes as she leaves the bathroom.

Thank God for that.

Arla may be a nightmare who constantly follows him around, but I don't want her blood on my hands. She has nothing to do with this.

I fiddle with the hilt of my blade stowed in the inner lining of my jacket, visualizing the assassination before it happens. The kill should be a simple hit, as all I need to do is sneak up behind Ronan and cut his throat before he notices me. It's my method, the method the man standing on the other side of this door taught me.

"Fucking bitch," Ronan grumbles to himself.

I hear him turn on the faucet at the sink, and that is my cue to act. My stomach churns as I push open the bathroom stall door slowly, stepping out with the knife in my hand. Time slows down as I creep toward my mentor, feeling my heart thump hard. Guilt is such a confusing emotion as I sneak up on my unwitting mentor, ready to take his life after everything he did for me.

For the first time in my life, I hesitate. Blood rushes in my ears as I tighten my grip on the knife, visualizing the image of cutting his throat open again.

Ronan glances up and notices me in the mirror. "What the fuck?" Tension coils through his body when he sees the knife in my hand.

I move fast, making sure he can't escape. One arm slides around his neck, gripping him. I bring the other hand to his neck, pressing the knife into his skin.

Ronan glares at me in the mirror, making the guilt almost unbearable. I can see the disappointment in his eyes. Disappointment that the young kid he took a chance on has turned against him to stab him in the back. "What are you doing, Gael," he spits out despite my grasp on his throat.

I shouldn't answer him. Hesitating could only lead to failure, and yet I have to explain myself to him. "I'm sorry, Ronan. It's the only way. Maeve is my world, and I won't let you marry her off to that Russian scum."

Ronan's gaze turns angry as he continues to glare at my reflection in the mirror. "You would kill your mentor for a piece of ass? Pathetic."

Rage courses through me, fueled by his sick remark. "You have no respect for your daughter."

I realize my stalling is dangerous. Ronan isn't stupid, and I know he'll fight if he gets the opportunity.

"Let me go, and we can talk about it," Ronan says.

I shake my head. "No, you aren't a reasonable man. I know I wouldn't live long, even if you agreed to a deal."

Ronan's elbow connects with my rib cage, shocking me.

"Fuck," I shout, trying to push the knife into his neck, but it's too late. The blade only nicks the skin, making a trickle of blood run down below his shirt.

He moves away from me. "You ungrateful son of a bitch," he says, eyes narrowing. "I took you in and ensured you didn't go to prison for that horrendous murder you committed." His hands ball into fists as he holds them out in front of himself. He shakes his head. "Looks like people don't change so much after all."

I tighten my grip on the knife, knowing I need to be creative before he raises the alarm. If his men come in here and find me, it is game over.

"You shouldn't have sold Maeve to the Russians

as if she is nothing more than a piece of meat." I move toward him, but he steps away.

"She is nothing more than a piece of meat. A mistake, that's what she is." Ronan is trying to wind me up and get under my skin. "I wish she were never fucking born. At least my brother would still be alive."

That comment makes my blood boil. "Your sick pedophile of a brother would still be alive? How great that would be. How can you blame Maeve for that psychopath's actions? She was five years old."

He holds his head high. "You thought you could get away with this, but you were wrong, Gael." He signals for me to come at him, holding his fists in front of him. "Let's see if the mentor still surpasses the student, aye?"

I know Ronan can't defeat me in a fistfight, not anymore. He has something else up his sleeve. I glance at the knife in my hand.

"Put it away and fight me like a man," he goads.

There is too much at stake. I won't risk everything I've worked for these three years. I only get one chance at this. "Sorry, Ronan. I know you too well." I grab the blade of the knife and throw it at him fast, catching him right in the throat. A trick that I learned in Europe, not from him. It's why he doesn't see it coming.

His wide eyes burn into my brain, making me sure I'll never forget the image as long as I'm alive. Ronan chokes on his blood as he falls to his knees on the floor, hands reaching for the blade protruding from his throat.

"I wish it could have been different, but I won't risk Maeve's happiness because you are too blind to see how amazing she truly is." I grab the hilt of the knife and pull it out before stabbing him hard in the heart, putting him out of his misery.

This is one occasion where I don't delight in the kill or watch the light leave his eyes. I wipe the knife clean and stow it in my pocket before turning my back on my dead mentor.

The heaviness of what I've done weighs me down as I walk calmly out of the bathroom, turning down a staff corridor toward a back exit. A few of the staff rush past me in a hurry. Ronan's blood splatters my dark suit, but no one bats an eyelid as I leave the club and my mentor dead in my wake.

I'm relieved it is done, but I know my actions today will haunt me in a way none of my other deeds ever have. Ronan deserved better from me, just like Maeve deserved better from him.

25

MAEVE

"Wake up, lass. Please wake up."

A panicked voice breaks through my unconscious state. My eyes flicker open only to shut as the light burns my irises. I groan and shift gently, bringing my hand up to my face.

"Thank God you're alive," Seamus exclaims, staring at me from outside the car.

I shade my eyes with my hand before opening them again. "Why wouldn't I be alive?"

He chuckles, holding a hand out to me. "Because I opened the damn trunk and you were unconscious, lass. You've been out for at least two minutes before I could wake you."

I take his hand, and he pulls me out of the trunk.

"What happened?" Seamus asks.

I shake my head. "I guess I do have claustrophobia after all." I swallow hard as the visions that wouldn't quit while I was in the dark, confined trunk return in flashes.

"You don't say?" Seamus nods toward a building. "Come on, lass. We need to get out of the open and inside the warehouse fast."

I nod in response, feeling a little shaky on my feet as I follow him down a broken up concrete path toward a dilapidated building. Seamus checks the vicinity before opening a side door and slipping inside, holding it open for me. A sense of unease sweeps over me as we walk into the dingy space. "This place gives me the creeps," I murmur.

He glances over his shoulder. "Don't worry, the place is creepy, but it's been empty for years. No Russians will come in here."

I take little comfort from his assurance. All I want is for this day to be over and Gael to return. We walk deeper into the building until we get to a large open space, which looks to be an old factory. "This is where I'm going to tie the both of you up. Gael should be here in…" He checks his watch. "thirty minutes approximately."

Thirty minutes is too long waiting to find out if

he succeeded. "Is he going to contact you once it's done?"

Seamus grabs a chair strewn to one side. "No, he has to keep contact to a minimum, even on the burner phone." He gestures for me to sit in the chair. "This will be yours. I'll find another one for Gael." Seamus doesn't wait for me to reply, walking in the opposite direction to the one we came.

I sigh heavily and sit, wrapping my arms around myself. The blood and gore of my visions are almost impossible to erase from my mind, and I can't understand where they've come from. The visions felt like distant memories, but that can't be possible. I've never seen those visions before.

Seamus returns with another chair and sets it a small distance from mine. "That should do, and I've got the rope here." He signals at the rope slung over his shoulder.

"Won't it be a little unbelievable because there are no guards?" I ask.

Seamus shakes his head. "Nah, we often leave prisoners to sweat it out alone for a while. It's not unheard of."

I breathe a sigh of relief. "Fair enough. I guess you guys have thought of everything." I swallow hard and glance at him. "Why isn't he going to let you know once it's done?"

His brow furrows. "I told you, Gael has to keep contact to a minimum. The smaller the trail left in our wake, the better."

I swallow my dread, trying to stop the anxiety clawing at my insides. "Do you believe he can pull it off?"

Seamus sighs heavily, glancing at me. "Yes, Gael can do anything if he is determined enough."

I think I'm getting on Seamus' nerves, even though he wouldn't admit it. It's impossible not to worry when the man I love is doing something so dangerous. "Sorry, I'm so nervous."

He nods. "It's understandable." He sits on the other chair he pulled up for Gael and fiddles with the rope. "The man knows what he's doing, and he'll be here." He glances at his watch. "Hopefully in fifteen minutes."

He sounds certain, but he can't be sure that Gael killed him without a hitch, let alone that he got out of the club without being caught.

I could cut the tension in the warehouse with a knife.

As silence fills the cavernous space, I hate that my mind returns to those bloody images. I can't believe I passed out in the trunk. The most haunting image from the visions was the man I didn't know, leering at me intimidatingly.

They felt like flashbacks I can't explain. I feared that man in another life or something, as if I knew him. What I can't explain is why I saw my father kill him.

My stomach churns as I try to push the questions out of my mind. This isn't the time to be dwelling on things I can't explain.

A bang at the far end of the warehouse catches my attention. I hold my breath, hoping it's Gael. My stomach sinks when two men enter the warehouse.

"Shit," Seamus mutters, crouching down behind a barrel to the left-hand side. "Stay quiet, lass. I'll handle this." Seamus pulls out a gun with a silencer fitted as I remain still in the chair, waiting for them to notice me.

When they do, their brows furrow. "Did Spartak order a prisoner to be brought here?" one asks.

The other looks confused. "Not to my knowledge. Shall I call him?"

The first man to speak nods in response, staring at me with uncertainty. Seamus hasn't even tied me up yet.

My stomach churns as Seamus slowly moves to

get a view around the barrel and shoots the man with the phone right in the head. He drops to the floor, and the other guy is so startled, he doesn't move before Seamus shoots him through the heart.

Seamus rushes over to the men, grabbing the cell phone. His shoulders relax the moment he picks it up. "He didn't ring him. Thank fuck for that." He stows the gun in his pocket, clearly unfazed that he murdered two men in cold blood.

I feel panic overwhelm me as the blood pools out of the man's head, the visions I'd had in that trunk returning to the forefront of my mind. "What are you going to do with them?"

Seamus scrubs a hand over his beard, shrugging. "I need them hidden for when your rescuers arrive."

Another bang startles both of us, and Seamus' eyes widen. "Shit, that better be Gael."

We both freeze, staring at the entryway.

My heart stutters in my chest as he steps into the factory, eyes finding mine in an instant.

All my anxiety melts away, only to be replaced with guilt at the haunted look in his eyes. He feels it too: the crippling guilt his actions today have caused.

I can't move to him as I'm frozen by the fear of facing reality. My father is dead.

His eyes finally break contact, and then his brow

furrows when he sees the two dead bodies. "What the fuck happened here?"

Seamus walks toward him. "Russians turned up unannounced. Luckily, they didn't have time to alert Spartak."

Gael runs a hand across the back of his neck. "We have to clean this up, fast."

"Aye," Seamus replies, glancing back at me. "I was about to ask Maeve to give me a hand."

Rage ignites in his eyes. "You leave Maeve the fuck out of this. I'm here now, and I'll handle it." Gael doesn't say a word to me, grabbing the guy's feet who Seamus shot in the head. "Come on."

I watch as they both drag the lifeless body away. My stomach twists with anxiety as Gael hasn't said a word to me yet. The fact he is here must mean my father is dead.

Deep down, I had a small hope that somehow he might have been able to reason with him, but I know that's a fantasy.

Gael and Seamus return and grab the other man without a word. I do not know where they are taking them, and I don't want to know. All I want is for Gael to acknowledge me.

The pool of blood in front of me is enough to make me feel sick. When they return, Gael finally looks my way again. "Seamus, clean up the blood as best you can." He walks toward me. "It's done, little dove. I'm sorry." I can see the regret in his eyes.

The pain clawing at my chest is an unusual sensation. The news almost feels unreal, as we've spoken about it enough times. "Was it fast?" I ask, standing.

Gael nods. "Fast and painless, which is better than he deserved."

I don't understand the vehement in his voice, and right now, I don't want to. Instead, I walk toward him and wrap my arms around his waist. "Thank God it's over."

Gael wraps his powerful arms around me in return, holding me tightly.

Tears fall freely down my cheeks as we remain like that for a few minutes until Seamus clears his throat. "We have to get this done, lad."

Gael breaks away from me and sighs. "You know your story, right?"

I nod in response, as I know I don't need to run over it anymore.

Gael turns and faces Seamus. "Come on then, lad. Do your worst."

Seamus looks hesitant before punching Gael hard in the face.

I gasp. "What are you doing?"

Gael glances at me. "Do you think they'd believe us if I'm not roughed up at all?" He shakes his head. "They wouldn't lay a hand on the Callaghan princess, but me... It may be a tough ask for your family to believe they wouldn't have just killed me, little dove."

I swallow hard and sink into the chair behind me, knowing that Gael is right. If the Russians had kidnapped us, then they would have killed Gael or, at the very least, tortured him for information. "What if they think you gave away my father, and that's why he's dead?"

Gael shakes his head. "Impossible, as they believe I've been gone for over a week. Your father only scheduled his visit to Podolka four days ago."

I nod and shut my mouth, as it is clear they have thought of every detail. Seamus balls his fists again, ready to beat Gael up. "Ready, lad?"

"As ready as I'll ever be."

Seamus beats him hard, and I can hardly watch as Gael takes punch after punch without making a sound. I can't understand how he can be so hardened to pain, but I feel it's all because of his childhood. I hate seeing him get hurt.

"I reckon that'll do. I'm sorry, Gael," Seamus says.

Gael turns around to take his seat, and I gasp at the sight of his face. "Oh my God."

"It's superficial, Maeve," he says.

It doesn't matter as he looks terrible. The bruises are already coming out all over his face, and his right eye is swollen shut. Blood drips from the crack in his busted lip.

"Now tie us both up, lad," Gael orders.

Seamus does as he says, tying me with rope first and then Gael. "All set. I'll see you both on the other side, aye?"

"Aye," Gael replies.

All I can do is nod as the weight of what we've all just done weighs on my shoulders. Within hours, I'll have to face my brothers and lie through my teeth to them.

26

GAEL

The gags in our mouths were necessary but irritating. The wait feels excruciating. For a short while, Maeve held my gaze. Now, she has her eyes shut and her head back, clearly struggling to come to terms with the decision we made. I wish there were some way I could console her.

Seamus and I dumped the two Russians in an old crate out the back, but it is only a matter of time until someone comes searching for them. Hopefully, the clan comes for us first.

A bang echoes through the factory. I groan as the sound makes my head hurt. I've got a royal headache since Seamus' beating, but there is no doubt the Russians would have been more brutal.

Rourke charges into the warehouse, a rage so acutely written all over his face. Killian follows close behind, a mask over his emotions. Last, Kieran rushes in, eyes red from crying as he zones in on Maeve. "Maeve," he shouts, rushing over to her.

The first thing he does is pull the gag out of her mouth before untying the rope around her wrists and ankles.

"Kieran," Maeve mutters, tears sparkling in her eyes. "Thank God you're here."

Rourke stops in front of Maeve. "What happened, Sis?"

I know how hard this will be for her, lying to her brothers. I sit, waiting for someone to untie me and remove the fucking gag from my mouth. No one even glances in my direction.

She shakes her head. "It all happened so fast," she says, shuddering slightly. "Gael found me in Madison and was about to bring me back to Chicago when the Russians ambushed us."

"Spartak," Rourke growls, clenching his fists by his side. "That son of a bitch."

Killian is the one to bring up the news to her. "We have some terrible news, Maeve." There isn't an ounce of emotion in his voice.

"What is it?" she asks, her voice shaky.

Kieran holds her hand as Rourke kneels in front of her. "Father is dead."

Killian steps forward when Rourke doesn't elaborate. "The Russians killed him at a club mere hours ago."

Maeve shakes her head. "Are you sure? He can't be dead."

Kieran allows tears to fall for their father. "Aye, he's dead. Stabbed in the throat and the heart. It was savage."

Maeve winces at the details, but tears don't fall. "Why would they kill him?"

Rourke draws in a deep breath. "Ever since he broke the pact to deliver you to Maxim, tensions have been at an all time high." He stands and crosses his arms over his chest.

Kieran steps in front of her again. "Don't blame yourself, though, Maeve. It wasn't your fault." He shakes his head. "I get why you ran."

Maeve swallows hard, tears spilling from her eyes. I know it's not the news that entices those tears, but her guilt. I feel it too. "I can't believe it." Maeve purposely keeps her eyes from me, focusing on the floor in front of her.

"Neither can we." Rourke cracks his neck. "It means we're at war with the Russians."

Killian steps closer to Maeve. "That's not important right now. Let's get you out of here, Sis." He glances at Kieran. "Go on, little brother. Get her out of here and wait for us outside." His eyes fix on me. "Gael, you have some explaining to do."

I notice panic cross Maeve's face momentarily as her younger brother ushers her away, leaving me with Rourke and Killian. She's worried about what her brothers might do to me, but I'm not. They'll question me, but I have an answer to anything they might throw my way.

Rourke strolls toward me, pulling the gag out of my mouth. "Yeah, how could you let this happen?"

My brow furrows. "I didn't let anything happen." I shake my head. "The Russians ambushed me about five minutes after I'd snatched an unwilling Maeve from the club she was working at."

Killian's eyes narrow. "You should have seen them coming."

I get they are doing their due diligence as the new leaders of the clan. "Right, I should have seen a white van swerving onto the sidewalk with four Russians who jumped out and circled us." I glare at Killian, who has always been the hardest of the three brothers to talk to. "He sent me straight into the wolf's den. It was a fucking trap."

Killian squints at me. "Why didn't they kill you, aye?"

He's not an easy man to convince, and I knew out of the three of them, he would be the toughest. "You tell me." I clench my jaw. "They kept questioning me about an acquisition that is supposedly taking place." I narrow my eyes. "Jackson Corp. Does that ring any bells? As I'd never fucking heard of it."

"Shit," Rourke says, stepping closer. "Are you saying they know about the acquisition?"

Seamus dug this gem up for me after a source close to Ronan found it out. A sign Ronan had lost his trust in me even before I made a move, as he hadn't mentioned this acquisition to me at all. Perhaps my working against him over the past three years hadn't gone unnoticed.

"I don't know what this acquisition is, but yes, if one exists, then the Russians are aware."

"Fuck," Rourke runs a hand through his hair. "Father was trying to expand the legitimate side of the clan business and move away from criminal activity." He paces the floor. "He intended to build a legitimate empire alongside the criminal one, just in case. If the Russians know about it, they'll try to stop us."

That's news to me, surprising news. Ronan didn't strike me as a man that wanted to move away from the underworld of Chicago, as he thrived in it and enjoyed digging himself a deeper hole in the dark underbelly. I don't understand why he wanted a legitimate side to the business.

"Why did he want to legitimize his empire?" I ask.

Killian glares at me. "That's not important right now. Why did they think you would know?"

My brow furrows. "I guess because I'm the clan chief."

"You were the clan chief," Killian says.

I had a feeling I'd get some resistance, particularly from Killian. He's never been too fond of me, even when he was a kid. "What's that supposed to mean?"

Rourke places his palm flat on Killian's chest. "Aye, what is that supposed to mean, Brother? Gael is a veteran Callaghan clan member and will remain in his position."

Killian's brow furrows. "Father wanted both of us to be involved in the clan's running."

"And we will be. It doesn't affect Gael's position." Rourke steps forward and pulls a knife out of his belt, slicing through my restraints. "Here, let me help you up."

I wince as Seamus bruised my ribs when he beat me. "Fuck," I hiss.

Rourke raises a brow. "You need to see a doctor, lad."

I shake my head. "I'll be alright after some rest."

"Nonsense. I'll send Jerry over to your place in an hour," Rourke says. "Kieran will give you a lift home."

"Thanks, lad."

Rourke helps me out of the warehouse where Kieran sits on a wall with his arm around Maeve. She looks broken, and I hate that I'm the reason for her anguish.

Rourke clears his throat. "Kieran, can you drive Gael home?"

His brow furrows, but he nods. "I'll be home soon, Maeve." He stands and nods toward the Mustang parked nearby. "That's me."

I slide into the passenger seat, resisting the urge to glance back at Maeve.

Kieran gets into the driver's seat and turns on the engine, pulling out of the parking lot. A heavy silence hangs in the air.

I glance at the youngest member of the Callaghan family. "I'm sorry about your father, Kieran."

His eyes mist with tears again. "I can't believe he's gone."

I swallow the lump in my throat, trying to ignore the image of Ronan choking on my knife, which won't stop replaying. "Neither can I."

I've killed countless men in my life ever since Ronan accepted me into the clan, but his death is the most poignant of them all. The image is one I'll never be able to erase from my mind. Or the disappointment in his eyes when he looked at me.

I know Ronan deserved better than the death his mentee inflicted on him, but he was the one that made a mistake when he trusted me.

There is no mending the darkness inside of me, which Ronan realized, and instead, he fed my darkness and became a casualty of it.

"What happened, exactly?" I ask.

Kieran shakes his head. "No one knows. He went into the bathroom at Spartak's club and was found twenty minutes later in a pool of blood." His grip tightens on the steering wheel. "The Bratva is trying to wipe their hands of it, but it's bullshit. They even wiped the CCTV." Kieran's eyes narrow. "No one else has access to it, so they think we're stupid."

I stare down at my hands. " He never should have trusted the Russians."

Kieran's brow furrows. "I thought you suggested it?"

I shake my head. "No, I didn't even know about the alliance he planned until the night of the announcement of Maeve and Maxim's engagement."

"Fuck's sake. Father was too stubborn, wasn't he?" Tears sparkle in his eyes, which are so similar to his sister's.

"Aye, but that's what made him such a great leader."

Kieran nods in reply as we fall silent, driving down the highway toward my home.

The guilt I feel for inflicting pain on this family should be worse, but remorse isn't something I easily feel. Ronan wouldn't have hesitated to set the police on me the moment he realized I'd run with Maeve, and I knew better than to chance it. The most overwhelming emotion I feel right now is relief. Ronan is dead, and Maeve is safe from the Bratva, as there is no way she'll marry Maxim now.

In the clan's eyes, they broke the pact the moment they killed the leader of the clan. Not to mention, they kidnapped Maeve.

Spartak will swear it wasn't him, but he has no proof, and the brothers won't listen to him now.

They are all angry and will direct their fury at the

Bratva, keeping the heat off of Maeve, Seamus, Tiernan, and me. I'm sure my two friends are enjoying a pint right now, and once at home, I intend to join them.

Life is too short for regrets. I intend to own my decision and help Maeve come to terms with it.

27

MAEVE

I sit with my head in my hands, feeling broken all over again.

The visions I had in the trunk of that car have haunted me ever since, but I can't work out what the hell they were. A figment of my imagination, perhaps.

"I can't believe he is dead," Kieran murmurs next to me.

Right now, I can't find it in me to cry, as the guilt is too consuming. I don't reply, knowing that silence is the best route to take right now. All I do is shake my head.

Rourke paces up and down next to the fireplace and has done for about an hour now. There's violence in his expression, and it scares me. He's always tended to lean toward violence, but right now, he's not thinking straight. "We need to strike back fast," he says.

Killian, my other brother, shakes his head in response. "That's not intelligent, Brother. We need to regroup and plan."

"Would you two shut up about revenge?" Kieran growls. "He died tonight, for fuck's sake."

"Kieran's right." I swallow hard. "He's hardly been dead five minutes, and you two are thinking about more bloodshed."

Rourke stops pacing. "That's my role now." He walks over to where we sit, eyes darting between the two of us. "If you have a problem with it, tough shit. I replace Father now he's gone, and sitting around for too long could cost us everything."

The door swings open, and Torin enters, looking devastated. "Tell me it's not true."

I wish Gael were here, but he wouldn't be expected to be at the family home so soon after such a tragic event, no matter what has happened. After my mom died, he explained what happened to her, but he gave me space at first. We both agreed it would raise suspicions if he were suddenly all over me, which means we have to give it time.

Rourke shakes his head. "We can't, I'm afraid."

Killian claps Torin on the shoulder. "The Russians will pay for this, Uncle. I promise you that."

"Fuck," Torin growls, running a hand over his head. "Two brothers dead and buried. How did it come to this?"

My brow furrows, and my heart pounds harder in my chest. "Two brothers?" I question, feeling an odd shiver race down my spine, the visions returning as a dark-haired man looms over me in the dark basement I remember as a child.

Torin's eyes widen when he sees me. "Maeve, I didn't know you were back." He glares at Rourke. "I guess you left that part out."

Killian's eyes narrow. "Aye, father's death distracted us. I forgot to tell you we got a tip-off from a Russian."

"The Bratva." Rourke glances at me. "They kidnapped Gael and Maeve and had them tied up in one of their warehouses." He runs a hand across the back of his neck. "It seems one of the Bratva members saw sense and tipped us off after they heard what happened to Father."

"Why did you say two brothers?" I ask, wondering why I've never heard of another uncle, even if he is dead.

"It isn't important," Torin says.

Killian moves toward me. "Certain things are better left buried, little sister."

I shake my head. "No." I glance around at all the faces staring at me. "How do all of you know about this brother and not me?"

Kieran stands. "Not all of us, as I don't know what's going on," he says.

Rourke glances at Killian. "Both of you sit down, and we'll explain."

Torin shakes his head. "The therapist said—"

"Fuck the therapist, Torin," Rourke says, crossing his arms over his chest. "If she insists on answers, then she'll get them."

Therapist.

I can't understand what is going on.

Killian is the one to speak next. "Torin and Father had another brother, and his name was Shane."

A shudder courses through me at the name, as it's a name that I fear. The image of that man's face appears in my mind again.

Could he have been my uncle?

"What happened to him?" I ask.

"Father murdered him when he found out what he did." A scream breaks through my memories as I remember the carnage in the basement, the horrific spray of blood running like a river over the floor as a knife protruded from his skull.

I see the image of my father glaring at him with blood splattered over his face. He has his fists clenched and his nostrils flared. My stomach churns, and I stand up, rushing to the nearby paper waste bin to throw up. It all comes charging back like a real-life horror story.

Shane.

All the memories down in that basement hit me at once: the abuse I received at my uncle's hand and the despicable things he made me do. Shane is a name I fear because he was the one that shut me in the basement and did things no man should do to a five-year-old girl.

My father never shut me in the basement, and I was never alone in that dark space. My head spins as Kieran places a gentle hand on my back. "Come on, Maeve. It's okay."

Kieran still does not know what I experienced, but from the pitiful looks on both Killian's and Rourke's faces, they do. Rourke clears his throat. "I guess you remember, then?" There's a sad glint in his eyes. "It was never Father that made you scared of confined spaces or the dark."

It feels like my world crumbles around me,

making what I did even harder to accept. "Why didn't anyone ever talk about this uncle?"

How the hell could I have forgotten something so huge?

Killian walks toward me and crouches down in front of me, showing an uncharacteristic sense of concern. He takes my hands in his. "When Mom found out about it, she went crazy and insisted on taking you to a psychiatrist to help you get over the trauma." His brow furrows. "However, they couldn't find any evidence you remembered the trauma at all. They diagnosed you with dissociative amnesia and said that you would only ever remember if you were ready."

Torin nods. "They told all of us not to mention him or anything about the event to you."

I demonized my father from such a young age, but he was only protecting me. "So, the story about Father disciplining us in a basement wasn't true?"

Rourke shakes his head. "No, you imagined that yourself. No one ever told you Father locked you in a basement, but we couldn't correct you."

I fall silent, wondering if anything I knew about my childhood was real. I related the trauma and night terrors to my father's methods of discipline, but they had nothing to do with him, other than the murder that I witnessed him commit when he found his brother down in the basement abusing me.

My stomach churns as I can't get Shane's face out of my mind. I shudder, wishing more than ever that Gael were here. I don't know how to handle this without him.

Kieran takes a seat next to me, placing a palm on my back. "Are you okay?"

I meet his gaze. "I just don't know, Kier."

He rubs my back in soothing circles, trying to calm me. "It's crazy adding this onto Father's death." His brow furrows. "I don't know what this uncle of ours did to you, but it must have been bad if Father killed his brother." Kieran swallows, his Adam's apple bobbing. "I'm sorry, Maeve."

I don't deserve his pity, not after what I've done. "I can't believe everyone knew about this."

Kieran shakes his head. "I don't know what the hell is going on. I'm as in the dark as you, Sis."

If the guilt of allowing Gael to kill my father isn't enough, the darkness surrounding my past feels like it could swallow me. It feels like the hole that I've dug myself is endless. A dark hollow pit that I'm free-falling into.

Killian lingers nearby. "You'll probably want to see the therapist, Maeve." His brow furrows. "I have her details somewhere, as Mom gave them to me a few years ago."

A therapist.

The idea of talking to anyone about my problems seems impossible. I can't reveal that I agreed to my lover murdering my father. It's a guilt I'll have to live with my entire life and never talk to anyone about, except for Gael.

Although I know Rourke loves me, I'm worried he may not agree with me being with him. I fear he takes after my father in too many ways. I know he's easier to talk to than Father, though.

"I'm not sure about that," I say, not meeting Killian's intense gaze.

"Think about it. The therapist insisted the moment you remembered you need to see someone."

Kieran glares at Killian. "Give it a rest, Killian. She has only remembered, and Father just died." He places an arm around me. "I think you ought to have a long hot bath, Maeve."

I shake my head. "I don't want to be alone right now."

"Alright. How about I fix us something to eat?" Kieran suggests.

I know he's only trying to help, but all his efforts

make the guilt deepen. "Not sure I could stomach anything, if I'm honest."

"Nonsense," Kieran says, helping me out of the chair. "Ally made brownies earlier, and there is ice cream in the freezer."

I let him guide me out of the living room as it beats sitting with the rest of my grieving family. At least with only one brother, my guilt is lessened. Ally, our cook, is busy preparing food despite what has happened. She never stops, even when our family has a crisis. It was the same after my mom died.

"I'm so sorry, Kieran and Maeve," she says as we walk in. "What can I get you?"

Kieran nods in acknowledgment. "How about a brownie and ice cream?"

She smiles, but it's wistful. "Coming right up. Sit yourselves down."

I sit at the central island, feeling numb. It's the only way to explain how I've felt ever since my dark past resurfaced.

Kieran turns the TV on in the kitchen, and the news flashes up. "Shit," he says.

"What is it?" I ask, noticing there's news of an explosion downtown.

"That's one of our pubs, Sis. The fucking Russians are rubbing it in." He shakes his head.

"Fucking bastards don't have the decency to allow us to grieve in peace." He stands, fists clenched.

The news doesn't make any sense. I'm well aware the Russians aren't the ones who killed Father, so why have they retaliated? Seamus, Tiernan, and Gael intended to meet up at one of the clan's pubs. My stomach churns as I hope it wasn't this one.

The images of the two dead Russians Gael and Seamus dragged away resurface to the forefront of my mind. I assume they think that was retaliation for Ronan and have hit back.

"Why would they do that?" I ask, staring at the screen as the carnage plays out on the broadcast. The headline states five dead and many more injured. Another result of our plan, but I'm sure Gael didn't expect this.

"Fuck knows."

Ally sets down the brownies in front of us. "There you go." She glances at the TV and places a hand on Kieran's shoulder. "Don't worry yourself about that. You have just lost your father." She takes the receiver and turns it off.

Kieran's jaw clenches, but he turns his attention to the brownie and delves in.

I do the same, trying to distract myself with it. My phone buzzes, and I dig it out of my pocket.

If you've seen the news, don't worry, we're okay.

I stow it back in my pocket and sigh in relief, eating the rest of my brownie. At least Gael is safe. I can't handle any more disasters today, even if I'm responsible for the chaos. I think I've had enough drama for the rest of my life.

28

GAEL

It's been four days since I saw Maeve, and I'm going out of my mind. I pace the floor of my kitchen, waiting.

She was supposed to be here twenty minutes ago.

As expected, Chicago is at war. Within the four days since Ronan's murder, the Russians and the clan have come to multiple deadly blows. A war has erupted as the bodies pile up on the streets. The feud with the Morrone family is now on the back burner, but I know better than anyone that it's only a matter of time until they get involved in the chaos.

Maeve has made sure she's kept her distance from me, rarely messaging. The only messages she has sent have been cryptic. It's driving me mad, but I know it's a necessity. The Callaghan brothers can't suspect anything. Otherwise, Ronan will have died in vain.

The doorbell sounds, cutting through my chaotic thoughts. I rush to open it, releasing a breath of relief when I see Maeve standing on the other side of the door. "I was getting worried, little dove."

Maeve's expression is vacant, which worries me all over again. "Sorry," she murmurs.

I step aside to allow her in. "Are you okay?"

Maeve shakes her head. "I honestly don't know."

I swallow hard, as I know she's blaming herself for her father's death, even though she never had a choice. I was always going to follow through with my plan. "I know it's hard, Maeve, but—"

"It's not that, Gael." She sinks into a seat at my kitchen table.

My brow furrows. "What is it, then?" I ask, sitting in the seat next to her and taking her hand in mine. Four days away from her felt like a lifetime, especially as I knew all the emotions she would have been dealing with alone. The fallout at home will have amplified her grief, trapped with the brothers she betrayed by allowing me to kill their father.

Her bright blue eyes meet mine, shining with unshed tears. "Did you know about Shane?"

Shane was Ronan's little brother. The same

brother who abused Maeve as a child and I watched Ronan murder when he stumbled across the two of them in that basement. A scene that was horrific enough for me to witness, let alone a five-year-old to see. That's not even mentioning the sick things Shane did to her. "Aye, lass." I nod. "I knew, but I wasn't allowed to say anything."

Her eyes narrow. "What happened to not wanting to keep anything from me?"

I shake my head and let go of her hands, standing. "This is different, Maeve. The psychiatrist said that only you could unveil the truth unaided when you were ready."

She laughs, but it's a frustrated sound. "That turned out great since Torin accidentally prompted me the day Father died."

I swallow hard, grabbing two glasses out of the cabinet and setting them on the countertops. "Do you want a drink?"

"Jameson?" she asks.

I nod. "Of course."

"Okay." She shuffles in the seat, watching me. "I wish you had told me, Gael."

I release a deep breath. "I'm sorry. I didn't think it was right to unveil it when the therapist said you may never remember it, anyway." I pour the two glasses of whiskey and hand her one, taking a seat next to her. "How do you feel now you know?"

Her eyes look a little distant as she stares into the whiskey glass. "More broken than I've ever felt before." Her eyes find mine. "And confused beyond belief."

I nod in reply. "Do you have questions?" My brow furrows. "I was there when your father found the two of you." My stomach twists with sickness as I remember the scared, teary-eyed little five-year-old girl.

Maeve's eyes widen. "You were there when Father killed him?" She confirms.

I nod. "Yes. What that man did to you is unspeakable, little dove."

"I don't remember seeing you there." Her expression hardens. "Torin said my father blamed me for his brother's death, even though he was the one to kill Shane."

I cast my mind back to the day, wondering if he blames Maeve for his brother's death. Ronan's attitude toward his daughter changed after that day. His words before he died repeat in my mind.

I wish she were never fucking born. At least my brother would still be alive.

The man was a disgrace. He harbored hatred

toward his daughter, which made no sense. I intend to protect her from his hatred, as no good will come of hurting her. "I don't think that's true, and I think his guilt ate away at him. He was angry about the way things turned out, is all."

Maeve sighs heavily. "I guess I'll never find out."

The timing of her remembering such a traumatic childhood experience isn't ideal after her father's death. I have a feeling that it can't be a coincidence. "How did it come back to you?"

Maeve shrugs. "It started in that trunk of the damn car. I had visions of the day." She shudders. "Then when Torin walked in and said *two brothers dead and buried*, it clicked into place. Especially when he mentioned the name Shane."

All I want is to take it all away from her. I know the heaviness of living with childhood abuse. It's hard to overcome, but I can't imagine what it's like to find out that most of your life you suppressed the memories. It's a crazy prospect, but one that the woman I love is experiencing. "I'm so sorry, Maeve."

I don't know what else to say. All I can do is remain strong for my little dove in her time of need. It irritates me that we have to keep our relationship a secret for now. Three years of waiting was long enough, but I know we can't move too fast as it may raise suspicion.

"How is everything else at home?" I ask.

Maeve huffs. "Not good. I broke my brothers." She glances at me, and I can see the guilt in her expression. "Rourke won't talk of anything other than revenge. Killian won't talk at all, shutting himself away, and Kieran is getting involved in clan business like he never has before." Maeve rests her head in her hands. "What have I done?"

I place a hand on her back, trying to console her. "You did nothing. It was all me."

She shakes her head and looks me in the eye. "I agreed to you killing him, so I may as well have stabbed him myself."

I clench my jaw, as her guilt doesn't make sense. "Remind yourself why you agreed, Maeve. He didn't care what happened to you and made that clear when he tried to give you to Maxim."

She nods. "I find it hard to believe Father protected me by killing his brother but then had no problem giving me to a man who is renowned for beating women."

"Another?" I ask, holding up the bottom of Jameson.

Maeve nods.

I top us both off and then take my seat again next to her. "You can't let this get to you, Maeve. You didn't kill him, and that's a fact."

She knocks back her whiskey and slams the glass down. "I know."

A silence falls between us as we sit at the table.

"Do you want something to eat?" I ask.

Maeve shakes her head. "I can't stomach food right now."

I narrow my eyes. "When did you last eat?"

"I had breakfast this morning." She glares at me. "Don't worry. I'm eating."

"Do you want to watch a movie, then?" I ask.

She shakes her head. "No, I want you."

I feel desire kick me in the gut at her declaration. My mind was staying out of the gutter as I didn't think she'd been in any state to be intimate. "Are you sure, little dove?"

She stands and straddles me. "I've never been more sure of anything in my life."

I capture her lips, feeling my cock harden beneath her instantly. Four days without tasting her was too long. Now that I've had her, I'm sure it would take someone murdering me to stop.

I lift her top off and unhook the bra at the front

before capturing her hard nipples in my mouth. "Fuck, I've missed you, baby," I murmur.

She moans softly, "I've missed you too."

I wrap my arms around her waist and stand, lifting her.

Maeve instinctively wraps her legs around my hips, clawing onto my shoulders.

I carry her to the bedroom, holding her lustful gaze. Gently, I set her down in the center of my four-poster bed. "Take off your pants."

Maeve doesn't hesitate, unzipping her jeans and wiggling out of them.

"Panties too," I order.

She tears them off her legs and chucks them on the floor, staring up at me expectantly.

I climb over her and grab her wrists one by one, clasping them in the inbuilt cuffs on my bed.

Maeve's eyes widen. "What are you doing?"

I move to her ankles and do the same, restraining her.

"Gael?" she questions.

I smirk, grabbing a spreader bar from under the bed.

Her lips purse together, and I fit it between her ankles. "I want you at my mercy, baby girl."

She swallows hard, eyes dilating as her pussy gets wetter.

I kneel between her spread legs and kiss her inner thighs softly.

Maeve moans, eyes rolling back in her head.

I move slowly toward her dripping wet center, longing to taste her again.

"Please, sir," Maeve begs, eyes finding mine.

I stop, smirking up at her. "Please, what?"

She bites her bottom lip temptingly. "I want to feel your tongue, please."

I groan and bury my tongue into her sweet as hell cunt.

Maeve writhes against the restraints as I lick her clit. Her pussy gushes as I devour her with an animalistic need. Anytime away from her now that I've had her is too long.

Maeve's moans are the music that feeds my soul, a sound I'll never tire of hearing. I slide my fingers inside of her, continuing to lick her throbbing clit. Maeve's hips jolt at the invasion as I plunge them in and out of her, driving her toward the edge.

I spank her thighs with my palm, making her moan louder. "Fuck me, please, sir," she cries.

My cock throbs in my boxer briefs at her begging. She doesn't have to ask twice as I'm struggling to retain control of the beast inside of me, trying to break free.

I pull my shirt over my head and toss it to the side. Then, I unzip my pants and drop them to the floor, followed by my boxer briefs.

Maeve gazes up at me with an adoration in her eyes I only ever dreamed of seeing. "Perfect," she muses, her eyes traveling slowly down my torso to the thick length jutting out between my thighs. Her eyes dilate as she tries to clench her thighs together, but the spreader bar stops her.

I smirk. "Did you forget about the bar, little dove?" I tease.

Her brow furrows in frustration, and she glares at me, writhing against the restraints. "Don't be a tease."

I shake my head and move toward her. "I'll be whatever I want, baby." I slide my finger through her soaking wet pussy before slipping my fingers into my mouth.

Maeve watches and groans, a gut-wrenching sound that satisfies me beyond compare.

"Tell me what you want," I order.

She licks her bottom lip. "I want you to fuck me, sir." Her eyes hold mine. "I want you to fuck me roughly, please."

Maeve is insatiable for rough sex, which I'd never have expected before we got intimate. The sweet, virgin Callaghan princess is a masochist at heart, and the other half fits the sadist I am deep down.

"Is that what you want, little dove?" I ask, fisting my cock in my hands.

"Yes, please, sir," she replies like the good little submissive she is.

I tilt my head to the side. "Since you asked so nicely." I step forward and kneel on the bed, positioning my cock at the entrance of her dripping wet pussy. "I might just give you what you want."

I reach under the bed and grab a bottle of lube. "First, though. I think you need something in your ass."

Maeve shudders, eyes dilating. "Yes, please, sir."

I grab a dildo from under the bed and smother it in lube. Using the spreader bar, I force her ass further forward and squirt lube onto it. Slowly, I work her ass free, stretching it with my fingers.

Maeve moans as her pussy gets wetter with each thrust of my fingers. "Fuck me, please," she begs.

I smirk at how eager she is. "Patience, little dove." I grab the dildo and slowly work her ass open, enjoying watching the tight ring of muscles stretch for me. "That's it, take it in your ass, baby girl."

Maeve's muscles shudder as she gets close to orgasm, and I haven't even fucked her yet. "Oh shit, I'm going to come," she screams.

I smirk. "Such a naughty girl, you can't even wait for my cock." I thrust the dildo further into her and make sure it's a tight fit before positioning the head of my cock with her dripping cunt. "Now I'm going to fuck that tight little pussy until you come all over my cock."

Maeve's eyes roll back in her head. "Yes, please, sir, fuck my pussy."

I slam into her hard, groaning at the tightness of her channel. The dildo in her ass remains in there as I move in and out of her, and it's unbelievable how tight it feels.

She groans. "Fuck, I feel so full."

I grab the spreader bar between her thighs, forcing her further back. My cock sinks in even deeper at this angle. "Do you like it, little dove?" I ask, watching her intently. "Do you like being stuffed with two cocks?"

Maeve nods. "Yes, sir, I love it."

I spank her thigh and plow into her with all my strength, feeling the dildo pressing against my cock. "You are so fucking dirty, Maeve."

Her beautiful blue eyes are dilated with lust as she

gazes up at me, her bottom lip caught between her teeth temptingly. I let my thumb brush over her throbbing clit.

She jolts at the sudden contact, letting out a soft *moan*. Her cunt grips me so tightly, as if she's trying to imprison my cock inside. I groan as my balls press against the dildo sticking out of her ass.

I pull my cock almost all the way out so only the swollen head is inside her wet heat before plunging back inside of her in one hard stroke.

"Fuck me harder, sir," she mutters.

I'll never believe how insatiable Maeve is. A woman who can take the darkest part of me and love it in ways I never knew possible. I dig my fingernails into her hips, drawing blood.

Maeve groans and enjoys it. Her pussy feels like heaven, fluttering and tightening around my throbbing dick. "That's it, baby girl. Take my cock in your pussy and the dildo in your ass," I growl, pumping into her deep.

Her eyes roll back in her head as pleasure takes over. Maeve lets out a deep cry as her juice floods around my cock, and her muscles grip me like a vice. I grunt as I keep fucking her through her orgasm, making her whimper and shake beneath me.

Her eyes open, and she gazes into mine, looking

deep into my soul. I keep fucking her, loving the way she moans and cries out.

I grab hold of her hips powerfully, pulling her tighter onto my throbbing cock and exploding deep inside of her. I roar as an earth-shattering release hits me, and I empty every drop of my seed deep inside of her.

"Fuck," Maeve says.

I'm panting for oxygen as I pull my cock from her tight cunt, watching my cum spill out of her pussy. It's a perfect sight. I pull the dildo from her ass and toss it to one side.

I unlock the restraints around her wrists and ankles, pulling them free. Maeve is limp as I lift her and lie down, pulling her against me. "Fuck, that was crazy," she says, shaking her head.

"It was so fucking good." I tighten my grip on her. "Give me ten minutes, and I'll fuck your tight little ass with that dildo in your pussy," I murmur.

Maeve groans. "I don't know if I can take it."

I smirk and kiss her forehead. "Don't be silly, baby girl. You'll love it."

Maeve rests her head on my chest with her eyes clamped shut. She doesn't say a word.

"I love you, Maeve," I murmur.

She makes a soft, exhausted groan. "I love you too."

I hold her tightly, feeling a deep sense of satisfaction that my plan worked. Three years led me to this moment. I claimed my prize, after all, despite bringing an entire city to it's knees. No matter the consequences, life has never been as good as it is right now.

29

MAEVE

uilt is an odd sensation.

I've been in limbo for a week, but it feels like longer. The revelation about my dark past clicking into place made sense of so many things about myself that I never understood.

It made me wonder if allowing Gael to kill my father was a mistake and a mistake that is irreversible now. I have to keep reminding myself that he would have discarded me to the Bratva without a second thought if we hadn't done what we did.

I can't stop asking myself one simple question.

How can I trust my memories as a child when I didn't remember such a terrible incident?

My recent memories of him are accurate, and he never gave me the time of day. Torin mentioned he resented me as I reminded him of Shane, the brother he murdered when he learned of his abuse. I can't understand how any of that was my fault.

It feels like déjà vu as I stare at a similar, ornate coffin that houses my father. His last resting place is right next door to my mother.

I swallow the lump in my throat as tears stream down my face. The pain is worse than when we lost her, but for different reasons. My amnesia is gone, but that makes it even harder. The trauma and guilt are trying to drown me. If it weren't for Gael, I don't think I'd survive.

The man lying in that coffin was my flesh and blood, and I stood by the decision to murder him. His expression after he killed his brother in that basement will haunt me forever. As I recall the image of his face, I know Torin is right. He blamed me for the death of his brother, even though what Shane did was out of my control. I was five years old, for fuck's sake.

I'll never learn the truth from him now. The clawing sensation in my chest has nothing to do with his loss but with my guilt that will haunt me forever.

Gael keeps his arm around me, hugging me against his side. I know he feels it too: the soul-crushing guilt that darkened his already black soul.

He was the one to stand in front of my father and take his life, an act I'm thankful I didn't witness.

Rourke, Killian, and Kieran no longer have a role model, and it's because of Gael and me, even if none of them realize it.

The tears fall down my face, but not because of my father's death. He would have shed no tears if it were me in that coffin after he sold me to a brutal Russian. It's because of the pain my choice has inflicted on the people I love. A choice that had selfish motives.

Torin stands and clears his throat. "My brother was a strong, fearless leader who stood up for his family above all." I can't help but feel that's not true. He stood up for power alone, as that is all my father cared about.

His eyes are sad, but Torin never cries. He's so much like my father was. Dark and depraved. I barely hear the words he says as he bids farewell to his older brother.

This is my fault.

A decision I'm going to live with for the rest of my life. It was my father or Gael. I chose him, but it doesn't mean it's a decision I'll be able to get over easily, especially when I saw the heartache it caused my brothers.

Rourke and Killian don't wear their hearts on their sleeves. Kieran is the only one who cries again, much like my mother's funeral. I don't understand why my father is even worthy of his tears, as he was nothing but cruel to Kieran. He singled Kieran out for his sensitive nature and always favored Rourke and Killian.

Torin finishes his farewell and steps back from the hole. The priest says a final blessing over him as my brothers and Torin ready themselves to lower him next to my mother.

We lost both our parents too early, but I'll always stand by my opinion. Father should have been in there instead of Mom three years ago.

The priest gestures to my brothers and Torin, who step forward and take an end of the emerald ties beneath the coffin.

A traditional Celtic song plays as they lower him into the ground to sleep next to Mom. I can't help but feel guilty that Father killing his brother is when everything changed for our family. Father disappeared from our lives. The key moment that I couldn't recall changed everything, and both Killian and Rourke were aware of it all this time. I find it hard to understand why Mom wasn't more resentful toward me.

My brothers say their goodbyes first, followed by Torin. I feel overwhelming guilt at the thought of even saying one word over his grave, and all I can say is sorry.

Gael ushers me forward once everyone else departs. "I know this is hard, little dove," he murmurs into my ear, always being a pillar of support. "You don't have to say anything if you don't want to."

I glance up to meet his amber gaze and sigh. "How can I not say something?" I glance back as my brothers walk slowly toward the cars parked nearby. "It would look suspect."

"Your brothers know you weren't close with him." Gael tightens his grip around my shoulders, providing the same emotional support as when Mom died. "Do what you feel is right."

I walk toward the hole, feeling the burden of my decision weighing heavily on my shoulders. "Sorry is all I can say, Father." I shake my head. "You didn't give us any choice. I couldn't risk you murdering the man I love." A lump forms in my throat as I stare into the dark hole. "I wish everything had been different."

Gael remains a few steps away from me, watching me with a torn expression. I know he blames himself for my guilt. Not to mention, he's guilty about killing his mentor too. A man that took a chance on him when no one else would.

"Sorry," I say again simply before turning my back on his grave. "I miss you, Mom," I mutter, glancing at her headstone.

There isn't a day that passes I don't think of her, even more since last week. It's crazy to think she's been gone three years, as it went so damn fast.

Gael keeps his distance between us as we walk back toward the cars, waiting to take us to the wake. Rourke's eyes are narrowed as he watches us walking over. "Alright, sis?"

I nod in reply.

"Come and ride with us." He glares at Gael. "See you at the wake."

Gael nods. "Aye, see you there."

I watch after him as he disappears toward the parking lot of the cemetery. Rourke opens the door to the town car for me, and Kieran and Killian are already sitting opposite. Rourke slips in next to me.

I stare out of the window, as a solemn silence fills the car as it moves toward our father's favorite pub. The same pub he announced my engagement to Maxim. The Shamrock.

Not one of us says a word until we get to the pub, where music is already playing. Irish wakes are supposed to be a celebration, but I never understood that. A celebration of life is difficult when the person who died is younger than they should have been. "Come on, Maeve. Let's sit down." Kieran nods toward a table, and Killian and Rourke follow.

We all sit down as Aisling comes over with whiskey. "Jamesons all around?" She asks.

Rourke nods. "Aye."

Aisling sets the glasses down. "I'm so sorry for your loss."

Kieran nods. "Thanks, Aisling."

She walks away, and Rourke proposes a toast. "To our father, may he rest in peace with our mother."

It's a simple toast that doesn't talk of revenge, but I sense it's only a matter of time.

"Aye," we all repeat and take a drink.

Kieran surprises me by clearing his throat. "Any thought on how we can get back at the Bratva for this?" His attention is fixed on Rourke as the next clan captain.

"I have an idea." He runs a hand across the back of his neck. "One that would make Father proud."

Killian sits up straighter. "Why haven't you run it by me then?"

Rourke's eyes narrow. "Because it was only an idea."

I sense that the play for power between those two will be a problem. Killian and Rourke are both headstrong and hate being told what to do. Kieran is used to being bossed around since he's the youngest of the four of us.

"Spill it then," Killian says.

Rourke glares at him. "I'm going to kidnap Viktoria Volkov and make Spartak sweat."

My stomach churns at the vicious tone of Rourke's voice. "Isn't that unfair? She has nothing to do with this."

Killian and Rourke roll their eyes. "Perhaps we shouldn't discuss clan business in front of you, Maeve, since you're so sensitive," Killian says.

I narrow my eyes at Killian. "And for a good reason. The Bratva kidnapped me, and it was horrible."

Killian's smirk drops, and he nods. "Aye, sorry, lass. It's just you have to be ruthless when you're dealing with people like Spartak Volkov."

It feels like no matter how much I try to ignore what Gael did, the consequences of our actions stretch so far and wide. Rourke is talking about destroying an innocent young girl's life by kidnapping her and torturing her. I know how the clan operates.

The door to the pub opens, and I glance over to

see Gael enter. He finds me across the crowd right away but doesn't come this way. It's torture having to keep a distance from him.

"Maeve, I know how you feel about the lad," Rourke says, shaking his head. "There's no use hiding it anymore, and you might as well find out if he feels the same."

My eyes widen. "What are you talking about?"

He shakes his head. "I'm not blind. I see the way you look at Gael." He sighs. "I've seen the way you look at him for years, remember."

I feel shaky as Rourke sees through my attempt to stay away from him so easily. Thankfully, he suspects nothing. "What about the engagement?"

"Are you insane?" Killian cuts in.

I frown at him. "What?"

"There's no way in hell you are marrying a Volkov after what they pulled," he replies.

"Aye, I'd die before you walk down the aisle and marry that son of a bitch," Rourke says.

I feel relief hearing that, but I knew they wouldn't make me marry Maxim, but I wasn't sure whether they'd want me to marry someone else. "I don't think Gael will be interested in me, anyway."

Kieran laughs. "Then you are blind, as the man has been in love with you for years."

Rourke nods. "Get him, Maeve."

I feel tears well in my eyes, as it doesn't help ease my guilt. They're supportive of me, but they wouldn't be if they knew what I'd done. "It's not the time or place."

"Life is too short, as this funeral shows," Kieran says. "At least speak with him."

I sigh heavily and wipe away my tears. "Okay." I stand to search the crowd, noticing him by the bar with Seamus. I walk over to him, feeling my heart pounding unevenly in my chest. It makes no sense that I'm nervous, as I already know how he feels about me.

"Gael, can we talk?" I ask.

Seamus' eyes widen when he sees me. "I'll give you two a moment." He turns away and walks in the opposite direction.

"What's wrong, little dove?" He murmurs.

I shake my head. "Nothing. My brothers insisted I come and talk to you because they think we both have feelings for each other."

Gael's eyes widen. "Shit. Do you think—"

I grab his arm and squeeze, stopping him from saying it. "No, they want me to be happy."

He nods toward the back of the pub, through the small dining space, with a security room in the back.

"Let's go somewhere more private." I follow him into the room, and he shuts the door. "So, they've given us their blessing?"

I nod in response, and he smiles, wrapping me in his arms. "That's good news."

"Yes," I say, tightening my grasp on him. "I love you, Gael."

"I love you too, little dove." He presses his lips to my forehead. "We've survived this, which means we can survive anything."

I break away from him and look into his eyes. "We have caused so much pain, though. Do you believe it was worth it?"

Gael looks uncertain about answering. "Yes, one hundred percent."

I swallow hard, as I'm not so certain. Love is blind has never been more true than now. "It's hard to forget the destruction our love has left in its wake."

Gael cups my cheeks in his hands and kisses me quickly. "Time will lessen the effects of the destruction, little dove. Give it time."

I wrap my arms around his waist and lean my head on his chest, allowing him to hold me. Gael has been my pillar of support for three years, and I'm thankful for it as I need him now more than ever.

30

EPILOGUE

MAEVE

Ten months later…

I stare into the mirror, admiring my beautiful A-line wedding gown. It's hard to believe this day is here, and I'm not marrying someone I don't know.

Rourke clears his throat behind me, startling me away from the mirror. "You look beautiful, Maeve."

I turn and smile at him. "Thank you. I'm nervous as hell."

He chuckles, smoothing down the fabric of his navy designer suit. "I never would have known by the way you almost jumped a mile."

I roll my eyes. "Sorry, I can't believe I'm getting married."

"Neither can I because you will always be my

baby sister." He moves closer. "I can't believe you're all grown up."

I roll my eyes. "I'm twenty-two years old, Rourke."

"Yeah, still a baby." His brow furrows. "Do you remember when I told you that you wouldn't be marrying Gael Ryan?"

I nod in response.

He holds his hands out. "Looks like I was very wrong."

I feel the heaviness of the comment weighing on my chest. The reason I'm marrying Gael is because our father is dead. "I wouldn't have been if Father were still alive."

The guilt continues to eat away at me daily for what Gael and I did to my brothers. I had no love for the man, but I know they felt differently about him. Rourke and Killian looked up to him in particular.

"Aye, but I can't deny I'm glad you are marrying an Irishman and not a fucking Russian." Rourke runs a hand across the back of his neck.

I raise a brow. "That's rich coming from you."

His lips turn into a smirk at my comment. "Shut it, little sis. Let's get this show on the road." He walks toward me and offers me his arm.

I take it, knowing that I'd rather Rourke walk me

down the aisle than my father any day. He's been more of a protector and father figure than our father ever was. "Thanks for offering to walk me down the aisle."

"Of course, who else would have?" Rourke rolls his eyes. "Killian isn't the type, and Kieran is younger than you."

I purse my lips together and don't say a word, as Rourke hates it when I get emotional. He may hide his emotions behind his tough exterior, but I know deep down he's got a heart bigger than anyone.

We walk down the corridor toward the main church, my heart thundering in my chest at a thousand miles an hour. "God, I'm nervous."

Rourke shakes his head. "You realize we're in a church right now?"

I laugh and shake my head. "Sorry, I'm so nervous."

Rourke stops at the open door and glances at me. "Don't be. You look like a million bucks."

I smile at my brother. "Okay, let's do this."

The music plays as Rourke leads me into the aisle. My heart is pounding in my ears as everyone's eyes land on me. All of our family and friends gathered here to celebrate our union.

My racing thoughts quiet the moment that I see

him. The other half of my whole. Gael's amber eyes find mine, and it feels like we're the only two people on this earth.

I allow Rourke to set the pace as I keep all my attention on my fiancé. I'm shaking with nerves, and my legs feel like jelly, but the only thing holding me together is the prospect of standing opposite him in a moment.

Finally, I make it to the end of the aisle, and the priest asks, "Who gives this woman away?"

Rourke smiles. "I do." He passes my hand into Gael's.

I tighten my grip on Gael's hand, squeezing hard. Gael smiles at me as I stand opposite him. My heart is pounding so hard as I stare into his beautiful eyes. This man is the only person who knows all of me, the bad and the good. He loves me despite it, and I love him despite his darkness.

The priest starts the ceremony, but I can hardly hear his words. Rourke insisted I get married at this church because it's a family tradition. I'd have preferred a smaller, more intimate wedding on a beach somewhere, but I'm thankful to be marrying my soul mate.

Gael's eyes bore into mine with such intensity. He makes me nervous.

I swallow hard as the priest asks Gael to place the wedding ring on my finger. My heart is pounding hard in my chest as Gael smiles easily, taking the ring from Tiernan, his best man.

"This ring is a symbol of my eternal love for you, little dove," Gael says, slipping it onto my ring finger. "I'll cherish you and protect you so long as I still have breath in my lungs and a beat in my chest."

Tears pool in my eyes at his words as they pierce through my heart and soul. He smiles at me, trying to reassure me.

The priest nods and glances at me. "Now you, Maeve."

I swallow hard and take the ring from Tiernan. "I give this ring to you as a symbol of my love." I slide the ring onto Gael's finger. "I vow to love you for as long as I live," I say, my voice cracking with emotion.

The priest speaks the final words, "I can now pronounce you man and wife. You may kiss the bride."

Gael's eyes flash as he steps forward and wraps an arm around my back, pulling me into him. His lips cover mine in a long, heartfelt kiss, and it feels like everyone else in the crowd melts away.

We're the only two people left on this earth.

When he finally breaks away, the crowd stands and cheers us.

Gael grabs my hand and glances at me. "Shall we, Mrs. Ryan?" he says.

I nod. "Yes, Mr. Ryan."

He leads me down the aisle past my brothers and two uncles, who are both smiling and clapping. The guilt is always there in the background, but Gael was right. Time has helped it fade.

We leave the church to find the wedding car waiting for us. Gael walks up to it and then freezes a few feet away.

"What's wrong?" I ask.

His eyes narrow as he scans the area before glancing at the car again. "I've got a bad feeling."

I shudder as I know that the Bratva could target us, especially since I was supposed to marry Maxim. "Shall we get the car checked?"

Gale nods. "Aye."

"What's wrong, lad?" Seamus, who is driving, asks.

"Check the car over. I've got a funny feeling."

Seamus' eyes widen, and he nods, opening the trunk to pull out a mirror to check under the car. He walks along each side and stops when he gets to the left side in the middle. "Fuck me."

"Bomb?" I ask.

"Aye, lad. You saved all three of our lives."

Rourke approaches with Viktoria on his arm. "I thought you two would be on your way to the reception by now."

I turn to face my brother. "They rigged the car."

Rourke turns rigid, eyes wide. "What?"

"It's rigged with explosives that could send the entire fucking car into space," Seamus confirms.

"Motherfuckers," Rourke growls.

Viktoria shakes her head. "This war is spiraling out of control."

Gael wraps an arm around my hip. "It's not far to the reception, and I say we walk it."

I nod in reply. "Sounds safer to me."

Rourke clears his throat. "I'll get the clan to check the vehicles here, and we'll all walk."

It's hard to believe that this is our reality now, as we're always expecting an attack. It's a result of our decision to leave chaos in our wake, although the fallout has been far worse than Gael ever expected.

If it weren't for Gael's intuition right now, we could both be dead. He wraps an arm around my shoulder and guides me in the pub's direction.

"Couldn't they try to get us at the pub?" I ask, glancing up at him.

Rourke doesn't give him a chance to answer. "I've had it swept for any bombs twice this morning, little sis. Don't worry."

Viktoria sighs. "I think I need to talk with my father."

Rourke growls. "Over my dead body, princess."

I smirk at the possessiveness in my brother's voice. It's surprising to see him so wrapped up in a woman since he's never been one for relationships in his thirty years.

Kieran and Killian follow in silence, as do my two uncles. There's a heaviness surrounding our wedding because of the war we are fighting, and I'm responsible for it, but I can't dwell on that right now.

Today has to be about celebrating our success, as I can't wait to start the rest of my life as Mrs. Ryan.

"How are you feeling, Mrs. Ryan?" Gael murmurs into my ear, tightening his arm around my shoulders as the limousine pulls away from the wedding party.

"Happy." I sigh and glance up at him. "At least, as happy as I can be."

Gael nods. "Me too."

I raise a brow. "I wish you would tell me where we're heading, though."

He shakes his head. "No, it's a suprise, little dove."

I huff as the car comes to a stop. "Where are we?" I ask.

"The airstrip. We're going abroad for our honeymoon."

I swallow hard as Gael gets out of the back and walks around to help me out. My wedding dress trails behind me, and I have to pick it up to stop it from getting dirty. Gael wraps an arm around me and leads me over to the step-up to the private jet. "Isn't this Rourke's jet?"

"Aye, he lent it to us." He ushers me up the steps into the aircraft, which I've been in before. It used to belong to my father.

"Can't you give me a hint of where we're going?" I ask.

He gives me a stern glare. "Stop trying to ruin the surprise."

I sigh and take a seat on the left-hand side. It's hard to believe that his plan worked. We're together and married, and no one is the wiser of our hand in Father's demise.

The underworld of the city of Chicago is at war.

A war unlike anyone has ever seen before. All the criminal gangs and organizations are butting heads. The Morrone Family and the Volkov Bratva are our number one enemies at the moment, as my brothers try to work with the Estrada Cartel, our only potential ally in this shit show of a war. The bikers are getting frustrated with us, even though they normally keep to themselves.

It's a dangerous time to be a Callaghan in the city of Chicago, which is why I'm thankful to be getting away for a few weeks. I glance at Gael, who is talking with the pilot at the front. He finishes speaking to him and then turns to join me, sitting down in the chair opposite.

"I need to know if I should get changed out of my dress or not. How long is the flight?"

Gael stands and walks toward me, placing his hands on the armrests of my chair. I love the way his dominance makes me feel, as it's addictive. "I'll have you out of that damn dress before we've even taken off, baby."

I swallow hard. "Is that right, sir?" I ask, knowing he loves it when I call him that.

He growls softly and grabs my hips, yanking me to stand in front of him. "Aye, it's right, little dove." He spins me around and unzips my dress.

The pilot clears his throat behind us, making me tense. "All set. We'll take off now." He shuts the door to the cockpit.

My stomach churns. "I didn't realize he was there."

Gael nibbles on the shell of my ear. "I did." He drags my dress down, and I step out of it. Gael throws it onto the chair before turning me back around. He takes a step backward. "A vision," Gael muses, admiring my ivory, lace bridal lingerie that I purchased. He steps forward again and slides his hand between my thighs, parting them. "Fucking sexy little minx, wearing crotchless panties." He shoves four fingers into my dripping wet pussy. "I'm going to fuck you with these on," he growls, moving his hand higher.

He stops the moment he feels the plug in my ass and growls. "Fucking hell, Maeve. Did you marry me with that plug in your ass?"

I love the utter disbelief in his voice but shake my head. "No, I went into the bathroom at the reception venue and put it in."

He unzips his pants, and I feel the length of his cock rest between my thighs. "I can't wait any longer. I'm going to fuck both of your holes and fill them with cum," he growls.

He doesn't even wait for a second, bending me over the arm of the chair and slamming his thick cock inside of me.

My knees buckle at the sudden rush of pleasure, but Gael holds me up. His arms are straining as he fucks into me with all his strength. I can't get enough of his insatiable dominance. He makes me feel like the most desired person on this earth.

Gael spanks my ass before grabbing the handle of the butt-plug and pulling it partially out, only to push it back in. "You're so fucking filthy, putting this butt-plug in your ass at our wedding reception."

I moan, and he spanks me again.

"Did you touch your pussy while you put it in?" he asks, stilling inside of me.

The desire inside of me heightens as I nod. "Yes, sir."

He growls. "That's very naughty. As you know, only I'm allowed to touch your pretty little cunt."

I bite my lip. "Sorry, sir. I had to get relaxed to put it in."

He spanks both my ass cheeks again with increased force, making me yelp. The pain only increases my arousal as I feel myself getting closer to the edge of no return. "Fuck, sir," I moan.

Gael groans. "Make that pretty little pussy come

for me, baby girl."

His dirty talking is all it takes to make me climax. My pussy muscles spasm around his cock, drawing him deeper as he plunges into me again, groaning as he comes along with me. My nipples are painful peaks as they rub against the leather of the armchair, a sensation that only heightens the explosive pleasure.

"One hole down, one more to go," he muses, applying pressure to the huge plug I lodged into my ass.

I groan as he pulls it out of me and spreads my ass cheeks wide. "You're so stretched and ready for my cock, Mrs. Ryan." I feel the cold lube as he applies it to my already gaping hole. "I'm going to make sure you're so fucking full of my cum by the time we arrive at our destination."

He gives me no warning, sliding the entire length of his throbbing dick deep into my ass with one thrust.

"Fuck," I cry, loving feeling so complete with him inside of me.

"That's right, baby girl, moan while I fuck that tight little asshole." He spanks my ass again, sending that tantalizing rush of pleasure through every one of my nerve endings.

His thick cock stretches me so much better than the plug as he plows into me with skilled precision, sending me toward another climax so damn fast.

"Oh fuck, Gael," I whine, shutting my eyes and fisting the throw pillow on the chair. "I love you fucking my ass."

He growls, and I know that I'm on the precipice of coming undone again.

"I think I'm going to come."

"Fuck, baby girl. Your ass is so fucking tight."

The orgasm hits me like a freight train, making my vision blur as I cry out.

Gael roars as his release hits him at the same time. "Fuck, take all of my cum, baby girl." He growls like a beast as he continues to thrust into me long after he came undone, making sure he's drained every drop of his seed inside my ass.

After a while, he finally slides his semi-hard cock out of my ass. Gael grabs the plug and slides it back inside of me, making sure his cum can't escape. "I want you full of my cum by the time we land, little dove."

It's crazy that despite the two mind-blowing orgasms he just gave me, I'm hungry for more from him.

Gael pulls me down onto his lap, wrapping a

muscular arm around my waist. He plants slow, gentle kisses along my shoulder, making goosebumps rise.

"Are you going to tell me how long this flight is yet?" I ask.

He smirks against my neck. "Don't worry, little dove. We still have enough time for about six more rounds of that."

My stomach churns at the thought of feeling that good six more times. "It must be a long flight then."

He bites the lobe of my ear. "Or maybe I'm going to keep fucking you non-stop, Mrs. Ryan."

I shake my head, smiling. "Be serious for a moment." I look up at him, and our eyes meet. "I think I'm officially the luckiest woman in the world."

Gael's brow furrows. "I'm the lucky one, little dove. You are way out of my league, if you didn't realize it already."

I shake my head. "No, we're both lucky. It's like you said, we're two pieces of a whole." I kiss his lips. "You complete me."

Gael smiles and kisses me deeply, pouring every ounce of his love into it. I know at that moment that it's the happiest I've ever felt.

Thank you for reading Merciless Traitor, the first book in the Callaghan Clan series.

I hope you enjoyed following Gael's and Maeve's story.

The next book in the Callaghan Clan series follows Rourke's and Viktoria's story.

You can pre-order the book now here

Violent Leader: A Dark Enemies to Lovers Captive Mafia Romance

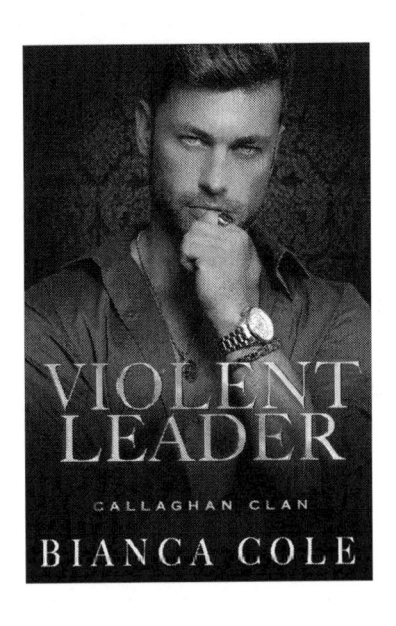

The city is in chaos, but I thrive in the aftermath.

Grief surrounds our family as we bury our father.

As the eldest son, leading the clan is my responsibility. The first task on my list: Make the Bratva pay for what they did.

I'll take the most precious thing from Spartak and defile her. *Viktoria Volkov.* Bratva princess and only daughter of Spartak. She will pay for the sins of her father.

Once I set my eyes on her, sticking to the plan becomes difficult. The Russian beauty calls to my primal urges. My desire for revenge twists into something else entirely. A dark, violent need rises to the surface.

I intended to give her back, broken and damaged. I'll break her and make her mine. I'm just not sure I can ever let her go. The question is, what will Spartak do once he realizes I'm keeping his princess forever?

Violent Leader is the second book in the Callaghan Clan series. This book is a dark mafia romance involving kidnapping, dark themes and certain subjects that may upset the reader. It has no cliff hanger a happily ever after ending, and can be read as a standalone. It features a dark, twisted Irish mob boss who takes what he wants no matter the consequences.

ALSO BY BIANCA COLE

Callaghan Clan Series

Violent Leader: A Dark Enemies to Lovers Captive Mafia Romance

Boston Mafia Dons Series

Cruel Daddy: A Dark Mafia Arranged Marriage Romance

Savage Daddy: A Dark Captive Mafia Roamnce

Ruthless Daddy: A Dark Forbidden Mafia Romance

Vicious Daddy: A Dark Brother's Best Friend Mafia Romance

Wicked Daddy: A Dark Captive Mafia Romance

New York Mafia Doms Series

Her Irish Daddy: A Dark Mafia Romance

Her Russian Daddy: A Dark Mafia Romance

Her Italian Daddy: A Dark Mafia Romance

Her Cartel Daddy: A Dark Mafia Romance

Romano Mafia Brother's Series

Her Mafia Daddy: A Dark Daddy Romance

Her Mafia Boss: A Dark Romance

Her Mafia King: A Dark Romance

Bratva Brotherhood Series

Bought by the Bratva: A Dark Mafia Romance

Captured by the Bratva: A Dark Mafia Romance

Claimed by the Bratva: A Dark Mafia Romance

Bound by the Bratva: A Dark Mafia Romance

Taken by the Bratva: A Dark Mafia Romance

Wynton Series

Filthy Boss: A Forbidden Office Romance

Filthy Professor: A First Time Professor And Student Romance

Filthy Lawyer: A Forbidden Hate to Love Romance

Filthy Doctor: A Fordbidden Romance

Royally Mated Series

Her Faerie King: A Faerie Royalty Paranormal Romance

Her Alpha King: A Royal Wolf Shifter Paranormal Romance

Her Dragon King: A Dragon Shifter Paranormal Romance

Her Vampire King: A Dark Vampire Romance

ABOUT THE AUTHOR

I love to write stories about over the top alpha bad boys who have heart beneath it all, fiery heroines, and happily-ever-after endings with heart and heat. My stories have twists and turns that will keep you flipping the pages and heat to set your kindle on fire.

For as long as I can remember, I've been a sucker for a good romance story. I've always loved to read. Suddenly, I realized why not combine my love of two things, books and romance?

My love of writing has grown over the past four years and I now publish on Amazon exclusively, weaving stories about dirty mafia bad boys and the women they fall head over heels in love with.

If you enjoyed this book please follow me on Amazon, Bookbub or any of the below social media platforms for alerts when more books are released.

Printed in Great Britain
by Amazon